UNSAFE HARBOR

The Rachel Porter Mysteries by Jessica Speart

GATOR AIDE
TORTOISE SOUP
BIRD BRAINED
BORDER PREY
BLACK DELTA NIGHT
A KILLING SEASON
COASTAL DISTURBANCE
BLUE TWILIGHT
RESTLESS WATERS *
UNSAFE HARBOR *

* available from Severn House

UNSAFE HARBOR

Jessica Speart

This first world edition published in Great Britain 2006 by
SEVERN HOUSE PUBLISHERS LTD of
9–15 High Street, Sutton, Surrey SM1 1DF.
This first world edition published in the USA 2006 by
SEVERN HOUSE PUBLISHERS INC of
595 Madison Avenue, New York, N.Y. 10022,
by arrangement with Harper Collins Publishers, Inc.

British Library Cataloguing in Publication Data

Speart,   Jessica
   Unsafe harbor
   1.   Porter, Rachel (Fictitious character) - Fiction
   2.   Women detectives - New Jersey - Fiction
   3.   Detective and mystery stories
   I.   Title
   813.5'4 [F]

   ISBN-13: 978-0-7278-6430-7
   ISBN-10: 0-7278-6430-0

Typeset by Palimpsest Book Production Ltd.,
Polmont, Stirlingshire, Scotland.
Printed and bound in Great Britain by
MPG Books Ltd., Bodmin, Cornwall.

Acknowledgements

Thanks go to John Meehan, Resident Agent in Charge with USFWS, Special Agent Carmine Sabia, and Supervisory Wildlife Inspector Laurel Zitowsky for their inside views of Newark Seaport; to Special Agent Tara Donn for sharing her knowledge of shahtoosh; to Susan Lieberman of World Wildlife Fund International for her insight on the ivory trade; and to Gerry Wachs for opening the Diamond District to an outsider.

One

The sound of a siren split the air, shrill as the cry of a prehistoric bird. I steered my vehicle to one side of the road as a set of flashing red lights appeared in my rearview mirror. Their reflection was dulled by the morning haze, the sky dingy as a soiled pillow case. I stifled a yawn and cranked up the radio, hoping the local shock jock would say something outrageous to jolt me awake.

The bumper-to-bumper traffic paid little heed to the blue-and-white Crown Vic that continued to screech angrily behind us. But that was the norm for this place. This stretch of the Turnpike lay between a couple of urban bullies, Newark and Elizabeth, the Mike Tyson and Evander Holyfield of industrial northern New Jersey. I'd quickly become acclimated to my new surroundings. In fact, perhaps a little too well. I gave the incident barely a thought until the Crown Vic's emblem caught my eye. Squeezing through morning rush hour traffic was a Port Authority police car. It clearly signaled that something was taking place in my territory. I watched as the squad car disappeared amid the crowd of vehicles, until even its call had been silenced.

Damn, I thought. *Why didn't I have one of those handy dandy sirens?* Instead, I continued to crawl along with the rest of the throng, like one more regular Joe. There was little to do but stare out the window as the scenery slowly slipped by. Vast warehouses gradually gave way to towering columns of colorful cargo containers. The metallic rainbows rose like giant Legos, their individual shells stacked high to the sky. Hidden from view lay a sprawling complex where goods from far-flung places arrived daily by ship. One if by air, two if by sea. Newark International Airport stretched along

1

one side of the road, while the Port of Elizabeth laid claim to the other. The Turnpike divided the two like a surgeon's knife separating a pair of Siamese twins. What both have in common is that each is a major hub of transportation. A massive blue and yellow structure appeared ahead like a concrete flag of Sweden. The Ikea building cheerfully announced that I'd reached my destination. Exit 13A swiftly approached and, as usual, my vehicle was stuck in the wrong lane. At times like this, I have no shame. The Trailblazer used its bulk to bully its way into the tiniest of spaces. What I hadn't counted on was hitting a patch of ice while swerving on to the exit.

My vehicle fishtailed, nearly colliding with another brawny SUV. That car did what no disc jockey this morning had so far achieved. Its blaring horn finally shocked me awake. I quickly over-corrected and, sliding to the other side of the road, brushed up against a border of tall graceful phragmites. Their feathery plumes shook their heads in distress as they valiantly buffered a small polluted creek. Taking a deep breath, I maintained my grip on the wheel and continued on, pretending not to notice the other cars that did their best to steer clear of me.

I'd been stationed at Port Elizabeth for only a few months, but the posting already felt like years. Perhaps it was due to the fact that winters on the East Coast were colder than I had remembered, the January days morbidly gray.

Things will be better once spring arrives, I thought, trying to bolster myself.

But the cold felt as though it would never go away. A gust of wind rounded a bend and shook the Trailblazer as if it were a toy. I must have been certifiable to have ever willingly left Hawaii. I tried to push that thought from my mind while passing the Jersey Garden Mall and drab hotels overlooking scenic oil tanks and chemical plants.

Turning on to North Avenue, I jostled my way between a line-up of trucks and entered Port Authority property. I felt like one more game piece on a board of Monopoly, my destination to pass Go, collect what I could, and land at the seaport.

Asphalt lots filled with truck wheels and empty containers

2

lined the roadway. This was the place where old semis go to die. A section of swampland up ahead caught my eye. It consisted only of weeds on which nothing had ever been built. However, plenty of action was taking place today.

Five Port Authority squad cars were parked in single file, their flashing lights simultaneously announcing that urgent business was underway. Sitting nearby was a silver 'roach coach', which best resembled a sardine can on wheels. A closer look revealed it was a mobile luncheonette truck that serviced the port.

My pulse sped up upon catching sight of the sign on its side. Whatever was going on obviously involved The Kielbasa House. It served some of the best homemade food in the area, and was owned and operated by a Polish woman that I'd befriended.

I parked behind the last car and got out. My hiking boots crunched through snow and weeds, the sound of my steps repeating the same message over and over. *Please don't let anything have happened to Magda.*

I nearly made it to the cordoned off area before finding myself stopped.

'Sorry, but this is official police business. You'll have to turn back around,' intoned an authoritative voice.

I stared at the Port Authority officer's badge. Then I looked at the man himself. Even through his clothes, I could tell that Officer Nunzio worked out diligently. His arms and legs were slightly bent, as if his muscles had sprouted muscles. He looked to be no more than thirty years old, sported a flat top, and was clearly gung-ho. My fingers clumsily fumbled while removing my own badge from my pocket.

'Special Agent Rachel Porter,' I responded, and quickly stashed the badge away, hoping that he hadn't seen the words US Fish and Wildlife.

Nunzio stepped aside and let me pass.

'What's going on?' I asked, as he walked beside me.

'There's been a homicide,' he coolly replied, as though murder were an everyday occurrence at the port.

But I heard the tinge of excitement lurking in his voice. I felt momentarily ill, certain that the victim had to be

3

Magda – why else was her lunch truck parked at the scene? Then I breathed a sigh of relief upon catching sight of her standing in the field with an officer.

A flowered babushka was tied around her head, and a threadbare coat pulled tightly about her body. Magda held both arms crossed against her chest, like a corpse in a coffin, with hands buried deep beneath the armpits. As for her face, it was chapped and raw from the cold and wind that whipped off Newark Bay and barreled through the seaport with a vengeance. Even from here I could see that her eyes were red and that she had been crying. Magda wiped her nose against her sleeve as the officer by her side offered a tissue.

'Is that woman somehow involved?' I asked, nodding towards Magda.

'Her? Yeah. She found the victim,' Nunzio said, and shifted his weight as though he were about to throw a baseball.

I moved closer and squeezed between a wall of blue uniforms, finding myself consumed by morbid curiosity. A small cluster of cops stood gathered around a blanket that had been thrown on the ground. Beneath it lay a body.

Man or woman? It would have been hard to tell but for the silky strands of blonde hair that formed a halo in the dingy snow. Their shade was so exquisitely golden that it couldn't have been natural; the hue so deliciously rich, no way had the color come from an over-the-counter bottle of hair dye. A few coarse weeds had already become entangled in the splayed tresses, as if determined to sully their gilded glory.

'Any idea who she is?' I asked, as Officer Nunzio continued to shadow me.

The paramedics anxiously stomped their feet against the cold, their shoes sinking through snow into wet earth. But the scene investigator refused to be rushed. He continued to carefully take photos while two officers scoured the ground for any telltale hairs and fibers. I stuffed my hands deep inside my pockets, cursing myself for having forgotten my gloves.

'Yeah. The perp was considerate enough to leave behind the victim's ID,' Nunzio answered. 'It's someone by the name of Bitsy von Falken.'

'*The* Bitsy von Falken?' I asked in surprise, knowing of only one woman by that name.

Bitsy von Falken was an esteemed member of Manhattan's highest society, one of the elite corps of the Ladies Who Lunch. She was equally famous for her extravagant parties thrown in the name of charity. Her husband, Gavin von Falken, gallantly underwrote their lifestyle as the Chief Financial Officer of a top investment firm.

'I wouldn't know. It sounds as if she was a little out of my social circle. My time is spent patrolling lovely Newark and Port Elizabeth,' Nunzio dryly replied. 'By the way, who'd you say you were with again?'

'US Fish and Wildlife,' I mumbled, fervently hoping he'd mistake my words for the FBI. 'How was she killed?'

But Nunzio had obviously heard me correctly. His response was to shrug and walk away, making it perfectly clear that I'd get no more information out of him.

I glanced around, having been left to my own devices. Aside from Magda's roach coach and the squad cars, my Trailblazer was the only other vehicle in sight. There was no sign of a Mercedes or Jaguar – the type of car that I imagined Bitsy von Falken would drive. That was, unless she'd journeyed here ensconced in the back of a limo.

The other possibility was that Bitsy hadn't come alone. Last night's snowfall would easily have covered up any tire tracks or footprints had she been unceremoniously dumped here against her will.

Nunzio joined the rest of his crew, a few of whom now turned and gave me the evil eye. Their message was clear. I wasn't welcome to hang around and snoop on their case anymore.

That was all right. The five-degree temperature was cold enough to discourage me from pursuing the matter further. Besides, they were right. Bitsy von Falken's death had nothing to do with my work. In any case, I'd probably hear all the lurid details on the news tonight.

I turned to leave, but not before glancing over at Magda once more. This time she met my gaze and I caught the gleam of fear in her eyes.

5

Two

I turned the heater on full blast, holding first one hand up to the vent and then the other. Having defrosted my fingers, I threw the SUV into gear and pulled away. Bitsy von Falken's ghost slipped quietly in beside me.

I couldn't imagine what she had possibly been doing here. I sincerely doubted that Bitsy secretly shopped at the outlet mall, and she certainly hadn't come to the port to sample its cuisine. But Bitsy's ghost merely smiled and sat primly in her seat, not giving anything away.

OK, if that's how you're going to be, I thought, and continued on to the office.

A passing plane gleamed like a silver jack thrown high in the sky, as the sun pushed through a cloud of industrial haze. The Trailblazer morphed into a vibrating chair as its wheels passed over a set of rumble strips designed to slow down trucks on dangerous curves. Even so, one leaned perilously close, as if threatening to topple on to me.

Port Elizabeth is the largest seaport on the East Coast, a mini-city that boasts streets lined with rows of warehouses and trucking companies. I passed a caravan of autos being driven off a car carrier that was longer than three football fields. A 958-foot floating garage, its interior is akin to a giant beehive. Port Elizabeth ships tons of scrap metal over to Japan and they send it back to us in the form of Toyotas.

I drove towards a herd of tall cranes that resembled a set of Tonka toys on steroids. The mechanical giraffes offload ships twenty-four hours a day, in a synchronized ballet, for entry into the most concentrated and affluent consumer marketplace in the world. Four-and-a-half million containers pour into the international seaport spanning Newark-

Elizabeth and New York Seaport each year, their contents ranging from Indian carpets to Spanish olives, to clothing, shoes, flammable gas, and everything else imaginable.

A train laden with containers squealed past the black-tinted windows of a three-story structure. My vehicle rounded Fleet and Corbin Street, also known as Suicide Corner, and approached the Sea Land Building. In addition to housing Fish and Wildlife, the edifice contains US Customs and Immigration, two agencies now under the umbrella of Homeland Security.

As usual, the guardbooth was unmanned and the entrance gate was up. It was good to know that the government was on its toes, protecting its federal employees.

I parked in the lot, stepped out, and took a deep breath. Ah! The pungent smell of jet fumes early in the morning. A fine spray from overhead planes immediately collected on my windshield. I slogged through snow and slush, using my key to enter the rear of the building.

My new territory didn't cover the Jersey of my childhood. I wasn't prowling the shore, canoeing through the silence of the Pine Barrens, or lolling in luscious fields of straw-berries. Rather, my beat consisted of Newark air and seaports, the rail yards and the airport mail facility, including FedEx and UPS.

Most ironic of all was that I'd actually requested the transfer. Well, not really. I'd asked to be assigned back home to New York, but that request had quickly been denied. Instead, I'd put my name on the list for Newark and – presto! – my wish was instantly granted. It had been easy. No one else had applied.

I slipped between the unpacked cartons and boxes still piled high in my office. They included not just my own, but those left behind by the last agent that had worked here. He'd returned to Idaho after only ten months in Newark. Rumor had it, he'd astutely observed that Fish and Wildlife was a sinking ship and he'd been smart enough to get off.

I had yet to delve into his boxes, knowing full well their contents. They were stacked with violations which he'd never bothered to write up. Most were fines against air shipping

7

companies that delivered wildlife products into the country without first getting them cleared. Tickets needed to be written and issued before the statute of limitations ran out.

My new boss had ordered me to get to it ASAP. We both knew what that would accomplish – it would bring much needed money into the agency's coffers, while keeping me out of any possible trouble and tied to my desk.

'Good morning, Grasshopper. I hear you rustling around in there. Stop whatever it is you're doing and get your rear end in here,' commanded a voice the texture of sandpaper.

I'd quickly learned that Jack Hogan likened himself to a wise sage and viewed his underlings as know-nothing minions. I went to see what was up with my master.

'You called?' I responded, sticking my head in his office.

Jack Hogan gazed back at me through bloodshot eyes. I swear, the man must never have slept. His clothes were always rumpled and he sported jowls that rivaled those of a bloodhound. But the clincher was long strands of hair carefully combed forward to cover an otherwise bald pate. When would guys ever learn that simply made them look like jackasses?

'How's it going with those tickets?' he asked, his eyes swimming in two scarlet pools.

'They're coming along,' I lied, having not yet started the process. 'By the way, there's a lot of activity going on at the south end of the port this morning. It seems there's been a murder.'

'Oh yeah?' he responded, perking right up.

Hogan was a former cop that admittedly cared little for wildlife. That being the case, Port Elizabeth suited him just fine. The only critters to be seen, other than rats and seagulls, arrived in the form of snakeskin boots, alligator skirts, mink handbags, and the occasional box of python crotchless panties. As far as I was concerned, those were reasons why no animal should ever have to die.

'So, who got knocked off? Anyone I know?' he inquired.

'I guess that depends on the crowd you hang out with,' I replied. 'The victim was a woman by the name of Bitsy von Falken. Her husband is the CFO of Hyde Barrow, an investment firm on Wall Street.'

8

'Sounds pretty hoity-toity to me. Way too rich for my blood,' Hogan commented and, taking a sip of coffee, smacked his lips.

'I'm just curious what she was doing at the port,' I continued, unable to erase the image of her blonde hair, defiled by snow and grime, from my mind.

'A rich broad like that? Who knows? Maybe slumming for the fun of it. Could be she was trying to score some recreational drugs,' Hogan ventured, lacing his hands behind his head. 'After all, that *is* Newark's main industry.'

Then he went back to doing what he loved best – staring out at the railyard and passing time until his retirement.

'So, boss. You got anything for me to work on yet?' I ventured, figuring I had little to lose.

Hogan turned and viewed me dispassionately. 'Yeah. Those damn violations that are piled up in your office.'

I didn't budge, but decided to stare him down.

'If you're planning a coup, you'd better first think of a way to kill the king,' he advised, in a tone that was clearly a warning.

We locked eyes and I realized that the man was much shrewder than I had thought.

'I'm not plotting anything,' I countered. 'I just think it's time I was given a real case.'

Hogan shook his head and smiled.

'You know what I don't like about you, Porter? You're a zealot, and I don't trust them,' he reflected. 'I gave you the lowdown when you first arrived. The Service only wants bodies here in Newark. That's the beauty of this place. It's a hidden gem. We're second banana to the New York office and in no way a priority. They're the star. That's why the best agents are sent over there rather than here.'

I felt my face begin to burn. Hogan knew how badly I'd wanted that station and had no qualms about rubbing it in.

'Now, how about you go and write up those tickets?' he suggested.

I didn't say a word but left as I came, damned if I'd play the well-behaved pupil.

I glanced in at the other Special Agent while walking back

9

to my office. Bill Saunders had transferred over from the Treasury Department about two years ago.

He had a criminal investigator's background and was a computer geek, capable of ferreting out a company's business records and bills of lading. The downside was that he was another with little emotion when it came to the plight of wildlife. Saunders was one more suit pulling in a paycheck whose philosophy seemed to be *do the bare minimum, punch the clock, and collect your pension.*

I was beginning to feel like a dinosaur within my own agency. I was definitely the odd woman out, as far as Hogan and Saunders were concerned.

I busied myself unpacking files until the two men headed off to lunch together. Only then did I stroll over to the Supervisory Wildlife Inspector's office.

'Hey, Connie. Got a minute?' I asked, leaning against her doorjamb.

Connie Fuca sat hunched over a stack of papers on a desk that was nearly as cluttered as my own. Petitely built, there was something imposing about the woman that gave her the presence of a powerful tornado – one that was ready to lash out.

'Not really. Why?' she brusquely responded, barely bothering to look up.

In her early forties, she had strands of white woven throughout a mane of black hair, and dark eyebrows that were furrowed in frustration. 'Harried' was a word I would have used had it been anyone else. But when it came to Connie, the most appropriate term was 'pissed off'.

'I was just wondering if you might have run across any illegal shipments lately,' I gingerly broached the topic, while taking a step into her room. 'I've talked to Hogan, but there don't seem to be many cases coming out of this office. From what I've heard, Special Agents at ports depend on inspectors to trip across things during the course of their examinations.'

Connie now took the time to peer at me. 'That's right. Inspectors are great, aren't they? Every agent should have one. We hand over the information that we gather from all our hard work, and you happily take the evidence, along with the credit for it. Isn't that what usually happens in such cases?' she responded, verbally biting my head off.

'I didn't mean it like that,' I feebly replied, attempting to defend myself.

'No? Well, it doesn't really matter since I don't have time to do inspections anyway,' she snapped. 'I'm too busy logging in entries, or haven't you noticed? The word *inspector* is a loosely-used term around here these days. My *real* job is collecting brokers' fees and clearing shipments as fast as I can, based only on paperwork. That's what DC wants, so that's what they get. Unlike Special Agents, we're actually expected to bring in money and pay our own way.'

I was prepared for a lightning bolt to be hurled as she glared at me, and then returned to her work. I quietly turned around and high-tailed it out the door.

What in the hell was that all about? I wondered, heading for the safety of my office.

I'd heard that relations between agents and inspectors at ports could sometimes be tense. However, I hadn't expected all-out war.

I pulled a handful of violations from a box and began to write up tickets, wondering if Connie's fate might not soon be my own. At times like this, I questioned why I'd ever become an agent in the first place. Then I remembered something my old boss, Charlie Hickok, had once told me.

'*We're all social misfits, Bronx. What kind of individual not only goes into law enforcement, but joins an agency where we work by ourselves? I'll tell you what kind. The ones that don't play well with others.*'

I was beginning to think he'd been right. At the moment, I was tempted to pick up my toys and go home. Instead, I waited for Hogan and Saunders to return and then announced that I was taking a late lunch.

The cold was invigorating as I escaped the confines of the office, jumped in my vehicle, and took off, free to roam. Even being stuck between a covey of trucks suddenly felt liberating. I hummed to myself as we traveled in a line down pockmarked roads.

11

Large oil storage tanks, softened by the snow, had been magically transformed into igloos, their steel staircases meandering silver vines. Mountains of rock salt were no longer simply waiting to be scattered on hazardous roadways, but had morphed into miniature versions of the Rockies, the Himalayas, and the Swiss Alps. As for Tripoli, Calcutta, and Neptune – each formerly dingy street suddenly seemed exotic and foreign. I soon spotted the same lunch truck that I'd seen earlier that morning.

The Kielbasa House sat parked in its usual spot where Magda was serving a few late afternoon customers. It was easy to see why her luncheonette was the busiest one at the port. She offered homemade kielbasa and pierogi rather than the usual tasteless fare. I could easily scarf down a plateful of the doughy pockets filled with either potato, cabbage or, my favorite, sweet farmers cheese. But right now, the aroma of Polish sausage was calling to me.

I waited until the last trucker was gone before walking over. Magda had her back turned, and was already hard at work closing up shop for the day.

'Hi, Magda. Have you anything left for a hungry customer?' I asked.

She jumped in surprise, as though a ghost had stealthily snuck up behind her. Whirling around, her hand flew to her heart and her complexion turned pale.

'My goodness, Rachel! You startled me,' she scolded and nervously glanced about. 'The pierogis are all gone. But there's still some kielbasa left. Wait a minute and I'll make you one.'

I watched as Magda placed a thick sausage on the grill, along with onions and sweet peppers. She looked so thin and frail, I could almost see her vertebrae sticking through her thin winter coat. Only something new had been added.

A large shawl lay draped about her shoulders and neck, its color that of rich red claret. It must have been warm because, for once, she wasn't shivering. Rather, Magda appeared to be perfectly comfortable working in the frigid cold. The shawl was probably about six feet in length, for it wound several times around her. Ragged fringe hung from its edge, and a set of initials were crudely embroidered in one corner. That seemed to imply that the stole had been hand made.

I tried to read the letters, but wasn't quick enough, as Magda turned back to face me. In any case, the wool seemed to be either pashmina or cashmere. The shawl was finely crafted, quite exquisite, and had obviously cost a good deal of money.

'That's a beautiful shawl, Magda,' I commented, as she handed me the kielbasa nestled in a roll.

'Yes, and it's very warm,' Magda replied, her fingers gently stroking the wool.

My own fingers eagerly clutched the bread, grateful for the warmth that emanated from the grilled sausage.

'Where did you get it?' I asked and bit into the meat, its sweet juices bursting inside my mouth.

'It's a gift from a friend,' Magda answered with a smile.

'You know, I saw you with the police this morning,' I followed up between bites, suddenly feeling quite ravenous.

I wanted to question the woman, but knew enough to be careful not to spook her. She already seemed to be on edge.

'Yes, I know,' Magda solemnly responded as her eyes filled with tears. 'Something terrible happened. It was a horrible thing. Horrible.'

'I heard you found a body,' I added, hoping that she would continue.

Magda's eyes once again began to dart around. I casually followed their course, wondering what could possibly be making her so nervous. However, rather than speak, she busied herself with cleaning, choosing not to respond. Only I wasn't yet ready to let go.

'What were you doing in that empty field at the crack of dawn?' I pursued, egged on by my curiosity.

She cleared her throat, stalling for time, her reluctance having become a palpable living thing.

'I've been parking my truck across the street at night. You know, in the warehouse lot that's filled with wheels. The owner said it would be all right. Oh, I hope he doesn't get angry now that the police are snooping around,' she anxiously replied.

'But don't you drive your truck home at the end of each day? Or does somebody give you a lift?' I questioned, having no idea where it was that she lived.

Magda bit her lip and lowered her head, as if in shame. 'The truck is my home now. I lost my apartment close to a month ago.'

I looked at her in astonishment, not having realized that Magda was in such dire straits.

'You're not saying that you sleep inside your truck?' I blurted in disbelief.

Magda nodded, her chin bobbing in and out of the folds of the shawl. 'I scrub it every day after work, and a friend lent me a sleeping bag.'

'But how can you possibly sleep out here in this cold?' I questioned, feeling both frustrated and embarrassed not to have known.

Magda stoically shrugged, which only made me feel all the worse. 'I run the heater full blast before going to sleep. If I wake up, I turn it on again for a while. That helps to take the chill off. It's really not so bad.'

I could scarcely believe what I heard. I wouldn't have left a dog or cat outside, no less a person.

'I'm sure there must be a shelter where you can sleep. At least temporarily, until you find another place to stay.'

But it was as if I'd suggested that Magda be locked up in prison.

'No! I won't go to one of those horrible places. They're filthy, and the people . . . they steal,' she vehemently declared, her voice trembling with rage.

Then she began to scrub the grill and ignored me, making it clear that the subject was off-limits.

'Fine. Just as long as you're all right,' I replied, and let a moment slide before returning to the topic of interest. 'So, you were parked across the street last night? Then you must have seen what happened.'

Magda slowly turned back again to face me. This time her expression was full of pain. 'No. It was dark. The sound of a car woke me up and then there was the glare of the headlights. They were so bright.'

'Did you hear anything? Voices, perhaps?' I continued to prod.

Magda quickly glanced around once more, and then leaned over the counter. She motioned to me and I followed, as if pulled by a string.

'I did see two people get out and open the trunk. They dragged something from inside and carried it into the field,' she revealed in a whisper. 'They stayed there for a while and then eventually left. I waited a long time after that. Maybe two or three hours. I lay listening to the pounding of my heart until the sky turned light. Only then did I go and take a look.'

It was now my turn to wait as Magda covered her face with her hands and drew a tremulous breath. I held my own, having become a captive audience.

'What did you find?' I finally asked, unable to wait any longer.

'I found a woman lying dead in the snow. Her skin was so white it didn't look real. And then there were her eyes and that mouth . . .' Magda shuddered at the memory.

'What about them?' I asked, dying to know.

Magda's eyes locked on to mine, as if afraid to let go. 'They'd been sewn shut with black thread. She couldn't have screamed no matter how hard she tried.'

We were both quiet, as if imagining her whimpering sobs locked in the back of her throat.

'Could you tell if she'd been shot?' I asked, eventually breaking the silence.

Magda continued to hold my eyes as if hanging on for dear life. 'No. There were no bullet wounds.'

'Maybe she'd been stabbed,' I lightly proposed.

But Magda brushed aside the suggestion. 'No. No knife marks. No blood. There were only purple bruises around her neck.' Her hand crept up to her throat, as if to make sure the blemishes hadn't spread to her own skin. 'I saw nothing else. After that, a police car drove by and I ran into the road and waved it down. That's all I can tell you.'

Purple bruises were something I knew about all too well. I'd nearly been choked to death while stationed in Texas. The experience had taught me an important lesson: never

15

wear a leather cord around my neck that could be used against me as a weapon. Ligature marks would most likely reveal that Bitsy von Falken had been strangled.

Magda's elbows remained planted on the counter where she buried her head. Soon she was covered in a sea of claret. It was as if the shawl were beckoning to me. I couldn't help but reach out and touch it. My fingers lingered in its folds, having never felt anything so luxurious in all of my life.

'I'm so sorry you had so see that,' I quietly said.

Magda raised her eyes and dried her tears. Then she grasped hold of my hand.

'Oh, you're so cold. Here, give me your other hand and I'll warm them up for you,' she offered.

I didn't protest, but let her wrap them in the stole.

My hands floated inside material that was light as gossamer and sinfully sensuous. Ultra-soft and thin, the wool could have been a mound of downy feathers; it weighed no more than air. Yet within minutes, my hands were so toasty that they nearly began to sweat.

'This shawl is so nice and warm. Where did you say that you got it again?' I asked.

Magda softly giggled, as if about to reveal a secret. 'I told you. A friend gave it to me. It's good for the cold. Yes?'

It *was* good for the cold. Which made me wonder why she hadn't been wearing it this morning.

'What kind of wool is it?' I asked, and gently rubbed the fabric against my cheek.

Perhaps Magda felt I was being too forward, for she abruptly unwrapped my hands and pulled the shawl away.

'I don't know. Wool is wool. I have to close up now,' she said.

She lowered the counter window, and I slowly walked back to my SUV.

Magda was right. Wool is wool is wool. Only some wools are vastly more expensive than others, and then there are those that are highly illegal.

A sickening feeling began to take hold. It was one that, for now, I didn't want to think about, much less know.

Three

I wrote up a few more tickets until four thirty rolled around and everyone promptly rushed out. It was as if a school bell had rung and officially announced dismissal. I hung back, choosing not to be part of the throng. Besides, I knew what awaited me on the road. I'd be swallowed up in a mob of cars. Finally, having no other choice, I climbed into my vehicle and gave way to being part of rush hour traffic.

My Trailblazer joined the horde that inched along the Jersey Turnpike. It gave me plenty of time to take in the local scenery. Row houses stood etched against clouds of smoke spewing from refinery stacks. It billowed like grimy scarves being pulled from a magician's sleeve. Then I looked to my right and my heart did a somersault. There was the place that I'd left for so long. I'd finally returned home to New York.

The Statue of Liberty seemed to welcome me back as it followed my Ford, never choosing to leave my sight. However, there was still a gap where the Twin Towers used to be. If I tried hard enough, I could almost paint them in once more with my mind. Then I'd look again only to find that they were really gone.

The city was where I'd been born and raised. It was the one true, solid thing in my life. Or, at least, that's what I'd always believed. But I'd been feeling lost of late, having bounced around for so many years. My friend, Terri, had suggested that maybe I needed to re-connect with my roots. Perhaps he'd been right. In this case, my Africa was New York City.

I followed the traffic into the Holland Tunnel and held my breath, anxious to reach the end. Once inside the tunnel,

I always had the same vision. I imagined one tile popping off the wall, followed by another and another. Then a trickle of water would begin to seep in. I'd watch in growing horror as the volume continued to swell until tiles shot off the walls like rockets. But, as in all good horror flicks, there was still more to come. That would only be the beginning.

A torrent of water next came hurtling in from the tunnel's opposite end. Then the crest would rise up along my tires. Soon it would slip into the car, and my feet would begin to get wet. The cold, dark liquid would tickle my ankles, climb past my calves, and scale my legs to slowly cover my thighs. All the while, I'd be pounding on the car door and windows knowing that I was going to die.

'*Don't be afraid,*' little fish would say, as they'd swim past with their mouths agape. '*Just take a last breath, and then swallow the water. For you, there is no escape.*'

Terrified screams would ring in a concerto of death as the tunnel walls began to cave in. We'd all be crushed beneath concrete and grime, buried in a watery grave. I had no doubt that my very last thought would be exactly the same as I had right now: *Life would be so much easier if only I didn't have to deal with lousy bumper-to-bumper rush hour traffic.*

The red tail lights of cars glowed eerily on porcelain white walls as I carefully checked the tunnel again. Their luminous splotches resembled splatters of blood, which only added to my catastrophic vision.

I expelled a sigh of relief as I exited on to the street, and was enveloped in a madcap swirl of activity. Gone was my nightmare, replaced by a multitude of people and noise. It was as if I'd been dropped in the middle of a movie.

The lights in high rise buildings beamed like stars in the night. They twinkled inside their concrete and steel constellations. Their reflection bathed the road so that taxis speeding by were immersed in their glow. The stream of vehicles morphed into glittering yellow chariots.

The city's pulse rippled through the air, and steam rose from beneath the street. It was as if Manhattan's very soul were being stoked. New York was twenty-three square miles of high-speed energy and non-stop performance art. And at the moment I was the only actor on stage, with one-and-a-half million residents comprising my audience.

An electric current raced beneath my tires, its vibration reaching up into my seat. A low roar announced that I was riding atop a subway train, and I knew right then and there that New York City was the greatest place on earth.

I drove the city's width to the Lower East Side, parked in the municipal garage on Essex, and briskly walked home. Sherlock Holmes could keep London, and Poirot could have Paris. As for me, I'd take Manhattan over either any day.

I'd chosen to live where New York first began, and where the term 'melting pot' had originally been coined. At one time, this spot had been deemed the most crowded place on earth. It was a neighborhood that had seen countless waves of immigrants come and go. In that sense, little had changed. People continued to move in and out, leaving traces of their passage along the way. What had become altered was mainly its exterior.

Formerly squalid tenements had recently been gentrified, with hefty rents to match. There was still McDonald's, with its ethnic offering of ranchero bagels, but the fast food chain was being steadily overrun by hip and expensive wine bars. My grandmother had once dreamed of escaping this neighborhood. Little would she believe what I was paying to live here today.

No matter. The area appealed to me with its eclectic mix of ethnic groups that merged into a unique native stew. Jews, Puerto Ricans, Dominicans and Chinese all crowded its streets in a concoction of young and old, hip and frumpy. The aroma of chicken soup from Jewish delis mingled with dumplings from Chinese restaurants, as Eastern European pickle shops vied for space with Turkish bakeries.

I took a deep whiff and the heady bouquet nearly carried me away. What brought me back to reality were a couple of roosters squaring off in an alley. The two cocks were about to duke it out over a piece of stale pizza crust. The scene managed to nail the Lower East Side's plucky personality.

I approached my apartment on Orchard Street. As far as I was concerned, it had the perfect location. My place was around the corner from El Sombrero Restaurant and Katz's Deli, with Il Laboratorio di Gelato just down the block. Entering the building, I walked upstairs to the third floor. There was something comforting in knowing that my grandmother and mother had done the same thing before me. Call me crazy, but it made me feel as if I were still surrounded by family.

I opened the door and walked in to find Santou and Spam stretched out on the couch together watching the news. Jake's arm rested on the fifty-pound pit bull, while Spam lay with his head nestled on his master's chest. I took in the scene and quietly chuckled. The two had bonded ever since we'd found the pooch as an abandoned pup in Hawaii.

'Hey, chère. You're just in time,' Jake said, gazing up at me from beneath a pair of hooded lids. 'Look at this. Did you know that a dead socialite was found at the port today?'

I followed to where he pointed at the TV. Damn! A reporter was broadcasting from the same exact spot where I'd been standing earlier this morning. Magda could be seen in the background wearing her flowered babushka. But the camera didn't stop there. It made sure to pan over to her silver tin can of a home, The Kielbasa House, with its name prominently displayed on the side. No wonder she'd been so nervous during our meeting. Why didn't the news crew just pin a big red bullseye on her?

'Oh, God. Why do they have to do that?' I groaned.

'What? Show the murder scene?' Santou asked, as I leaned over and gave him a kiss.

But he wasn't about to let me off that easy.

'Come back here, woman,' he said, and pulled me down for another as Spam joined in to lick my face.

I curled up in Jake's arms and jockeyed with Spam for space.

'No. Make sure to show the one possible witness to the crime,' I explained. 'See the woman in the babushka? That's Magda, and The Kielbasa House is her mobile luncheonette. She's been sleeping inside there. Magda had a bird's-eye view of what went on when the body was dumped.'

Jake gave a low whistle and shook his disheveled black

curls. 'The press. You've got to love them. By the way, did you know that the victim was Bitsy von Falken?'

I nodded, my face rubbing against his stubbled cheek.

'Interesting timing,' he continued. 'There are rumors that her husband's company is in trouble.'

'What kind of trouble?' I immediately followed up.

I admit it. Part of my interest was purely professional, while the other half was because I loved gossip.

'Hyde Barrow is about to come under investigation for investor fraud,' he explained.

Santou was again working for the FBI, having spent a year in Hawaii recovering from a back injury. He'd been assigned to the Manhattan office after I'd put in my own request for a transfer. My superiors in DC had been more than happy to comply, and promptly planted me in Newark.

My new boss, Jack Hogan, had been right. The station wasn't just low-key, but completely off the radar. The New York office was the superstar. All high-profile cases in the area wound up there. It was a sore point that continued to eat away at me.

New York had been a hard adjustment for Santou to make, though he was happy to be in the field again. He'd grown up in Louisiana with its bayous, gators, and Cajun food. New York was a completely different world for him. But it was one that Spam and I both loved.

Spam was thrilled with all the new odors to be sniffed on each corner, and there was a park just around the block. As for me, I was once again mastering the fine art of dashing between moving cars, using my horn too much, and viewing eye contact as an act of overt aggression.

It was true. Living in a city apartment did take some getting used to. Santou still referred to our place as the equivalent of a veal pen. I considered that a small price to pay for any number of reasons, not the least of which was its sentimental value.

The apartment had not only been my grandmother's, but was also where my mother had grown up. Besides, it did have a certain amount of charm. The place boasted wide plank hardwood floors and taller-than-average windows.

Granted, there wasn't enough hot water and the radiators pumped way too much heat. But that's what windows were for. I simply cracked them open and let the cool air blow in. The only drawback was that the apartment also came with the city's very own version of wildlife – cockroaches, a creature that I'd always detested.

I left Jake and Spam on the couch and walked toward the kitchen, my antennae set on high alert. If the apartment was a veal pen, then the kitchen was the size of a thimble. No problem. Few people cooked in the city anyway. It was a shortcoming that suited me just fine. After all, this was the land of take-out. Which was why I was surprised to spot a large round Tupperware container sitting on the counter.

'What's this?' I called to Jake.

'Gerda dropped it off. It's half of a cake that she baked,' he responded.

Gerda wasn't only our neighbor, but so much more. She and my grandmother had been in a concentration camp together. Gerda was a young girl at the time – part of a group of youngsters that had drawn butterflies on their barrack walls using fingernails, pebbles, and whatever else was available. My grandmother, who'd been a few years older, had done what she could to keep them all safe.

After liberation, the two were inseparable and had immigrated to New York together. They'd shared this apartment until Ida got married. Then Gerda had moved next door.

'Of course, it looked much different back then,' Gerda once laughingly told me. 'I think the word "hovel" would have best described it.'

I used to sit as a child and listen to her tales of pushcart vendors and Yiddish theatre, entranced as she played the piano and slipped pieces of candy into my eager hands. If I listened closely, I could hear strains of music coming from her place even now.

After my grandmother died, an aunt took over the apartment. But she'd been getting on in years and had recently decided to move in with her daughter. I'd come back just in time to claim it as my own. Upon arriving, I'd immediately been adopted by Gerda. Or maybe we simply picked up where we'd left off so long ago.

'Oh, yeah. And Terri's going to join us tonight for dinner. Apparently, Eric's working late and Lily has a date. I guess he's feeling a little blue,' Santou informed me.

No sooner had he said the words than our buzzer rang.

'Let me in before I freeze to death out here,' Terri wailed over the intercom.

I buzzed him up and unlocked the door.

'For chrissakes, Rach. Tell me again why it is that you live all the way downtown?' Terri groused, as he breezed inside. 'It's certainly not for the charm. I swear to God, sometimes I think that you're bound and determined to channel your dead grandmother. Not a good idea. So let me save you some time and trouble and perform a quickie exorcism.'

Terri threw his arms wide open, as if he were about to placate the gods.

'Ida, for the love of Abraham, Isaac, and Moses, please let your granddaughter go! There, that ought to do it. Now maybe you and Santou can move closer to civilization.'

Terri was apparently feeling close to the spirit world tonight. His blond curls bounced on the collar of his faux rabbit fur coat, as he sank into my latest Salvation Army got-it-for-a-steal chair.

Terri Tune had been my former landlord in New Orleans. Since that time we'd become fast friends. Stylish, well mannered, musically talented, and with the skill of a make-up artist, Terri was the girl that my mother had always hoped I would grow up to be. Instead, she'd ended up with a daughter who'd gone into law enforcement, lived in jeans, and carried a gun.

Terri had recently moved to New York with his significant other, Eric. I'd helped them out a few years ago when Eric's daughter, Lily, had run away. Now the three of them lived as a family in Chelsea, a section of Manhattan famous for its brownstones, hot new art galleries, and gorgeous men.

Terri removed his coat and I took a closer look at my friend. He'd already been tan, but was now as brown as a tobacco leaf.

23

'What's going on? Did you take a trip to Miami that I don't know about?' I asked, secretly envious that he might have escaped someplace warm in the middle of winter.

Terri preened in his chair with the insouciance of a Vogue model. 'It looks pretty natural, huh? I didn't go anywhere other than the local tanning salon on my block.'

'Actually you're looking a little too well-baked,' Jake astutely observed. 'Maybe you should think about laying off the sun lamp for a while.'

Terry glared at him as though he were nuts. 'Don't be ridiculous. Being this tan is all the rage. Besides, I have to do something to combat the winter doldrums. And I'll have you know that I don't use a sun lamp, but the latest cutting edge technique – UV free airbrush tanning, which doesn't harm or age the skin. Speaking of which, you could stand a dose of it yourself,' he advised Santou. 'Anyway, what else can I do? I'm chained to a phone in a windowless office five nights a week. It's not like I can get away. My boss keeps promising that we're going to move, but so far I haven't envisioned myself in new headquarters any time in the near future.'

'Maybe what you need is a new crystal ball,' Jake wryly commented.

Terri was working as a telephone psychic these days. In fact, he was in such high demand that his company had recently given him a hefty raise. Terri swore that he'd inherited the gift of second sight from his mother. True or not, he'd clearly tapped into something astounding. '*Mr T*', as he was professionally known, had become so popular that there was talk of putting him on his own cable TV show.

'On the bright side, I'll still be in show business. And who knows? Maybe it'll help me to get a decent gig as a female impersonator again. I'd thought San Francisco was tough, but New York is totally ridiculous,' Terri had complained. 'Sure, I could work in a schlock club for next to nothing. But Eric and I are planning to get a weekend house, and my boss just agreed to give me a 401k.'

Even I could foresee there were going to be bright things in his future.

Spam began to whine as we walked out the door without

24

him. The poor pooch couldn't understand why we didn't just cook dinner on the beach anymore.

As for Terri, he needn't have attempted to exorcise Ida. The neighborhood had already done that pretty much on its own. We hit the street and were immediately swept up into cool pop heaven.

We passed a café where a muffin and tea cost an easy ten bucks. Unbelievably, teenage kids were its main clientele. I used to wonder how they could afford it until, one day, I saw them glued to their laptops. They sipped tea while buying and selling items on eBay for profit.

Equally strange was that the formerly staid Ludlow and Rivington Streets were now the main axis of hip. It's there that chi-chi clubs drew crowds every night of the week. And while one could still haggle for bargains on clothes and leather goods, the old Jewish stores were rapidly being replaced by trendy designer boutiques. Anything to do with Ellis Island was suddenly *très chic*.

We strolled by a pickle store where the smell of brine rolled over me in a wave of remembrance. I used to come with my grandmother when a pickle cost only a nickel. The store owner liked to joke that was still the case today. The only difference was that they now had to charge forty-five cents in tax.

'Let me guess. We're going to that Dominican dive that you like so much,' Terri predicted as we rounded a corner.

'That's amazing. You got it on the first try,' I replied with a grin.

This was what I considered to be the Lower East Side at its best – a place where the cost of each dish was under twelve bucks. We feasted on garlic shrimp, fried pork chops, rice with Dominican sausage, and bananas drenched in honey.

'Next time I get to choose the place,' Terry said, popping a breath mint into his mouth after dinner. 'Now I have to head off for the salt mines.'

'Don't worry. I predict that some day soon you'll be rich and famous,' I assured him. 'Just wait and see. Word of your psychic ability is going to spread, and all New York society will be clamoring at your door.'

'Brad Pitt, I'll make time for. The others will just have to wait their turn,' Terri responded and gave me a kiss.

'But we'll get our fortunes told for free, of course,' Santou joked.

'For Rachel, yes. As for you, I'll probably charge double,' Terri saucily retorted, and grabbed a cab to work.

Jake and I slowly made our way back home. It didn't matter that it was cold. Santou pulled me close and my world became warm.

'You haven't mentioned how work is going lately,' Jake said in passing conversation.

He should have known by now that was enough to open a can of worms.

'Same old, same old,' I replied. 'I'm not allowed to take a case unless a perp walks into my office, slaps down a few dozen dead endangered species on my desk and says, *Here. This is just so you'll know that I'm smuggling.* And we can both guess the likelihood of that.'

I looked off to my left while crossing Delancy. The Williamsburg Bridge loomed, with its cables as taut and strong as the muscular arms of a construction worker. We continued past weathered tenements on narrow streets. Each was decorated with vine-like trellises of old fire escapes. It wasn't necessary to peek around them to see that behind each lay New York's version of an urban backyard. I already knew because I had one of my own.

'Sometimes I feel like I'm just treading water and trying to minimize whatever loss I can. The problem is that I'm not making any headway,' I groused.

What I didn't say was that deep down I was bone-tired of constantly fighting, and worried that my fire was beginning to die out.

Santou was wise enough to not say a word. Instead, he continued to hold me close, and I knew that he had unspoken worries of his own.

What gnawed at me was being stuck in an office where I was viewed as nothing more than window dressing. How was I supposed to develop cases when I felt so trapped?

My foot struck something hard and I tripped, nearly falling

flat on my face. It was Santou's steadying arm that saved me. I examined the offending item with my toe. It was a tree root that had pushed its way up through the snow and ice from beneath the brick strewn soil. The message couldn't have been any more clear. Adapt and thrive. Otherwise, leave or die. There was simply no other choice.

Four

Jake and I headed out together early the next morning. Only I made my way toward the parking garage while he took Spam for a walk. I stopped at a nearby news stand and bought the daily paper. There it was in bold, black letters strewn across the front page. The headline blared: BITSY VON FALKEN FOUND DEAD IN ABANDONED JERSEY LOT.

Just terrific, I thought.

I quickly read the article. Sure enough, Magda was mentioned, though not by name. Instead, the piece revealed there was a possible eyewitness that owned a luncheonette truck at the port. That should make it easy enough for any wily predator to hunt her down.

Idiots, I fumed, while climbing into the Trailblazer.

I was still cursing to myself as I parked in front of Kossar's Bialys and picked up a bag of fresh bagels. I'd become spoiled since returning to New York. These weren't the sad lumps I'd gotten used to while away, the out-of-town imposters baked with blueberries and sun-dried tomatoes, among other offenses. Rather, they were honest-to-goodness firm-on-the-outside, chewy-on-the-inside New York bagels topped with sesame, poppy seeds, garlic and salt, just as God had intended. I stashed the bag inside my Trailblazer and took off.

I drove as quickly as possible through the Holland Tunnel, all the while watching to make certain that tiles didn't pop off. I safely emerged into a different world.

Industrial New Jersey lay spread out before me. I sped past abandoned factories, their windows covered with sheet metal like pennies on a dead man's eyes. It made me think back once more to what Magda had told me. The image was now permanently seared in my brain. What kind of maniac would have sewn Bitsy von Falken's eyelids and mouth shut? I couldn't stop shivering, though the heat in the vehicle was turned up full blast.

I tried to occupy my thoughts by staring out the window. No problem there. I found plenty to look at. New Jersey has the densest railroad and highway system in the country. But that's not where it stops. The state also contains one hundred and eight toxic waste dumps.

A flock of seagulls flew over one now, and I wondered if Jonathon Livingston ever realized that he was hovering above a strip of oil refineries. It's earned the area an apt nickname: Oilfield U.S.A., boasting the largest petroleum containment system outside the Middle East.

But this section of New Jersey has gained additional fame as well. Terrorism experts recently dubbed the stretch between Newark Airport and the seaport to be the most dangerous two miles in America. The strip is a chemical juggernaut possessing more than one hundred potential targets. Among them are chlorine gas processing plants. An attack on one could be lethal to twelve million people within a fourteen-mile radius.

I approached Newark. Its disjointed skyline resembled a mouthful of jagged teeth. My own choppers were tightly on edge as I continued to think about Bitsy von Falken. The lot where she'd been found was one hell of a bleak, unmemorable place to be dumped in.

I wondered if her death had been a tragic act of passion, perhaps a love affair gone awry. Or had it been a deliberate crime, as cold and heinous as the black thread that pierced her eyelids? There were always clues left behind. It was just a matter of connecting the dots. In which case, I couldn't help but wonder what the Port Authority police might have discovered.

I parked, still stewing over this morning's article as I made my way into the office and sat down. The red light on my answering machine repeatedly blinked in frustration, as if worried it might be overlooked. I hit the play button, leaned back, and listened to the message.

'I see that Bitsy von Falken was found at the seaport yesterday. That's funny, considering I'd never have dreamt she'd be caught dead in such a place. In any case, she might have been wearing a shawl. If so, you'll want to check it out. The thing is shahtoosh, which I understand is illegal. It's also worth a fortune. Oh, yes. By the way, she wasn't the only Park Avenue bitch that's wearing them around town. Those shawls could be the unofficial flag of the Upper East Side. Ta ta, and happy hunting!' the woman's voice cheerfully signed off.

I copied down my 'anonymous' informant's name, along with her phone number. It didn't matter that she hadn't volunteered the information. It was conveniently stored on my caller ID. You'd think by now everyone would have known not to make an anonymous call from their home, thanks to shows like *Law and Order* and *CSI*. Evidently, Tiffany Stewart didn't watch a lot of TV.

Hmm. Although Ms Stewart had a Manhattan area code, her accent had sounded southern. I gave it no more than a passing thought. All I cared about right now was that I might finally have a case on my hot little hands. With that in mind, I picked up the phone and dialed Officer Nunzio, my friendly Port Authority cop.

'This is Special Agent Rachel Porter,' I announced, once he was on the line. I only hoped the title Special Agent made me sound kick-ass official. 'We met at the crime scene yesterday.'

'Yeah, I remember you,' he said, sounding thoroughly unimpressed. 'I'm kinda busy right now. What's up?'

So much for the exchange of any pleasantries.

'I was just wondering if you could possibly answer a question,' I replied.

But Nunzio obviously wasn't one to waste time.

'Probably not,' he responded.

'Well, let's give it a try anyway,' I suggested, and proceeded to launch into my inquiry. 'I just received a tip that Bitsy von Falken might have been wearing an unusual shawl. The wool for it is from endangered Tibetan antelopes that are protected under international law in over one hundred and forty-seven countries,' I said, purposely piling on the facts.

'What do you think? Can you help me out here?'

I knew he was still on the line because I could hear him breathing.

'Did she have one on?' I pressed.

'A woman's been killed and this is what you're calling me about? Some Goddamn shawl?' he replied. 'Where in the hell are your priorities?'

'You have your job and I have mine,' I replied, feeling slightly guilty until I remembered the excitement in his voice at having found a dead body yesterday. 'So, did you find one or not?'

Nunzio cleared his throat of morning phlegm, as if giving himself time to think.

'Come on. It's not like I'm asking about the murder weapon or vital evidence from the crime scene,' I continued to plead.

'Yeah, but you know the rules. This is an active investigation. I'm not supposed to talk about anything,' Nunzio said, as if reciting from an official police handbook.

'And I'm not the press. I'm a federal agent. I swear not to interfere or step on your toes as far as the case is concerned. So, how about it?' I would have promised the moon to get what I wanted.

'Aw, what the hell,' Nunzio finally relented. 'The press already knows just about everything on this case anyway. I don't see how giving you this information will make any difference.'

Yes! I silently rejoiced. Then I held my breath, waiting to hear that Bitsy von Falken had indeed gone to meet her Maker draped in a shahtoosh shawl.

'Nope, we didn't find anything like that,' he responded.

Damn!

I thanked him and hung up. But I wasn't yet ready to call it quits. Instead, I high-tailed it into Jack Hogan's office.

'What's up, Grasshopper?' he asked, without raising his head from his newspaper.

It gave me quite the view. The few wispy strands of hair that clung to his scalp for dear life were still damp from their morning shower.

'I just had an interesting message on my answering

31

machine,' I informed him. 'A tip was left that Bitsy von Falken might have been wearing a shahtoosh shawl when she died. Do you know if any shipments of shahtoosh have ever been smuggled into this port?'

'Sure. We found one a couple of years ago,' Hogan matter-of-factly retorted. 'Some company here in Jersey was bringing them in.'

Bingo! If *that* wasn't hard-core proof of smuggling, then I didn't know what was. There was no way that Hogan could stop me from opening a case now.

'Great. I take it that the owner was convicted,' I said, my pulse beginning to stir.

'Nah. We couldn't prove that the company knowingly violated the law. The owner claimed they thought the stuff was cashmere. He swore he'd never even heard of shah-toosh. So we slapped them with a three-hundred-and-fifty-dollar fine and told them not to make that same mistake again. That was it. Case closed,' Hogan replied.

Terrific. A 350-dollar fine amounted to no more than a speeding ticket. But then Fish and Wildlife's penalty system was routinely used by companies as a cost of doing busi-ness. Get caught, pay a fine, and continue on with trade as usual. It was cynically referred to, by both agents and inspec-tors alike, as *Monty Hall Justice,* or *Let's Make A Deal.* The message that it sent was loud and clear: This is American commerce, where everything can be negotiated away.

'Well then, they're probably at it again,' I surmised. 'Bitsy von Falken had to get that shawl from somewhere. And evidently she wasn't the only socialite that's running around town wearing one.'

'If you're trying to open an investigation, forget about it, Porter. That company closed up shop two years ago. They're long gone. Besides, one shawl on a dead socialite does not a case make,' he shrewdly observed. 'Did you bother to even ask the PA police if they knew anything about it?'

'Yes,' I reluctantly responded.

'And? What was the upshot?' Hogan inquired. 'Do they have the damn thing?'

'No. They said it wasn't there,' I was forced to admit.

'Then there's your answer,' Hogan said, and returned to his newspaper.

But I had a pretty good idea as to where I could find it.

I went back to my desk, grabbed the bag of bagels, and stuck my head inside Wildlife Inspector Fuca's office.

'Good morning. How about trying the best bagel in New York?' I offered, and shook the bag as a peace offering.

Connie looked up from over her pile of papers and hesitantly smiled.

'Sure. Why not?'

I plunked the bag on her desk and we each took a bagel.

'Sorry to have snapped at you yesterday,' she said after the first bite. 'It's just that sometimes this whole thing really hits me. I've become nothing more than a paper pusher and it's frustrating as hell. I begin to forget why I ever took this job.'

'I can relate to that,' I told her. 'I'm itching to do a case, and instead wind up writing violations all day like some kind of glorified meter maid. Newark isn't turning out to be my dream station, either.'

'That's odd. Everyone else here seems content with having their ass planted behind a desk. You got some kind of problem with that?' Connie wryly joked.

'Yeah. It makes me edgy when I'm not digging into things. But then, I've never worked at a port before,' I replied.

'Get used to it,' she advised. Her fingers gathered stray poppy seeds into a neat little pile. 'You're one of us now.'

'How do you figure that?' I asked.

'Because we're both forced to operate under an identical set of rules. We only do inspections when there's major suspicion of smuggling, the same as agents. Otherwise, we're totally bogged down with paperwork,' she responded, and waved a hand at her desk. 'Do you want to guess how often I'm able to go into the field and examine what comes in?'

I hadn't realized the situation was equally bad for inspectors. The thought was appalling. Wildlife imports into Newark had increased 332 percent over the past six years. Without a doubt, the US was now every wildlife trafficker's number one destination.

Creatures were routinely sliced and diced into jewelry, turned into Chinese medicines, and transformed into ornamental statues, lamps, shoes, and belts. Then there was the black market live-animal trade that supplied pet stores, circuses, collectors and laboratories. Add those together and illegal trafficking came to a staggering twelve billion dollars a year, all moving through an underground pipeline of flesh, feathers, and fur. Yet almost no inspections were being conducted.

'How can that be?' I asked in astonishment.

'Easy. Think about it. A million containers come into this port every year, of which about seven thousand are specifically reported to contain wildlife. And each of *those* shipments can hold up to fifteen hundred boxes apiece,' she explained, while grabbing a second bagel. 'If we *do* inspect anything, all we're likely find are only minor violations. That's because the real smugglers are smart enough to mark their shipments as containing something other than wildlife. They're listed instead as clothing, cookware, or pottery. Which means those containers are able to simply sail right on through. Much as I hate to admit it, not all the blame can be pinned on Hogan. It's the big wigs in D.C. that won't allow us to do our job.'

'But what about Customs Inspectors? Won't they catch those items that we don't?' I questioned, beginning to feel totally impotent.

'What, are you kidding? Most of them wouldn't know an elephant if it bit them on the butt,' Connie retorted with a sharp laugh. 'Not that it matters. Ocean cargo has always had the lowest rate of inspection in this country. I mean, come on. Ninety-eight percent of all containers are electronically cleared before they even land here. Sure, there used to be a random check of goods at one time. But not anymore. The truth is, Customs' attention is focused on just one thing these days. Terrorism is their only priority,' she said, setting me straight.

I had to concede it was certainly understandable. Ocean ports are deemed to be the soft underbelly of the nation's security, with six million containers flowing into the US

34

every year. Bin Laden knows this as well. He covertly owns a shipping fleet and has used it in the past to transport stockpiles of weapons. It's why cargo containers are now viewed as potential terror vehicles – the Trojan horses of the twenty-first century. Most experts predict it's the way in which the next terror attack will be launched.

Equally disturbing was that Newark is rumored to be the number one port on the terrorist hit list. A dirty bomb set off inside one container would successfully disrupt rail lines, oil refineries, the air traffic system, and highways, essentially crippling the economy.

'Even drug cases are way down since 9/11,' Connie revealed. 'We have no choice but to depend on the general public's honesty and integrity.'

'In other words, we're screwed,' I morosely summed up.

'You got it,' Connie agreed with a tight grin. 'Meanwhile, what little security we have here is pretty much of a joke. But then, what can you expect when Montana receives three times more money from the government than the Port of New York and New Jersey, and Houston gets five times as much?'

It was due to Homeland Security's financing formula, better known as 'follow the pork.' Money wasn't being allocated based on risk of attack, but rather on which politicians have the most clout. It's why Wyoming was granted thirty-eight dollars per person in anti-terrorism funds last year, while New Yorkers received just a measly five dollars and fifty cents apiece.

Not to mention ports in Martha's Vineyard and Arkansas that received funds, though they didn't even meet requirements for eligibility. It was enough to make me start drinking at ten o'clock in the morning.

'Sorry to have chewed your ear off,' she proffered.

'Don't be silly. It's interesting, even if its does make me want to go out and slit my wrists,' I joked. 'But now let me tell you the reason why I came in here.'

'You mean it was more than just to offer me a bagel?' Connie asked, playing the wide-eyed innocent.

'I'm afraid so. You heard about the woman that was found at the port yesterday?'

Connie nodded.

'Well, I received a tip this morning that she might have been wearing a shahtoosh shawl. The problem is, I have no idea how to differentiate it from cashmere or pashmina,' I explained. 'I'm not sure I could even identify shahtoosh if I saw it.'

'Shahtoosh, huh?' Connie seemed to think about it for a minute. 'OK. Let me give you a tip. Try this if you find a shawl and think that it might possibly be shahtoosh.'

Connie pointed to a ring on my right hand that had originally belonged to my grandmother.

'Take your ring off, and see if you can pull the shawl through it,' she suggested.

'An entire shawl?' I skeptically asked.

'Uh huh. There shouldn't be a problem if it's the real thing. Shahtoosh wool is about seven times finer than human hair. The fibers are so soft that they'll collapse into nothing. That's why a six-foot shawl can easily pass through a woman's ring without getting snagged.'

'Thanks for your help,' I said, and headed straight back to Hogan's office.

He sat picking at a sad looking donut on his desk.

'Here, why don't you try one of these?' I offered. 'I bought them fresh this morning on the Lower East Side.'

He gazed at me through a haze of red, and I wondered whether he'd drunk too much or just couldn't fall asleep last night.

'Thanks, Grasshopper,' he said, and plucked out a plump garlic bagel.

Perhaps Connie was right. Maybe Hogan wasn't such a bad guy, after all. But now wasn't the time to find out. I decided, rather than tell the truth, to play it safe and lie.

'An express shipping company just called from their office at the airport. They received a package containing snakeskin boots that don't have the proper permit. They asked if I'd drive by and pick them up. Do you mind?'

Hogan hesitated, and I knew that I had only one shot.

'What do you think of the bagel?' I asked.

'It's terrific. I can't get 'em like this in Jersey,' Hogan replied.

My fingers slid the paper sack across his desk. 'Here. Why don't you keep the whole bag? I'll be happy to bring in more whenever you like.'

Hogan slowly blinked and, for one brief moment, I wasn't certain what his decision would be. Then his stomach rumbled and a muscle twitched under his eye.

'Sure. Go ahead,' he said, and took the bribe.

Five

I got into my Trailblazer, turned on the heat, and pulled out on to Fleet Street. But rather than head for the airport, I went in search of Magda. The feeling that had been eating away at me since yesterday had only grown stronger. If Bitsy von Falken had been wearing a shahtoosh shawl, I was determined to know about it.

In Persian, *shahtoosh* means 'king of wool,' and that's exactly what it is – the most expensive and luxurious wool in the world, approaching near-mythic quality. The fibers are so fine, they're almost as soft as baby's skin. The shawls have been prized items in the dowries of well-to-do Indian brides, valued by that country's elite and much loved by maharajas for centuries. Legend has it that Napoleon gave one to Josephine, who was so enthralled she immediately ordered four hundred more. Even so, the animals still managed to survive. They were placed on the road to extinction in the mid-eighties. That was when designers discovered the shawls and fueled a craze, making them the most coveted garments on earth. Elevated from dowry treasures to 'must have' accessories, the stoles became the status symbols *par excellence* of the globe-trotting set. Tibetan antelopes, their fashion victims, have been sacrificed on the altar of human vanity ever since. A shy, sloe-eyed creature, also called a chiru, the antelope stands four feet tall, weighs eighty pounds, and has long elegant horns that rise almost vertically. Endowed with striking black markings and a swift, graceful gait, the animal and its fur have become legendary.

The chiru is native to the windswept plateaus and thin air on the roof of the world. It's there, eighteen thousand feet up in Tibet, that the small antelope braves blizzards, and forty-degree-below temperatures. Inaccessible as that seems, it hasn't stopped poachers from going after their prey and turning the area into the wild, wild West.

Organized gangs travel in high-speed jeeps, across barren and rocky plateaus, in order to reach the chiru's remote habitat. They hunt the antelope year round, filling the voracious demand for shawls in Europe, America, Hong Kong, and Japan. However, the Tibetan antelope can't be sheared for shahtoosh, unlike goats whose wool is made into pashmina and cashmere. The chirus' hair is too short and the only way to obtain it is by killing them.

In a grim twist of fate, hunters recently discovered chiru calving grounds high in the mountains, where pregnant females gather every summer with their young. It's in the midst of giving birth that vehicles surround them at night, switch on their headlights, and blind the animals in their glare. Poachers then open fire with automatic rifles and slaughter them by the thousands.

Those that manage to break away are chased by jeeps until they literally drop dead of stress and exhaustion. Afterwards, hunters skin them on the spot, leaving behind nothing but bloody carcasses. The pelts are sold for eighty-five dollars apiece to black marketers. Then merchants transport the wool by yak over remote Himalayan passes, through Nepal, and into Kashmir, where traders barter and buy the pelts in exchange for items such as tiger bones and drugs. Five pelts are required to make one six-foot shawl that is spun, woven, and embroidered with exquisite filigree, by an ancient weaving industry. From there the shawls are smuggled to fashion hot spots like Paris, Milan, and New York, where they're easily sold for twenty thousand dollars apiece.

Only a century ago, chiru numbered over one million strong. But fashion demand has driven them to the brink, reducing their population by ninety percent. Tibetan antelope are now on the endangered species list, having joined the ranks of tigers, rhinos, and great apes. In another ten years, the chiru will no longer exist. Apparently, the ultimate cost of fashion is the extinction of a species.

However, one other thing is helping to fuel their demise.

Profits from their pelts are also being used to buy arms. Tibetan antelopes have become the helpless pawns in a deadly trade of guns that are funneled to Islamic militants.

I spotted Magda's truck parked alongside the road and quickly pulled over. She was already busy setting up for the day. Even from here I could see the claret shawl that lay draped over her shoulders. 'Good morning, Rachel,' she cheerfully called, upon catching sight of me. 'How about a cup of coffee? I'll make you some.'

I got out and slowly walked towards her, each step feeling heavier than the last.

'Good morning, Magda. How are you today?' I asked, as her reddened fingers placed the cup in my hands.

I wondered if her skin would forever remain coarse and chafed from working outside in this weather. 'I'm fine,' she said, and raised her shoulders so that the shawl rose up to meet her chin. 'Things are much better now that I'm warm.'

I had never felt more cold, partly due to the bitter wind, and partly because I knew what was about to happen next.

'Has the shawl helped with that?' I inquired.

'Yes,' Magda replied, her face beaming like a child.

'Where did you say you got it again?' I asked, hoping for a different answer this time; something to placate my misgivings.

But Magda's demeanor quickly changed, confirming my worst suspicions. 'I already told you. It was a gift from a friend,' she responded, her fingers nervously plucking at the fringe.

'Would you mind taking it off for a minute? I'd like to have a closer look at the wool.'

For the first time, I truly hated my job. But I also knew there was no other choice. Magda stared at me as a look of fear crept back into her eyes.

'What for?' she asked dubiously.

'I need to check something. That's all,' I replied, my voice sounding flat to my ears. The woman crossed her arms defensively, and pulled the shawl about her tight as a cocoon.

'I'm sorry, Magda. But I really must insist. Please don't make me use my legal authority,' I said.

But I felt like a total bitch.

Magda reluctantly removed the shawl and handed it over, as her eyes welled up with tears.

I was once again struck by the shawl's weight. It felt as though I were holding nothing more than a cloud. Then, following Connie's instructions, I removed the ring from my finger; something I rarely did these days.

In the ring's center was a diamond, one that held special meaning. My grandfather had sewn a few gems into his coat during his rush to escape the Nazis. This was the only one that remained when he arrived in the US. He'd had it set in a ring when he married my grandmother.

I cherished it, not for the stone, but for what the ring revealed of my family history. It also held an important lesson. Power can be a dangerous aphrodisiac that must be used carefully.

I hoped I was doing so now as I slid one corner of the shawl inside the ring and easily pulled it through. I could scarcely believe my eyes and drew it through once again.

I looked up to see that Magda's mouth was trembling.

'Magda, this is a very expensive shawl that's called shahtoosh. You need to tell me the truth. How did you get hold of it?' I gently questioned.

But Magda refused to give in.

'How many times must I tell you? My friend is very generous. It was a gift. Why are you doing this to me?' she demanded, and burst into tears. The droplets froze like tiny icicles on her skin.

'Can you give me your friend's name? I'll need to ask her a few questions,' I said.

Magda shook her head and began to sob even harder. My throat tightened as she hugged her body through the thin winter coat, her shoulders furiously quivering.

'You won't tell me? Or you don't know?' I persisted. 'Please talk to me, Magda. If you help me, I promise that everything will be all right.'

However, Magda refused to listen to reason. 'You're confusing me. Please, just go away.'

I only wished it could have been that simple. I would have liked nothing more than to walk off and pretend I'd never seen the damn shawl in the first place. However, things had gone too far for that now.

'I'm sorry, Magda. I'm going to have to take the shawl with me. It has to be sent to our lab for testing. Shahtoosh is illegal. If that's what this turns out to be, and you're hiding something, you could wind up in trouble. Do you understand?'

Magda said nothing, but stared at me through a veil of tears. I'd never felt so wracked with guilt in all my life.

'Listen, Magda. There's one more thing you should know. This shawl costs twenty thousand dollars.'

Her eyes grew wide in surprise, but she continued to remain silent.

'Only someone very rich could afford to buy it. Even then, it would have to be purchased on the black market. Is that something you really want to be involved in? Think about it and give me a call,' I suggested.

I pulled out a business card bearing my office and cell-phone number, and placed it on the counter. Then I turned and walked back to my vehicle.

I returned to work, haunted by the image of Magda shivering in that poor excuse for a winter coat. Still, I couldn't stop my fingers from wandering over to the shawl. Its allure was undeniable. So much so, that I threw it over my shoulders in the Fish and Wildlife parking lot. Then I quickly took it off, realizing that I had draped myself in a bloody shroud.

I stashed it in my bag, hurried inside, and buried myself in paperwork. I remained there the rest of the morning until Hogan left for an early dental appointment. Only then did I scurry out of my room to show the shawl to Connie. I knocked on the door and walked into her office.

'What's up?' she asked, from behind a stack of papers that must have mushroomed overnight.

'You know that talk we had before? Well, I found something, and need your expert opinion. Hogan said you tripped across some shipments of shahtoosh here a few years ago. What do you think? Is that what this is?' I asked.

The shawl unfurled in my hands like fine wine spilling from a glass.

Connie stood up and walked over, a soft whistle escaping

her lips. The material seemed to float in the air as she examined the fringe and embroidered letters.

'You'll have to send it to the lab for positive ID. But my guess is yes. You can see the shawl is hand-woven, and these are probably the weaver's initials. Where did you get it?' she inquired.

'Possibly from a dead woman,' I grimly revealed.

Connie quizzically raised an eyebrow. 'The one found here at the port?'

'That's what I'm thinking. There are still a lot of unanswered questions. Do me a favor and don't tell Hogan. He doesn't know about it, and I'd like it to stay that way until I'm able to get more proof,' I explained.

'Don't worry. Your secret is safe with me. All I ask is that you keep me in the loop,' Connie requested.

'You've got a deal,' I agreed.

Then I packed up the shawl and sent it to our forensic lab in Oregon, along with a note. The director, Ken, was a friend and I knew that he wouldn't betray me. With that out of the way, this seemed a good time to pay Ms Tiffany Stewart a visit. I tracked down her address and took off for Manhattan.

My Trailblazer sped along the Jersey Turnpike, running parallel to the wind-swept waves of the Hudson River. Their scalloped edges deftly ensnared the light. Even from here I could see old abandoned piers and the rusted girders of twisted jetties, their skeletal remains disintegrating where they dotted the banks on the other side.

I took the Lincoln Tunnel, hoping to escape downtown traffic and, instead, landed smack in the bowels of Midtown. Fortunately, my city driving skills instinctively came back to me.

I always play by my fellow drivers' rules – ignore the traffic lanes, drive as fast as you can between lights, and don't stop until pedestrians get within an inch or two of your bumper. My success was duly noted in a variety of non-verbal ways, also known as how New Yorkers say *Have a nice day*. Jaywalkers flipped me the bird, while cab drivers flicked their hands beneath their chins and rudely cut me off.

I paid little heed, too caught up in all the activity going on around me. If car alarms and construction are the music of the city, then bike messengers are its chorus boys. I watched entranced as they wove in and out of traffic with the grace and ease of Broadway dancers, while taxis battled like schools of salmon struggling to swim upstream.

I hit Broadway, a long-ago Indian trail, and headed north toward Central Park. This was my oasis in the middle of the city. It was where I escaped Manhattan's feeling of twenty-four hour restlessness. I turned on a cross street, entered the park's confines, and was immediately engulfed in silence, embraced by an island within an island at the center of the world.

Snow-laden trees posed in winter garb, their limbs as gnarled as Martha Graham dancers. Beaux Arts lampposts regally stood planted every few yards, their frames tall and thin as Ichabod Crane. A hawk soared overhead and I wondered how many people knew this was a stopover for birds on the North American flyway. Probably not as many as those that still identified the park with muggers and crime.

I exited the park all too soon and crossed Fifth Avenue, the Continental Divide that separates the east from the west side. And just like that, the city once again changed. I turned on Park Avenue, and entered New York's bastion of privilege and wealth.

This is the heart of the Upper East Side where the oh-so-proper and the filthy rich reside. I drove past blocks of fancy townhouses and snooty boutiques in which I could never afford to shop. Like it or not, here I would forever be viewed as nothing more than another intruder.

Spotting a parking space, I refused to concede until I'd managed to squeeze in my SUV. Then I grabbed my cell-phone and called Tiffany Stewart's number.

'Hello?' answered a low, husky voice with a slightly Southern twang.

It was the kind of voice I'd always wanted – half Marlboros, half booze, and oozing with sex. No question but that this was the same person I'd heard on my answering machine.

'Is this Tiffany Stewart?' I inquired.

'Yes, it is. Why? Who is this?' she asked, as if poised to hang up on a telemarketer.

'I'm Agent Rachel Porter, with the US Fish and Wildlife Service. You left a message for me this morning.'

There was a moment of silence before she finally replied.

'I'm sorry, but you must have mistaken me for somebody else,' she stiffly responded.

'Not a chance. This is definitely the right number. You called to inform me of Bitsy von Falken's shahtoosh shawl. There's something I need to ask you. What color is it?' I pressed. My question was followed by an even longer pause than before.

'Listen, you can't squirm out of this. So let's stop playing games. Your name and number were recorded on my caller ID,' I informed her.

'Damn, I hate those things,' she muttered half to herself. 'Oh, all right. So, it was me. Big deal. I was just being a good citizen. You want to know the color of her shawl? It's claret. There. Are you satisfied now?' she asked, dropping all pretense.

'Not quite. I'd like to speak with you in person. Would it be all right if I come by?' I asked, fully prepared to knock down her door if necessary.

'Hmm. Let's see. Today is out. In fact, it looks as if my entire week is fully booked,' she responded, clearly stalling for time.

I was damned if I'd be placed at the back of her social calendar. 'OK, then. How about right now?' I countered, blatantly ignoring her response.

'Didn't you hear what I just said? I told you that today's out,' she repeated in annoyance.

'Well, you're obviously home at the moment, and I'm just around the corner. You'd be doing me a big favor. I promise to only take a few minutes of your time,' I replied, refusing to take *no* for an answer.

'My place is a mess,' she volleyed, in a half-hearted dodge.

'Don't worry. It can't be nearly as bad as mine,' I countered.

'I'd rather not,' she continued to resist.

'Let me make myself clear. I can come up now. Or you can travel to Newark with your lawyer,' I responded.

'For chrissake, what do they do? Give you people a course on how to harangue your way into someone's home?' she complained in exasperation.

'Yeah. As a matter of fact, it's called *Learn to be a Pushy Bitch 101,*' I blithely retorted.

I was caught off-guard as Tiffany Stewart suddenly started to laugh.

'OK, Sergeant Pepper. You've made your point. Come on up.'

'Rachel Porter,' I corrected.

'Yeah, yeah. Whatever. I take it you already have the address. I'll tell my doorman to let you in,' she replied, and hung up.

What a pleasant surprise. This was turning out to be easier than I'd expected. Perhaps dealing with Tiffany Stewart wouldn't be so difficult, after all.

I walked down the block to a brand new high-rise that reeked of opulence, style and class. Its crisp green awning formally announced that I'd reached *THE BUCKINGHAM.* Catchy title. I half expected to see a Changing of the Guard. Instead, I was greeted by a doorman in a dark blue pea coat and a stiff-brimmed cap.

'May I help you?' he asked, his eyes perusing my scruffy jacket, denim jeans, and kick-ass boots.

I immediately guessed he was about to suggest that I use the delivery entrance.

'I'm here to see Tiffany Stewart,' I quickly said, in order to spare him any embarrassment.

But his expression clearly stated, *I doubt that.*

'Your name?' he asked with a sniff, as if I were a vagrant that had wandered over from the wrong side of town.

'Special Agent Rachel Porter,' I replied in my haughtiest tone.

'Oh yes,' he said, and one-upped me with a slow blink and the barest hint of a nod. 'Mrs Stewart is expecting you. She's in apartment 30B on the thirtieth floor.'

I stepped into an elevator that was bigger than my apartment. New York was definitely a city of haves and have-nots and, at the moment, I was feeling pretty low on the economic food chain. In simple terms, I was on par with *Oriental Cup-of-Noodles* while Tiffany Stewart was unquestionably New Zealand rack-of-lamb.

The elevator effortlessly rose thirty floors without a hitch or a jerk, as if used to conveying valuable cargo. Its doors silently parted and I entered a hallway whose plush gray carpet muffled the sound of my footsteps.

Eenie, Meenie, Minie, Moe. I figured 30B should be easy enough to find since there were only four apartments on each floor. I rang its bell knowing that Tiffany Stewart was probably already standing behind the door.

The entrance opened, and I felt as if I'd been transported to Never Neverland. Donald Trump, eat your heart out. My eyes didn't know where to land first – on the enormous crystal chandeliers, the French-cut glass mirrors, or the fortyish, fit, and fabulous-looking woman that stood before me.

Tiffany Stewart was a combination of Dolly Parton, Pamela Anderson and Madonna all rolled into one. In fact, it was if she'd bought a few of their body parts and had her chassis reassembled.

Long blonde hair fell below her shoulders, its color the same glorious shade as that on Bitsy von Falken's corpse. Tiffany Stewart stood attired in a sweater laden with enough sequins to have blinded an army of onlookers. Even so, it was impossible not to notice her twin assets that rose majestic as the Himalayas beneath her skin tight top. Tiffany was either naturally well-endowed, or had found herself one heck of a good plastic surgeon.

The next thing to grab my eye was the humongous diamond choker that encircled her throat. The woman had more money hanging around her neck than I made in a single year. I was tempted to count the stones, but there were far too many. Besides it would have depressed me with thoughts of my all-too-minuscule savings account.

The remainder of her outfit consisted of black stretch pants over a pair of legs as long as two exclamation points, punctuated by blood-red Manolo Blahnik spike heels. The final fashion accoutrement was the teacup white poodle that lay in her arms. The pooch was about as large as the diamond on her ring.

Though I hadn't known what to expect, this certainly wasn't it. Tiffany Stewart was far from your average run-of-the-mill tight-ass socialite.

'Well, come in. Just kick your boots off on the mat, and hang your jacket on the rack,' she instructed, and motioning with her lit cigarillo.

Only then did I dare to step on her spotless white carpet.

'How about a drink?' she asked.

I followed her cigarillo to where a glass of scotch sat on a garish gold coffee table. The lipstick on its rim perfectly matched the color on her lips.

'No, thanks. It's a little early for me yet,' I replied. 'Besides . . .'

'Yeah, yeah. I know. You're on the job,' she brusquely retorted, cutting me off. 'Having to work for a living really sucks.'

Maybe so. But it was the phrase she'd so casually dropped that caught my attention. *On the job* was inside lingo used to convey you knew someone on the force. It came in particularly handy when stopped by a cop for something like a speeding ticket. I took note of the term, but chose to say nothing. Instead, I asked a question that had been eating at me ever since her phone call.

'How did you find me anyway?' I inquired. 'Most people don't know what a Fish and Wildife agent is, let alone how to track one down.'

Tiffany Stewart sank into a gold brocade couch while indicating that I was to sit in a nearby chair. The poodle buried its head in her lap as she took another drag on her cigarillo.

'Have you ever heard of a little thing called the Discovery Channel? They had a special on agents like you. Who else am I going to call about shahtoosh? The NYPD?' she retorted with a sharp laugh. 'After that, I let my fingers do the walking through the phone book.'

'But why Newark? Why not call the New York office?' I asked, still somewhat perturbed.

'I don't know. Why? Is there a problem?' she archly responded.

'No. Of course not,' I replied, not wanting to put her off before we even got started.

'All right. So then, exactly what is it that you want from me?' she asked.

The words wafted in the air on a billowy cloud of smoke.

'How do you know that Bitsy von Falken owned a shah-toosh shawl?' I inquired, getting straight to the point.

Tiffany rattled the cubes in her glass, and stared at them as though they were precious gems. Then she took a long, leisurely sip of scotch.

'Are you kidding? Who doesn't own one of those things in this town?'

'I don't know. You tell me. Do you have one of them?' I countered.

'Not on your life. I spend my money on more substantial items. I believe in only buying articles that maintain their value and are rock solid investments,' she archly replied.

'Such as?' I asked, curious to know what those might be.

Tiffany raised a hand and wiggled her diamond ring at me. The gem caught a ray of light and emitted sparks, as if there were a fire burning inside.

'Ice, baby, ice. These little beauties never lose their worth. Turns out Marilyn Monroe was right. Diamonds *are* a girl's best friend. Worse comes to worse, you can always drop 'em in your pocket and run.'

Her fingers wandered up to her throat and grazed the choker, as if to reassure herself that it was still there for when the time was right.

'I'm not one of those pretentious *grandes dames* around here that locks up their jewels and takes them out only on special occasions. What good does that do? Next thing you know, you're dead and somebody else is enjoying them. I firmly believe in wearing my commodities.' I was getting the distinct impression that Tiffany didn't much care for her social peers. To my mind, that made her an even better informant. She'd have no qualms about gathering dirt on them.

'So then it's true. A number of women in your circle *do* have shahtoosh shawls,' I remarked, and waited to hear what she had to say.

'Not *my* circle, honey. Don't get me wrong. I may live up here, but that doesn't mean I have to hobnob with this stuck-up crew. I wouldn't let one of those snooty bitches trounce her bony ass through my door,' Tiffany snapped, with obvious disdain in her voice.

Whatever had happened between these women was definitely personal. That made me all the more curious as to Tiffany Stewart's back story.

The poodle let out a sharp yap.

'Is this what Chardonnay wants?' Tiffany asked, and reached for a candy bowl.

Except rather than sweets, it held doggy treats. Only then did I notice the poodle's collar. It was a Hermès crocodile-and-calfskin number that was handcrafted in Paris, and cost around fourteen hundred dollars. Only the best for this little Upper East Side pooch. Apparently, Chardonnay also believed in wearing her commodities.

The pooch nearly nipped Tiffany's finger as she popped a treat into its mouth. Spam could easily have swallowed this runt in a single gulp.

'Sorry about that. I just assumed . . .' I began, only to be cut off once again.

'Yeah, yeah, I know. You figured I must be part of their clique because I live like this. Well, maybe I was for a while. But all that ended the day my dear departed husby kicked the bucket. Once Andrew was gone, those broads wasted no time in showing their true colors,' she revealed.

Tiffany was clearly not to the manor born, but had married into her social circle. I decided to do some prospecting of my own and see what I could find out.

'Do you mind if I ask what you did before you were married?' I inquired, figuring that she'd probably been her husband's secretary.

'I was an artist,' Tiffany revealed.

50

'Do you mean like a painter, or an illustrator?' I continued to press.

'No, an exotic dancer,' Tiffany matter-of-factly replied. 'My body was my art form. That's how I met my sweetie. He used to come to the club where I worked. He was so smitten with my talent that he gave me a present the very next day after we met. It came in one of those pretty little blue boxes. Cute, huh? Something from Tiffany's for Tiffany. Soon, I had so many of those boxes that I could have built a damn castle out of them.'

I could only imagine how impressive her talent must have been. That helped to explain all of the bling. It also revealed why she was considered a pariah within the Upper East Side community. I didn't hesitate, but jumped right in.

'Do you happen to know where all these women are buying their shawls?' I asked.

'Sorry, but I can't help you there.'

Damn! I watched as Tiffany fed her dog another treat. Maybe if I was really good in this life, I'd come back as a spoiled Upper East Side pooch in the next.

'Then how about giving me the names of any other women you know that own shahtoosh shawls,' I suggested.

She petulantly shook the ice in her glass, as if wondering where all the scotch could have gone.

'What do you think I am? Some sort of frigging computer? It's not like I have a printed list inside my head,' she snapped.

Maybe not. But she'd certainly produced Bitsy von Falken's name fast enough. Surely she knew at least one or two others. I was beginning to wonder if I'd only been given Bitsy because she was already dead. Perhaps Tiffany still felt a twinge of loyalty to the rest.

She poured a hefty dash of Chivas into her glass and took a sip, which seemed to calm her down. I caught Tiffany's gaze and held it, letting her know that I wasn't about to go anywhere. At least, not until I'd received further information.

'OK. Maybe I can give you a lead in the right direction,' she finally relented.

Tiffany slipped out of the Manolo Blahniks, and I saw that her toenails were painted to match the color of her shoes.

'Bitsy threw one of those big charity wingdings that she was always so good at – oh, I guess it must have been about a year ago. This one was to raise money for cancer awareness. Bitsy wanted to do something different, so she decided to auction off shahtoosh shawls.'

'Did you attend?' I asked.

Tiffany wrinkled her nose and leaned back against the brocade couch. 'Andrew was already dead. I was told that my invitation got lost in the mail. Fat chance. In any case, I hear that people snapped them up like so much beluga caviar.'

'That's great. The problem is, dead women don't talk, and Bitsy had the invitation list,' I pointed out.

'You're right about that. Except for the PR firm that co-ordinated the event. I bet they still have a record of all the attendees,' she slyly revealed.

Beneath that mound of sequins, Tiffany was proving to be a lot sharper than she'd originally let on.

'I don't suppose you'd happen to have the company's name, would you?' I asked.

That last glass of scotch had apparently done the trick.

'I just might,' she said and, standing up, dumped the pooch on the couch. I watched as she walked over to a French provincial desk and opened the top drawer. What do you know? The name and number of the firm had already been neatly written out on a plain piece of paper. She picked it up and then walked me to the door. 'I have only one request. That you don't use my name. I had nothing to do with where you got this information,' she said, and handed me the creamy white sheet of paper.

'No problem. By the way, that's some rock you're wearing,' I said, getting a better view.

It made my own diamond look puny by comparison.

'Thanks. It's a fifty-six carat, emerald-cut, D color stone,' she disclosed, and held it forward for closer inspection.

'D color? What does that mean?' I asked.

'That it's the top of the line. The very best there is,' She proudly told me. 'See? The color is icy white.'

The diamond appeared to be absolutely flawless. Its fifty-eight facets sparkled intensely, producing a myriad of tiny rainbows.

'Believe me, honey. I worked hard for this stone and everything else that I have. Andrew was OK, but he was certainly no angel,' she commented. 'Come to think of it, Bitsy always wore quite a boulder of her own. I wonder whatever happened to it? Probably some cop, or whoever knocked her off, slipped the ring from her finger and into their pocket.'

This was the first I'd heard of any diamond. Perhaps the shawl hadn't been all that Magda had snatched. The ring could very well be stashed away inside The Kielbasa House at this very moment. If so, Magda was in bigger trouble than she could have ever imagined.

Six

Everyone has a scam. No one turns informant for no reason. So, what was Tiffany Stewart's stake in the game? Why had she come forward? And why give me the information? What did she have to gain?

I thought back again to her phone call. She'd had no hesitation in supplying Bitsy von Falken's name. Then why the reluctance in tapping the other women? Not only that, but Tiffany must have planned to tell me about the PR firm all along. Why else had it been written down and so readily available? Just who was playing who, anyway? One thing for certain was that sainthood wasn't running rampant on the Upper East Side these days.

I shelved all such thoughts for the moment and focused on what I had in hand – the phone number for Haller and Associates Public Relations Firm. Pulling out my cellphone, I quickly placed the call.

'Haller and Associates. This is Joy speaking,' answered a woman in a professionally cheerful manner.

'Hello, Joy. This is Chrissy Hilton. I'm going to be throwing an event to raise awareness for Hashimoto disease, and I'd like your firm to handle it,' I began, launching into my spiel.

'Excuse me, but are you a member of *the* Hilton family?' she inquired, unable to contain the excitement in her voice.

'I'm sorry, but I'd rather not comment on that. I don't like to flaunt my family connections. I'm sure you understand,' I evasively responded.

Sometimes I felt as if I were the creator of my very own reality show. Why should I simply *want* to be a Hilton, when I could actually pretend to be one?

'Oh, of course. Please forgive my rudeness. It's just that I'm thrilled to have you call. Now what can we do for you?' she asked, bouncing back like a real pro.

'As I said, I'm planning to host a charity event. Bitsy von Falken, who was a very dear friend, used to just rave about the way you handled her party,' I explained.

'You were a friend of Mrs von Falken's?' Joy asked in a hushed tone. 'Oh, my goodness, wasn't that dreadful news? Please accept my condolences. What a horrible thing to have happen. It must be just terrible for you.'

Actually, I felt fairly certain that it was far worse for Bitsy.

'Thank you. Yes, my days just haven't been the same ever since. Which is why I plan to hold this event in her memory. I want to invite all the very same people that came to her fundraiser. Would you possibly still have that attendance list?' I asked, careful to sound appropriately disconsolate.

'Exactly which party would that be, my dear?' Joy inquired.

Which party? I could count the number of parties I'd thrown in my life on one hand – and those had all been pot luck dinners.

'The charity event that Bitsy held for cancer awareness. I believe it was about a year ago. It was the one at which shawls were auctioned,' I said, going for nonchalant. But in truth, my anticipation was about to overflow.

'Well now, let's find out, shall we? I'll just check the computer,' Joy said.

Click, click, click.

My nerves tagged along for the ride as her fingertips pranced on the keyboard.

'Ah, yes. Here it is. That won't be any problem at all. Naturally, we'll be happy to send out the invitations for you,' she informed me.

'That would be wonderful. However, would you mind emailing that list to me first? I'd like to go over the names, and then we can take it from there,' I replied.

Either someone had snuck up from behind and slapped a gag on her, or Joy had suddenly become mute. My request was met with dead silence.

'Is anything wrong?' I finally asked, hoping to move

things along. Joy responded with a sigh as deep as the Grand Canyon.

'Oh dear. I'm afraid we *do* have a problem. I can't release this information. Privacy issues and that sort of thing, you know. It goes totally against our policy,' she disclosed.

'I can appreciate that. But I have a problem of my own. An unpleasant incident took place a few weeks ago involving some of the women. Nothing I can discuss of course, but it upset Bitsy terribly. I want to make certain that their names aren't on the list,' I blatantly lied.

'Well, that's easily solved. Just give me their names and I'll cross them off,' Joy replied in obvious relief.

'That's the problem. I can't seem to remember them. I'll need to see the list in order to jog my memory. Couldn't you make an exception just this once?' I cajoled.

'I'd really rather not,' she resisted.

It was time to pull out the big guns.

'Just between you and me, I know that Paris is planning a big soirée and is looking for a new PR firm to handle all the details. She wasn't pleased with the last company that she used. I'd be happy to put in a good word for you.' I had no qualms about providing Joy with a little imaginary incentive.

'Paris Hilton? Planning a party? Really?' she asked, just about panting. 'That would be absolutely divine.'

I could nearly hear her ticking off all the new names to be added to her contact list.

'Well . . . I suppose we could make an exception just this once,' Joy complied. 'In fact, I also have a separate list of those women that bought shawls, and exactly how many. The auction was a huge success. Mrs von Falken wanted a record kept for the next time she planned a similar event. You might consider doing something along the same line, yourself. If so, would you be interested in seeing that list as well?'

'What a brilliant suggestion. Let me just give you my email address,' I said, and reeled off an undercover addy that I kept for such purposes. 'Could you send those to me right away? I'd like to go over both lists tonight.'

'Of course,' she amiably agreed. That was followed by an awkward pause. 'Hmm. This is rather odd. I can't seem to find your name on either of these lists.'

Joy had caught me off-guard. I hadn't planned on the woman being quite so thorough.

'How strange. Oh, wait. Now I remember. I told Bitsy not to bother with an invitation since I was going to be out of the country. I was on safari with Paris in Botswana and then went to a friend's tea plantation in Rwanda,' I replied, nimbly tap dancing my way out of that one.

I figured I might as well hit her up again while she still had Paris Hilton on the brain.

'By the way, I'll need one more favor. Seeing that Bitsy was so successful, I think I *will* try auctioning those shawls. Thank you again for the marvelous suggestion. No wonder she used your firm. You're an absolute lifesaver. Of course, I'll need to place an order right away for a few hundred of them. Would you mind providing me with the name of the supplier?' I congratulated myself on being oh-so-clever.

'I'm sorry, Ms Hilton, but I'm afraid we had nothing to do with the shawls. Mrs von Falken took full charge of obtaining those herself. Perhaps her husband might be able to help you,' she suggested. 'Although I suppose this probably isn't the proper time to ask.'

'No, I'm sure you're quite right about that,' I agreed. 'In any case, it shouldn't be a problem. I'll just call around and ask a few people. Please don't forget to email those lists to me. I'll be back in touch tomorrow.'

'Don't worry. They're already on their way,' she assured me.

I thanked her, gave her my email address and hung up. Then I got into my Trailblazer, and a number of vehicles prowling the street immediately homed in on my primo parking space. I was tempted to sell it to the highest bidder but instead rushed home, anxious to peruse the list.

I parked in my garage, and then dashed across to the old Essex Street Market. More than likely, there wasn't any food in my fridge.

The market was opened in 1930 to accommodate all the

pushcart vendors. Now it sprawled across an entire city block. These days stalls offered everything from canned goods to fresh produce, dumplings, tripe, pigs feet, and rib bellies in an edible cultural explosion. I made my way down the aisles, along with a parade of local Latinos, Chinese and Jews, where I was tempted by assorted cheeses, fish, spices, nuts, and fresh fruit. There were even a variety of services available.

JCC Electronics had once fixed my TV, and I'd had pants hemmed by Mr Smith Expert Tailor of Piccadilly, London. Both stalls were next to a *botanica* that offered aerosol cans of Money Attracting Spray, breast-enhancing cream, laminated portraits of Pope John Paul II, and Virgin Mary statuettes. I passed them by and ducked into Schapiro's Wines to grab a bottle of cheap kosher burgundy. Then I left, having forgotten what I'd come in for in the first place.

High-tailing it home, I jogged up to the third floor, and unlocked the door. Spam raced toward me with the determination of a homicidal linebacker. It was one thing to be loved; quite another to be mauled as the dog nearly knocked me over.

'Down, Spam! Down!' I ordered.

But the pit bull continued to lick my face as he pinned me against the wall. So much for my home-schooled course in obedience training.

Otherwise, the place was bursting with silence. I was more aware of the quiet than I'd ever been while living alone. I glanced up at the clock, knowing that it was too early for Jake to come home, yet wishing that he were already here. I suppose that's what happens when you get used to spending time together. The only problem was that we were doing less and less of that these days. *Quit worrying,* I reprimanded myself, and locked any misgivings away.

Then I turned my attention to the work at hand.

'Good boy, Spam. Just give me a minute and then I promise that we'll go out,' I told the pooch, knowing he would understand, as I booted up the computer.

He lay back down and rested his chin on my foot, as I entered my password.

Two emails from Haller and Associates immediately

popped up on the screen. I downloaded the attachments, and printed out both lists.

My, my, but Joy was well organized. Not only did they provide a bounty of names, but also included their contact phone numbers.

I quickly scanned them and could scarcely believe my eyes. I didn't need to know about charity balls to instantly recognize the crème de la crème of New York high society. Included was everyone from socialites and supermodels, to actresses, countesses, heiresses, and trophy wives. It was a virtual Who's Who of anybody who was considered to be anyone in Manhattan. At one time, I would have swooned to spot my name among such a celebrated group. But times change, dreams shift, and now these people were on my hit list.

I was musing about life's strange twists and turns when the telephone rang.

'I predict we're having dinner together this evening,' Terri said in place of hello.

'Uh huh. And I knew it was you before I picked up the phone,' I jokingly responded.

'Seriously, if I catch a sleigh downtown can we snowshoe out and grab a bite to eat?'

'Are you trying to tell me that you don't like my home cooking?' I teased.

'And what home cooking would that be? A Swanson's Frozen Dinner or take-out?' he parried.

'I just got a bottle of Schapiro's finest kosher burgundy. Care to come up for a drink before we head out?' I asked.

'Rach, surely you jest. That crap is pure rot gut. I don't know how you can drink the stuff. For God's sake, even *they* advertise it as wine so thick you can cut it with a knife. The only thing it's good for is cleaning out clogged pipes. I'll come up for a while, but you're going to have to do better than that. Besides, I'm afraid if I stay too long I'll thaw out and won't be able to leave until spring.'

Terri was having a hard time adjusting to the cold. All the ice and snow just didn't go with what he liked to call his tropical personality.

'Why couldn't Eric have found a new job some place more suitable? Say in Hawaii, perhaps?' he'd moaned after experiencing his first bout of snow.

In truth, I was beginning to worry about their relationship. Eric was a workaholic and homebody, while Terri still liked to party. Throw a rebellious teenage girl into the mix and they were beginning to have trouble.

'See you soon,' I said, and hung up.

Then I walked into the kitchen and flicked on the light, only to have a shriek tear from my throat. Every horror film I'd ever seen came rushing back to haunt me. There on the counter was my worst nightmare – a roving gang of cockroaches.

A group of oval brown bodies were gathered in a shiny mass of twitching antennas, and skittering limbs. Santou had left a slice of Gerda's cake out, and the bugs were rockin' and rollin' all over it. Unbelievable. The damn things didn't have the decency to run away and hide from me, even though they were faster than cheetahs.

I quickly transformed from my normal animal loving self into a vindictive Terminator.

Yeah, yeah. I know. I'm supposed to protect every living creature. But truth be told, we all have our limits. Besides, these were the least endangered critters on the planet. Not only can they survive decapitation, but the frigging bugs regenerate their own body parts. *I* should have had such talents. Even the Army could have learned a thing or two from them. Cockroaches are the perfect survivors, able to live on a drop of water, a sliver of soap, strands of hair, and fingernail clippings.

The only thing worse than encountering one was actually having to kill it. No way was I going to smash them on the counter and hear their tiny exoskeletons crunch. And then there was all that goo that would have to be cleaned up. Instead, I chose to do the only rational thing in such a situation. I closed the kitchen door, grabbed a can of Raid, and furiously began to spray the room.

A sickly sweet scent permeated the air, but I didn't care. To hell with the fine mist that fell on my dishes, pots and pans. What were a few toxins and chemicals when it was a matter of self-preservation? The bugs were mini-weapons of mass destruction and this was all out war.

It was only when the can of Raid was finally empty that I knew the battle was temporarily over. I quickly cleaned up the mess, grabbed hold of Spam and left, unable to stand the smell any longer.

I didn't take a deep breath until we were standing outside and Spam began to pull me around the block. We went for our ritual walk where I pretended to be my secret fantasy. I morphed into Michelle Kwan while slipping and sliding along on the ice.

I eventually had no choice but to go back inside the building. However, I wisely made tracks for Gerda's rather than enter my own apartment.

Nailed to the right-hand side of her doorpost was the *mezuzah* I'd first seen as a child. I'd always loved its silver and blue rectangular case adorned with mysterious Hebrew lettering. Only later did I learn that two handwritten chapters of the Torah were tightly rolled up inside. I'd always wondered how someone managed to do that.

The *mezuzah* was nailed to the post at an angle, and I used to try my best to straighten it. Gerda had caught me once and laughed at my mistake.

'Rachel, not everything in this life can be exactly as you want it. *Mezuzahs* are supposed to hang that way. Do you know why?'

I shook my head, not having the slightest idea.

'Then I'll tell you, my darling. The rabbis couldn't agree on whether *mezuzahs* should be horizontal or vertical, so they decided to compromise. Remember that as you go through life.'

I touched the *mezuzah*, and kissed my fingers, before knocking on her door.

Gerda answered my tap looking particularly spiffy tonight. She wore a deep blue dress offset by a beautiful diamond brooch. The stones reflected the twinkle in her eyes. Gerda had carefully applied her make-up so that the rouge on her cheeks matched the color of her lips. They both comple-

mented her freshly-dyed hair, which was red as ripe straw-
berries.

She took one look at me and started to *tsk, tsk, tsk* with
her tongue.

'Rachel. What's the matter? You seem a little frazzled, my
dear.'

I leaned in to give her a kiss, and a flood of memories
washed over me. I took a deep whiff and realized it was the
scent of Gerda's skin. The smell was exactly the same as
that which I associated with my grandmother. It was a mixture
of powder, and soap, and perfume. I wasn't yet ready to
release my breath, but rather chose to float on a soothing
sea of remembrance. Though it was too comforting to immediately exhale, it was also too bittersweet to stay for very
long.

My childhood hadn't been all that easy. It had been filled
with pain and loss and regret. Only at my grandmother and
Gerda's had I been able to escape into a different world, one
filled with laughter and music and happiness.

I could still smell the tantalizing aroma of Passover meals
cooking in their kitchens, and nearly taste the holiday sweets.
My grandmother, my mother, and my sister were all gone now
and Gerda was the only family that I had left. It was one of
the reasons why I had chosen to come home to New York.

'It's those damn cockroaches,' I said, and stepped inside
her door. 'They're driving me crazy, Gerda. I don't know
what your secret is, but I can't seem to get rid of them.'

'I already told you what to do, my darling,' she replied,
while fingering the diamond studs in her ears. 'First you
have to keep your apartment spic-and-span clean. Those *cock-
a-roaches* will eat anything. Grease on the kettle, crumbs
under your toaster, even food particles on a dishrag.'

Good luck with that, I thought.

Between Spam, Santou and myself, the roaches were
clearly having a field day. Besides, I knew that nothing
would ever totally stop them. The little beasties not only eat
their own dead, but also dine on their living when food
becomes scarce.

'If that doesn't work, then stick some bread in a jar and

smear the inside lip with Vaseline,' Gerda instructed. 'They'll climb down inside the jar, but they won't be able to climb back out. After that, screw the top on and walk down to Chinatown where you can spin the jar around and let them loose. They'll be so dizzy that they'll never find their way back home again.'

Gerda was incredibly humane, even when it came to something as minuscule as bugs. I wondered if it had anything to do with her time spent in a concentration camp. Though her homespun remedies were fun, I still preferred my tried and true method – a few good shots of Raid. At least that way I knew for certain that they were gone.

'You look so pretty tonight, Gerda. Are you going out?' I inquired.

'Yes. David is coming by and taking me to dinner. We're going to Sammy's Romanian. Why don't you join us?' she suggested with a sly smile.

That would be terrific, if I was trying to boost my cholesterol level and wanted to risk *plotzing* from a heart attack. Sammy's was famous for enormous slabs of beef slathered in chicken fat. Jugs of additional rendered *schmaltz* were placed on each table as if in a dare. Dinner required that a bottle of iced vodka be consumed just to help Roto-Rooter your arteries.

However, Gerda had an ulterior motive for inviting me to dinner. She knew that Jake and I were involved, but still hoped that one day her grandson and I would become an item.

'You're a nice Jewish girl and David is a nice Jewish boy. Besides, he's a gem dealer in the Diamond District. What could be better?' she'd ask with a shake of her tightly-permed curls. 'So what if you're a little older? That doesn't really matter. Men tend to die earlier. Think of it as a bonus. You'll have him around a bit longer.'

'Thanks, but I already have plans with Terri tonight,' I told her.

'That *fagellah*?' she asked and wrinkled her nose, as if wondering why we were friends. 'Oh, well. What do I know about young people these days? The world is a different place. Who's to say? Maybe it's a good thing.'

'Would you mind if Spam stayed here with you while I'm gone? I just launched a roach attack in my apartment, and it smells like the inside of a Raid can.'

'Of course, he's welcome. At this point, he's the closest thing that I have to a grandchild.' Gerda leaned down and gave the pooch a pat. 'For you, I have some pot roast,' she said.

No wonder her place smelled so good and brought back so many memories. Spam apparently felt the same way. He let out a bark and merrily wagged his tail.

Seven

I walked into the hallway only to hear the buzzer insistently ringing from downstairs. I didn't bother to let Terri in, but quickly raced down to meet him. He stood shivering in the cold as I headed outside.

'Hey, I thought you were going to buzz me up,' he complained. 'What's the problem? Cockroaches again?'

'Wow, you really are psychic,' I answered, duly impressed.

'Oh, please. Don't cheapen my psychic abilities. You know perfectly well it's the fragrant scent of Eau de Raid that you're wearing,' he wisecracked. 'So, where are we off to?'

I glanced at my friend. Terri had on a heavy winter jacket and thick woolen cap. Dressed like that, I figured he could withstand a few blocks of hiking in this weather.

'What say we do a little shopping before dinner?' I suggested.

'Oh, my God. Hell *has* frozen over! You're finally going to hit some of those cute little boutiques around here that I've been telling you about,' he crowed.

'Don't get so excited. This excursion isn't for me, but for a woman that owns a luncheonette truck at the port. She's in bad need of a decent winter coat, and I've decided to buy her one.'

Terri looked at me in surprise. 'Well, aren't you turning out to be the good Samaritan. And here I thought all you cared about were creatures with a minimum of four legs and fur,' he replied, linking his arm through mine.

I would have loved to be viewed as genuinely benevolent, but my conscience wouldn't allow it.

'I'm afraid it's a bit more complicated than that. Magda had a beautiful warm shawl. The only problem was that the wool turned out to be illegal. I also suspect that it was taken off a dead woman. So, I had to confiscate it,' I explained.

'Your friend took it off a dead woman? Honey, maybe it's time you started hanging out with a better class of people. So then, this is a pure guilt shopping trip,' he surmised.

'Well, yes. But there's something else,' I replied. 'I went to see a very wealthy woman today. I swear, she looked like an over-the-top ad for Tiffany's. In fact, that was her name. Even her dog wore designer accessories. It made me wonder what the hell's wrong with this picture? I figure if her dog can wear an Hermès collar, then Magda shouldn't have to suffer and shiver in the cold.'

'See? Now that's more in line with what I'm talking about. People of that economic caliber. An Hermès collar? I'd love one of those things myself,' he said, and gave my arm a squeeze. 'Ooh, I'm definitely beginning to see exciting new things for you.'

'I hope so,' I replied, feeling less certain of my fate.

It was an emotion I'd been experiencing of late, and had yet to figure out why. I pushed it to the back of my mind and, instead, tried to focus on all the stores around me.

Common wisdom is that the Lower East Side has already been fully co-opted, white-washed and stripped of all its personality. That isn't quite the case. True, the neighborhood is going through a period of transition. However, there are still a few unique pockets to be found.

We passed by historic buildings that had been constructed to pack a maximum number of people into a minimum amount of space. Individuals now occupy the same tenements that once housed entire families.

Soon we wandered past a line of boutiques so ultra-cool that I couldn't even tell what they were selling. Terri gave a disappointed sigh as we continued on and headed for a strip of bargain clothing stores. The owners stood outside where they hawked their wares like carnival barkers. It's here that I entered a shop that had been around since my grandmother's days.

'Great. They should call this place *Schmata Central*. I

should have known we'd end up at discount heaven,' Terri griped.

Terri might consider their wares to be 'rags,' but to me they were hidden treasures. I went in the back and picked through the racks until I found exactly what I was looking for – a winter coat in Magda's size.

'That coat is one of our most fashionable items and made of the very best material. Here, let me help you try it on. I'm sure you'll look lovely in it,' the saleswoman schmoozed, turning on the charm.

'I just want to make sure that it's warm,' I said, slipping my arms through the sleeves and zipping it up.

'Trust me. Nothing will keep you more toasty. And check out the price. You've got yourself quite a bargain there,' she added, piling it on.

'Hmm. I have to be honest with you. The material feels a little chintzy. My aunt said I could probably find a better deal a few doors down,' I replied, making my opening gambit.

'How can you say such a thing? You might as well cut my heart out right now and get it over with,' the woman groaned.

'Don't get me wrong. The coat is fine. It's just a little too expensive for the quality. Can you possibly do better?' I asked, hoping to snag her on my line.

The woman folded her arms across her chest and firmly shook her head. 'I'm sorry, but you're already getting a very good deal. You'd be wise to buy it at that price.'

'Thanks, but I'll take my aunt's advice,' I replied, and began to walk out of the store.

'All right. Perhaps I *can* take off just a few dollars more,' she said before I passed through the doorway.

I waited as she checked the coat's tag and then entered some numbers into a calculator. I would have thought the woman was figuring the speed of light as she ran through a series of complex mathematical equations. She finally wrote down a number and slid the paper towards me. I looked at it, crossed out the figure, and replaced it with one of my own. We went through another round of haggling before each of us was satisfied. Then I paid the woman, took my package, and Terri and I left the store.

'I never knew you were such a world-class bargain shopper, Rach,' Terri said in admiration as we set our sights on Chinatown.

'And I thought you would have seen that in your crystal ball,' I answered with a grin.

No two ways about it. Bargain shopping was what I liked best after catching smugglers and poachers.

There's something about the air on a night that's cold. It brings back the area's ghosts. A beguiling sound began to float towards me on infinitesimal flakes of snow.

It was the faint tinkling of show tunes that Gerda used to play. She and my grandmother had liked to boast that Al Jolson, Irving Berlin, and the Gershwin brothers had all once lived in the neighborhood.

Goose bumps pricked at my skin as the distant echo of a scratchy recording now reached my ears. I glanced around, curious as to its source, and found myself suddenly transported back into old New York.

I blinked and discovered that all the cars had mysteriously disappeared. In their place, the street was now jammed with a series of pushcart peddlers. Their wagons were filled with every imaginable item from hot potatoes, to fish, to produce, to dry goods, and clothes as they hawked their wares.

'A quart of peaches for a penny! Damage eggs for a song!' vendors trilled, as I looked on in stunned amazement.

Something hard bumped against me, and I turned to find a laundryman heaving a sack filled with wet, clean towels and sheets, on his back. He delivered them from door to door where women hung them to dry on their fire escapes. But that was only part of the hustle and bustle in this city-within-a-city.

Men in long coats and hats had their shoes shined by bootblacks, as cheeky young newsboys stopped to shoot craps in the middle of the street.

A rag-picker scavenged for junk to be re-sold near a sweatshop, while another peddler sang of tin cups and bandanas for sale at only two pennies apiece. The stench and the noise of it all were nearly overwhelming.

I became lost among a crowd that jostled and shoved, as

people shouted to each other in a Babel of foreign tongues. And, for one crystalline moment, I felt sure I'd caught sight of my grandmother – or a woman that looked exceptionally like her. She was as she must have appeared upon first arriving in New York – heartbreakingly young and filled with boundless hope. I could almost have sworn that the woman smiled at me. And then she was gone. Just as quickly, as we entered Chinatown, the vision vanished.

It struck me that Chinatown was exactly the same as the Lower East Side must have been nearly a century ago. Vendors and stores stood tightly crammed around the ramparts of the Manhattan Bridge as we picked our way through a never-ending stream of pedestrians. Most were Asian immigrants speaking in their native tongues – Mandarin, Cantonese, Cambodian, Thai, and Vietnamese, with Laotian and Filipino thrown in for good measure.

Turning on to Canal Street, we were swept up in a colorful bazaar of knock-off Louis Vuitton bags, Gucci wallets, and Chanel sunglasses. Terri was torn between purchasing a 'Rolex' watch, or an 'Hermès' scarf, when my cellphone rang.

'Hey, there. What's all that racket I hear in the background? Don't tell me that you're out trying to pick up some guy in a bar, are you?' Jake teased.

'I make no promises when you leave me alone at night,' I returned the banter. 'Are you home yet? Terri and I are in Chinatown. We're on our way to grab something to eat. Why don't you come join us?'

'I'm afraid I won't be able to. I almost hate to say it after your warning, but I have to work late again tonight,' Santou informed me.

My stomach automatically tightened into a knot. Most of Santou's time was spent on counter-terrorism and homeland security these days. But I was beginning to worry there might be another reason why he was continually coming home late.

'Is everything all right?' I asked, even though I knew he'd never be able to tell me.

'Yeah. All's quiet on the New York front. There's just something I have to check out,' he replied.

I only hoped whatever it was didn't have voluptuous curves and two legs.

'What's the color code tonight?' I asked, attempting to lightly jest, though my heart was beginning to ache.

'How about blue for missing me?' Santou replied, with a low, sexy growl.

It didn't matter how long I'd been with the man. He always knew exactly how to make my pulse race.

'That goes without saying,' I responded, trying out my best imitation of Angelina Jolie. 'See you later?'

'I'll be home as soon as I can,' Jake promised.

By the time I hung up, Terri had settled on both the watch and the scarf and I firmly put any doubts about Jake behind me.

'Maybe bargain shopping isn't so bad after all,' Terri declared, as we headed off to Doyers Street.

This was the heart of old Chinatown. The tiny alley curved with the insouciance of a charming European lane, its storefronts filled with restaurants and barbershops. But it hadn't always been so quaint. The bend in the road had once been known as the 'Bloody Angle,' due to all the bodies that lined its gutters, the victims of violent ambushes and Chinese gang fights. Perhaps even their ghosts were here tonight.

We entered our favorite Chinese restaurant and slid on to a red plastic banquette. The place didn't look like much. The décor bore the usual black velvet paintings of tigers, white Formica tables, and bright bare bulbs. But the food was terrific, even if the waiters hardly spoke any English. Two large bowls of Shanghai dumpling soup were placed before us, followed by a platter of kung pao shrimp. However, I only picked, finding that I wasn't really all that hungry this evening.

'So, how are things going with you and Eric these days?' I asked, attempting to delicately broach the subject.

'What do you want to hear? The good, the bad, or the ugly?' Terri glumly responded, in his own unique version of Clint Eastwood.

'How about all three?' I suggested.

'Well, the good thing is that I'm not alone, I suppose.

Although Eric is rarely at home anymore. The man seems to do nothing but constantly work all the time. And when he is around, we no longer have very much in common. I'm all glitter and boas, while he's into button downs and J. Crew,' Terri complained.

'Well, you wouldn't want a clone of yourself, would you?' I responded, hoping Terri wasn't about to jump ship once more.

'No. But I also have no intention of growing old gracefully. Whatever the hell that means. Whoever came up with that sad-ass saying must have been trying to sell annuity funds,' Terri griped. 'I mean, *really*, Rach. These days, Eric's idea of a good time is sitting at home and watching *The Apprentice* on TV. I'm not ready to spend my evenings bundled in a blanket and drinking hot chocolate. This is the Big Apple. I want to have fun!'

Actually, a down comforter and a cup of hot cocoa sounded pretty good to me. However, I wisely kept my mouth shut.

'And then there's Lily. That girl is getting way out of line. Granted she's a teenager, and has had her fair share of problems. But she has more than a dozen different boyfriends and is out partying all night. For chrissakes, she's having a better time than I am.'

'Hmm. I wonder which one of you she takes after,' I joked, but decided maybe it was time that I had a talk with her. 'I have an idea. Why don't you tell me about some of Eric's good points?'

Terri took a sip of his tea. 'Well, he's kind and certainly generous. And he believes in my psychic ability. In fact, he thinks I ought to quit *Psychics-On-Call* and go freelance. He wants to come up with an advertising campaign and market me as the Psychic to the Stars. Can you imagine it, Rach? I could tell Whitney Houston to cut out the drugs, drop that low-life Bobby Brown, and put her daughter on a diet,' he said with glee.

'Eric doesn't sound half bad to me,' I responded. 'In fact, he really seems to care about you.'

Terri smiled and the worry lines on his brow began to

soften a bit. 'Yeah, I guess when I look at it that way, you're probably right. Maybe things really are better than I imagined.'

I felt as if I'd done my good deed for the day.

'And what about you and Jake? Is he happier now that he's back at work once again?' Terri asked.

'Yes. Everything's fine,' I said, and stopped any further conversation by popping a shrimp in my mouth. Only rather than a shrimp, it turned out to be a red hot chili pepper. Damn! It felt as though my mouth were on fire. Grabbing a mouthful of white rice, I promptly put out the flames.

'See? That's what happens when you lie,' Terri responded.

'What are you talking about?' I growled, finding myself inexplicably angry at both Jake and the chili pepper at the same time.

'I know you too well, Rach. You've barely touched your food. And you've been distracted ever since that call came in from Jake,' he observed. 'What's the matter? You can give me advice but can't talk about your own problems?'

Oh, what the hell. I suppose that's what friends were for.

'I'm not certain that anything's actually wrong. It's just that Jake keeps coming home late. Maybe it's the job, or it could be that he's seeing someone.' I viciously stabbed a dumpling with my chopstick, having voiced my fears.

Terri stared at me with his big blue eyes, and then broke into laughter. 'You really are crazy, Rach. But that's what I love about you. Why on earth would you think that he's playing around?'

I squirmed in my seat, growing increasingly uncomfortable with the subject. 'Let's just say that our nocturnal activities have fallen off of late.'

'For chrissakes, Rach. The guy's probably tired from working day and night. Besides, how many years have the two of you been together? Tell me. In all that time have you ever tried spicing up your sex life?' Terri quizzed, morphing into Dr. Ruth.

I didn't respond, fairly certain that Terri and I viewed 'spicing it up' from two entirely different perspectives.

'Your silence speaks volumes. Here. I suggest that you

give these a try,' he said, and pulled two pairs of fuzzy red handcuffs from out of his bag.

'You carry those around with you?' I asked in surprise.

'I believe in being prepared,' he replied, and handed me the cuffs.

'Thanks, but I already have a pair,' I informed Terri, and promptly gave them back to him.

'Uh huh. And are they for work or play?' he asked.

'Well, Fish and Wildlife issues the fuzzy blue ones for use on the street,' I said, making a face at Terri. 'They're regular handcuffs for work. What do you think? That I'd actually use something like those on a lawbreaker?'

'Of course not. Which is exactly why you need a separate pair for fun. Oh, come on, Rach. Loosen up. For chrissakes, don't be so stuffy,' he scolded, and slipped them into my bag.

I was about to respond when my cellphone rang. I quickly picked it up, hoping it was Santou with news that he was on his way.

'Agent Porter,' I answered.

'Hello? Is that you, Rachel?' responded a woman with a heavy eastern European accent.

What came through loud and clear was the fear in her voice, and I immediately knew the identity of my caller.

'Magda?' I asked. 'What's wrong?'

'There's something I have to tell you,' she nervously imparted.

'You can tell me anything, Magda,' I tried to reassure her. 'No matter the problem, it will be all right.'

'No, it won't. What I did is terrible. It's very, very bad.'

'Don't worry. I'm sure we can fix whatever it is. The important thing is that you've called,' I soothingly replied, having a fairly good idea what she was about to confess.

'That shawl I was wearing? I lied,' Magda said, and took a deep, jagged breath. 'My friend? She didn't give it to me.'

Magda exhaled as though she'd swallowed a handful of broken glass.

'All right then. Where did you get it from?' I asked, trying to make the process as easy as possible.

There was a long pause, during which Magda began to whimper.

'I picked it up in the field the other morning,' she reluctantly admitted.

'What morning was that?' I pressed, trying to coax her along.

'You know. The morning that the dead woman was found,' Magda whispered, as though afraid of Bitsy's ghost.

A sob began deep in her chest and worked its way up into her throat, as if a panicked animal were clawing to get out.

'I'm sorry, but I was so cold and the woman was already dead. I know it was wrong, but I didn't think it would do any harm.' Magda wailed, as if in mourning for her soul. 'I hid the shawl in my truck, but someone must have been watching. And now I'm afraid that they're coming back to get me.'

She said something else, but it was lost in a flood of blubbering.

'What are you talking about, Magda? Who's coming to get you?' I asked, trying to make sense of her gibberish. 'Have you seen someone hanging around or following you?'

Magda sniffled and blew her nose. 'No. No one. It's just a feeling I have.'

She added something else again, but this time in Polish.

'Magda, I can't understand what you're saying. Please, you've got to speak to me in English,' I snapped in frustration, and quickly realized the words came out sounding too brusque.

She muffled her whimpering, and I knew that I'd hurt her feelings.

'Magda, listen to me. I think you should go to a shelter tonight. There'll be people around and you'll feel safe,' I gently advised.

But it was Magda's turn to vent. 'No! No shelter. I already told you. I won't stay in a place like that. What would people say?'

'They'd say that's what shelters are for. To help those in need,' I tried to persuade her.

But Magda's mulish pride bristled straight through the

74

phone. 'I'm not in need, thank you. I'm fine on my own.'

'All right then. How about if I drive out and pick you up? You can come back to the city and stay with me,' I suggested.

There was a pause, and I knew that Magda was seriously considering my proposal.

'You have a boyfriend, don't you?' she hesitantly questioned.

'Yes, but that won't be a problem,' I said, thinking little of it.

'He lives with you, as well?' she asked, with the slightest trace of disapproval.

'Yes, we live together. But I have a very comfortable couch that you can sleep on,' I responded, still not quite getting it.

Then I heard the giveaway – the clucking of her tongue.

'No, no. It's beginning to snow again. There's no need for you to come. Besides, I'm just being a silly woman. Everything is fine,' Magda insisted.

This time, she didn't bother to disguise the coolness in her voice, and I became frustrated, angry, and embarrassed all at once.

How dare Magda judge me as if I were some kind of scarlet woman? To hell with it. Let her sleep in her damn truck with her precious pride and morals for all I care, I fumed.

'Fine. Do as you wish. But I want you to call the Port Authority police and ask them to keep an eye on you tonight. Will you do that for me?' I asked.

'I'll get in trouble if I call,' she replied. 'They told me the other day that I can't sleep in my truck anymore. Some silly rule about my being a vagrant, whatever that means.'

It means that you should be sleeping at a shelter, I wanted to scream.

'All right. Then tell them that you're staying somewhere else, but are worried about your truck. Say a suspicious looking character has been hanging around,' I instructed.

There was a momentary silence, as if Magda were purposely trying to bait me.

'Magda, did you hear what I just said?' I impatiently asked.

75

'Yes, I heard you. All right, I'll call,' she reluctantly responded in a tight voice.

'Promise me,' I pressed, feeling as though I were dealing with a pigheaded child.

'Yes, yes. I promise,' Magda grudgingly agreed.

'OK, then. I have a gift for you. I'll bring it by first thing in the morning,' I revealed, hoping that might help patch things up between us.

'A gift for me?'

Magda sounded genuinely pleased, and I wondered how many presents she had received in her life.

'Rachel, I'm so sorry,' she said between tearful gulps that nearly swallowed each word.

'That's all right,' I replied, knowing what she meant.

She may have stolen the shawl, and disapproved of my lifestyle. But we were still friends. I got off the phone and realized that Terri was staring at me.

'What was that all about?' he questioned.

'It has to do with a case I'm working on. It's the one I told you about earlier. That was Magda, the woman that stole the shawl,' I replied.

'Oh,' Terri simply responded. That single utterance was enough to send shivers racing down my spine, though I didn't know why.

We finished our dinner in silence.

'I'd better head off to work,' Terri finally said, having become unusually quiet.

We parted outside the restaurant and I walked home alone.

Eight

The streets felt oddly deserted and the sidewalks were covered with snow. The city was so still that I could actually feel its pulse pounding beneath my feet.

Ba boom, ba boom, ba boom.

The steady rhythm was abruptly interrupted by the sudden flapping of wings. Startled, I jumped, afraid that the Angel of Death was hovering above me.

I glanced up, but saw nothing at first. Then ghostly silhouettes gradually emerged. A flock of Canada geese passed by, flying through the night.

I took a deep breath and then slowly let go. However, a sense of disquiet had already taken root in my soul. Even the streetlights seemed to sense my nebulous fear. Their elongated shadows proceeded to taunt me.

The shops on Orchard Street were closed. Their shuttered forms loomed ominously in the dark as I neared home. I hurried past and anxiously let myself inside my building. Then I dashed up to the third floor, the stairs groaning like the rattling of bones beneath my boots.

I pulled out Gerda's spare key, and opened her door. It wasn't that I was being rude. I simply knew that she wouldn't be home. Dinner at Sammy's Romanian Restaurant was an all night event.

This time, I greeted Spam with an overabundance of fanfare by wrapping my arms around his neck. If there were ghosts lurking nearby, we'd face them together.

We strode down the hall and slipped into my apartment, after which I hastily closed and locked the door.

Home, sweet home. Damn, but the place was cold! Then I remembered. I'd left the windows wide open. Gone was the scent of Raid, replaced by a smattering of snow.

I quickly brushed the flakes off the sill and lowered the sash. Then I set about disposing of what dead cockroaches were left. Next, I washed down the counter and cleaned all the exposed dishware. But I didn't stop there. I proceeded to scrub the pots and pans, hoping to keep my demons at bay. However, nothing could shake the feeling of dread that continued to grow inside me.

'Come on, Spam. Let's go for a walk,' I said, in an attempt to escape.

We trudged out into the cold, but still my bogeyman wouldn't let go. Rather, he held on tight as the snow began to come down even harder.

Back upstairs, I plugged my cellphone phone into its recharger. Then Spam, my sense of foreboding, and I all climbed into bed together.

I closed my eyes and the dread now began to take form. It was Magda removing the shroud from a corpse. I peered down at the body, and was stunned to find that the face was my own. The flesh slowly began to disintegrate until nothing was left but bone. I cried out in horror, causing Spam to spring up with a growl.

'That's OK, boy. It's only me.' Santou's voice floated in the air, as if in a dream.

It became reality as he slid into bed and nestled beside me. Jake laid his arm across my body and I felt safe once more. That is, until the phone on my nightstand began to ring. I immediately sat bolt upright, as if I had been touched by a ghost.

'Hello?' I mumbled into the phone, my voice sounding strange to my own ears.

Apparently, I wasn't the only one to whom it seemed foreign.

'Rach, is that you?' someone asked.

'Yes. Is this Terri?' I responded, slowly beginning to wake from my fog.

'Yeah, it's me. Are you all right?' he questioned, clearly concerned.

'I'm fine. Why?' I asked, and then immediately panicked.

Some sort of disaster must have happened. The thought was automatic. The events of 9/11 were never far from my mind. I grabbed the remote and turned on the TV, hoping not to see a calamity.

'I'm sorry,' Terri swiftly apologized. 'Don't be alarmed. It's just that I'm sitting here at work and keep envisioning the color red all around you. I finally decided to call and make sure that everything is all right.'

'Yes. Thanks for checking. Everything's fine,' I assured him.

However, I knew that wasn't true. I hung up the phone, turned off the TV, and lay back down not knowing what else to do. Though the room was cold, the bedsheet clung to my back which was laden with sweat.

'Who was that, chère?' Santou asked, his breath nuzzling at my neck.

'It was Terri. He had a feeling that something might be wrong and just called to check,' I replied.

'I hate to say it, but he's getting crazier by the day with that new job of his. He's actually beginning to believe all that crap he feeds everyone,' Jake intoned, and pulled me close.

He quickly fell back to sleep, while I remained wide awake. I finally slipped out of bed, still feeling the impression of his body against my back, my legs, and heels. Grabbing my clothes, I pulled them on and quietly slipped outside.

The snow was deeper than before, the night even more silent. The stillness was broken only by the occasional snarl of a car, or the whine of a snowplow chugging by. I kept my eyes glued to the ground, finding myself on a time-killing mission – making fresh footprints in the snow.

If mammals sleep longer in the winter, then why can't I? I pondered, feeling decidedly envious.

Though my body was sluggish as a bear, my mind was racing a mile a minute. By the time I reached the parking garage, I finally knew what I had to do. I climbed into my Trailblazer, turned on the engine, and let it idle for a few minutes. Then I pulled out into the street and took off for the seaport, my vague unease having distilled into specific concern.

79

There was no fighting traffic at this hour, as I cut across town to the Holland Tunnel. The tube stood waiting for me, its mouth wide open in a languid yawn. Only I knew it was a blatant dare.

I approached, tightly gripping the steering wheel, and then floored the pedal to the metal. The Trailblazer shot through like a rocket, clear to the other side. The tunnel took it in stride, knowing that I'd eventually have to return.

I emerged to a string of gas stations, each brightly lit as a Christmas tree. Sunoco, Exxon, Amoco, and Shell all seductively called to me. I paid no heed, but continued on my way. The world was white as I pulled on to the Jersey Turnpike and, for a moment, I was lost in a flurry of snow. Then I glanced to my left to see that the Hudson River was twinkling at me. The river was vibrantly alive with thousands of downtown lights, and I knew that New York City would always survive.

I followed my Yellow Brick road dotted with refinery stacks blowing smoke. Their vapors formed lunar cobwebs that daintily laced the night sky. Ever so slowly they morphed into winged devils with tails and horns. Then the wraiths turned to me with what seemed to be blood red eyes.

Go back home, go back home, they distinctly warned.

Instead, I stepped on the gas and took off, a sense of urgency spurring me forward. My wheels hit a patch of ice and the rear end fishtailed, first left and then right. Next thing I knew, I was heading for the center guardrail on the Turnpike. I'd become a deer caught in the headlights of the oncoming cars that blinded me.

I could scarcely see as my adrenaline kicked into high. I spun the wheel into the direction of the skid with all my might. Only at the very last second did I finally seem to get my vehicle under control.

Phew. That was a close call, I thought, as the guardrail began to drift away from me.

But my relief instantly died as I realized that my Trailblazer had instead begun to slide toward the opposite side of the road.

A bevy of horns angrily screeched as I skidded across all

three lanes of traffic. My pulse raced as fast as my tires, which spun helplessly on the ice.

Congratulations, you've just crossed the line. This is the night that you're finally going to die, my demons gleefully informed me.

Like hell I will, I snarled, my adrenaline ratcheting up another notch.

I quickly swung the steering wheel hard once more, piloting my vehicle on a different course. However rather than straighten out, my SUV began to skid in a 360-degree turn.

Round and round and round she goes. Where she'll stop, nobody knows.

The rhyme danced in my mind as the road continued to revolve around me. Never had I felt more out of control in my life. I prayed that I'd somehow survive the night. When my vehicle finally stopped, it stood perfectly parked on the shoulder of the road. Except that it now faced approaching traffic.

I sat, not daring to move a muscle, until my hands finally stopped shaking. Even so, my heart continued to pound with unknown fear. Taking a deep breath, I threw my Trailblazer into gear, turned the vehicle around, and slowly continued to drive down the Turnpike. The SUV crawled the rest of the way before pulling off at the seaport exit.

Only then did I look up at the sky. The firmament had grown abnormally bright. I wondered if it was due to a full moon. But there wasn't a star to be seen in the night.

My pulse had begun to throb. It was as if I were silently being called. I looked up once more and found that the color red was now staining the air all around me.

The sky began to ooze, and then gush, in a massive visual rush, almost as if an artery had been cut open and the heavens were hemorrhaging blood. And I suddenly knew exactly what I'd been fearing all along.

I no longer cared about slipping and sliding as I tore at breakneck speed past hotels and the outlet mall, and hooked a right on to North Street. It was there that I finally caught sight of the fire that torched the night.

Magda's silver truck was being consumed by an angry

mob of flames. Their red-hot tongues greedily lapped up the falling snow, as though the flakes were fuel, as they mercilessly turned The Kielbasa House into a funeral pyre.

'Magda!' I screamed, and frantically scrambled out of the Trailblazer.

But my calls were drowned by the deafening roar of sirens as fire engines rushed to the scene.

'There's a woman inside that truck! You've got to get her out!' I cried to all that passed by.

The men heard my pleas, but there was little they could do other than to battle the fire.

I'd lose my mind if I had to stand by and wait. Instead, I began my own investigation, carefully combing every square inch of the area for some sign of the woman. But I came up with nothing other than a few empty food containers and beer cans that lay strewn about the ground. All the while, smoke filled my lungs, and burned my eyes, until tears streamed down my face. Still, I refused to give up hope as firefighters fought to put out the flames.

I was so distraught that I didn't even notice Officer Nunzio standing nearby, until he tapped me on the shoulder.

'Seems like we were here just yesterday,' he remarked as casually as if we were at a football game. 'What are you doing back again tonight?'

So much for the caring, sensitive man that had questioned my priorities.

'Remember the woman that found Bitsy von Falken's body? Well she called me earlier this evening. Magda was afraid someone might be following her. I came out because I began to worry that something might be wrong,' I explained.

'Then it's a good thing that she wasn't sleeping in her truck tonight,' Nunzio commented.

'What do you mean?' I asked, praying that he was right and she'd been found safe and sound.

'We warned her not to sleep there again, or she'd be given a ticket. Besides, if she was so afraid why didn't she call the police?' Nunzio logically questioned.

A firefighter walked over before I could answer, having

caught the last part of our conversation. He was dressed in full firefighting gear, and furrows of dirt streaked his face.

'You had good reason to be concerned,' he confirmed. 'It looks as though the fire was due to kerosene. Either this was arson, or a dangerous appliance was being used in there.'

My heart sank and my conscience grew heavy with guilt. I should have driven here right away and dragged Magda back to my place, whether she liked it or not.

'Has anyone been found inside?' I asked, barely able to get the words out of my mouth.

The firefighter removed his helmet, revealing thin strands of hair that lay plastered to his scalp with sweat. He wiped an arm against his face and the soot spread like war paint across his flesh.

'We haven't been able to search in there yet,' he disclosed. 'But I doubt anyone would have been in that truck at this time of night.'

'That's what I've been telling her,' Nunzio confirmed.

I checked my watch. It was three thirty-three a.m. My own personal witching hour.

'Magda lost her apartment a while ago. She'd been sleeping in that truck ever since. I know she planned to stay there tonight, because I spoke to her earlier this evening,' I revealed.

I didn't want to think about what the last moments of her life had probably been like. But Magda had clearly had a premonition. She'd been right, and had called to ask for my help. Only, I'd let her down.

What had stopped me from immediately rushing out here? Her stubborn protests that everything was all right? The fact that she refused to go to a shelter? Or my own foolish pride? So what if she hadn't condoned my lifestyle? I couldn't help but feel partially responsible for her death.

The firefighter walked away and I realized that Officer Nunzio had been staring at me the entire time. I wondered if I looked guilty enough to be arrested for negligence.

'You never answered my question. Why did she phone you instead of the police?' he probed.

'I don't know,' I responded with a shrug. 'I told her that she should call you.'

What I didn't say was, *what good would that have done?*

'She was probably afraid that you'd force her to go to a shelter,' I added. 'And she was adamant about staying in her truck.'

'OK. So then tell me what you think. Was someone really after her? And if so, why?' Nunzio continued to dig.

I wasn't yet ready to reveal that Magda had stolen Bitsy von Falken's shawl. First of all, I'd be reamed over the coals for not reporting it immediately to the police. Secondly, Hogan might end my investigation.

'Once again, I don't know. But I suppose she could have been murdered if someone thought that she'd actually witnessed a crime,' I surmised.

'Yeah. Except why wait a few days? If the perp was gonna kill her, he'd probably have done it right away. Then she wouldn't have a chance to talk. Here's another question for you.'

Nunzio's face resembled that of a harlequin. Half of it remained in shadow, while the other half was illuminated by the light of the flames.

'Do you have any idea how she kept warm at night in that thing?' he queried.

'Magda said that she ran the truck's heater on full blast before going to sleep. If she woke up at night and was cold, then she'd turn it back on for a while,' I revealed.

'OK. But what did she do for light?' Nunzio asked, in what distinctly sounded like a dare.

I instantly knew what he was getting at. Nunzio was hoping to prove that the fire was an accident.

'Maybe she had a flashlight,' I said.

'Or maybe she had a kerosene lamp. If so, she could have easily knocked it over in her sleep,' he suggested. 'For all you know, she even kept a kerosene heater in there. Those things are notorious for starting fires.'

While that was true, I also knew in my heart that Nunzio was dead wrong. I had no doubt that the flames were the result of foul play. Magda had clearly realized she was in danger. So why had she insisted on spending the night in her truck?

Then I heard the words that I'd been dreading all along. *'Officer Nunzio, over here! A body's been found.'*

There was one last thing I knew. I didn't need an autopsy to prove that the charred bones were all that remained of Magda.

Nine

Dawn was already beginning to break by the time I left the scene. Its dim rays tentatively spread across the sky, intermingled with waning streaks of red still visible from last night's tumultuous fire.

I didn't bother to go home, but drove straight to the office. Once there, I pulled Magda's new coat over myself. Then I conked out on Hogan's couch for a couple of hours. My sleep was interrupted by a series of vivid dreams. In one, Magda deftly wrapped her shahtoosh shawl around me like a winding sheet. It was just about to cover my nose and mouth when something hard jabbed at my arm and I let out a startled shriek.

'For chrissakes, Porter. What are you doing sleeping here in my office?' Hogan asked, leaning over me.

His breath smelled bitter and stale, and I wondered if the man ever considered brushing his teeth. Or, maybe I was still dreaming. I sat up and rubbed my eyes.

'What the hell happened to you, anyway? You look like shit,' he pronounced, catching a better glimpse of me.

'There was a fire at the port last night. The lunch truck, The Kielbasa House, was purposely set aflame along with the woman that owned it,' I dully reported, still not wanting to believe it was anything more than a nightmare.

'Well, whaddaya know? This port is really turning into a hopping place these days,' Hogan replied with a snort. 'First there's that socialite's death, and now this. You better watch yourself, Grasshopper. Other agents will soon be fighting to come here and take your job.'

I shot him a withering look.

'Did you hear what I just said? The woman in the truck? She's dead,' I repeated, wondering if he'd understood.

'Yeah, well. It's probably because she didn't pay her Mob tax or something,' Hogan retorted, and sat down behind his desk.

I watched as he pulled a donut and a small cup of coffee from a paper sack.

'Mob tax? What's that?' I asked, still feeling half asleep.

Hogan gazed at me as though I were a total moron.

'Don't you know anything, Porter? And you call yourself a New Yorker,' he scoffed, and bit into his donut. 'Haven't you ever noticed those big black limos that pull up to the piers like clockwork every month?'

'Yes,' I replied, though I'd never given it much thought.

'Well, what do you think they're doing out here? You should try using your powers of observation next time you spot one. You'll notice a couple of guys get out with brief-cases. It's not legal briefs they've got stuffed in there. Those jerks are mopes with the Jersey Mob. They're collecting their monthly fees from the shipping companies,' he explained.

'And what do the shipping companies get in return?' I naively questioned.

Hogan took a sip of coffee, and wiped a stray drip of it off his chin.

'In return, the Mob lets them stay open and continue to do business,' he revealed. 'Think of it as kickback money. More than nine thousand people work at this port. What do you think would happen if the longshoremen suddenly decided to go out on strike?'

'Big trouble,' I responded.

'Big, big trouble, all right,' he agreed. 'Car dealers wouldn't receive their brand new automobiles, clothes wouldn't reach department stores, and there'd be a nasty jolt to the economy. It's just the nature of the beast. That's how this port is run. Could be your friend refused to play ball. In which case, the fire was probably set to teach anyone thinking of doing the same thing a lesson.'

'Or perhaps it was something else,' I proposed.

'And what would that be?' Hogan gamely questioned.

87

'Remember that anonymous phone call I received the other day? The one about Bitsy von Falken owning a shahtoosh shawl?' I reminded him.

'Yeah, and I told you that one shawl on a dead socialite does not a case make,' he responded, quoting himself verbatim.

Score one for Hogan, I thought. At least the guy still had his memory.

'Well, the woman that died in the fire last night is the very same person that discovered her body. But that's not all. She also found Bitsy von Falken wrapped in a shawl,' I revealed.

'And how do you know that?' he asked.

'Because the woman, Magda, told me,' I responded, doling out this minuscule scrap of information.

'Right. And then, of course, she was also killed. So naturally, it must all be tied together. I think you've got shahtoosh on the brain,' Hogan said, with a dismissive flick of his hand. 'Besides, we already talked about this and you said that the cops didn't find anything.'

'That's true. They didn't,' I replied, knowing that the shawl was safely at the forensics lab.

I had no intention of tipping my hand until I was certain the wool was shahtoosh and had some idea of exactly what I was up against.

'So then, the police must have it now,' Hogan assumed.

'No. Magda found the shawl and kept it,' I lied. 'Perhaps her murder is somehow connected.'

'To a shawl? Earth to Grasshopper. Come on, Porter. What do you think is going on? Wait. I've got it. Another socialite was filled with shahtoosh envy and decided to whack von Falken for it. Unfortunately, she forgot to take the shawl along with her and your lunch lady got her hands on it. That's why your friend was killed, right?' Hogan shook his head in amazement. 'Sometimes I wonder how you ever made it to Special Agent in the first place. Talk about your crazy conspiracy theories. That's the worst crock of shit I've heard yet.'

'Of course, I don't believe that the killer was another socialite . . .' I began to explain.

But Hogan cut me off, holding up a single finger.

'That's enough. And don't you dare think of prying into this thing either. You know damn well about our budget cuts. We're not going to waste one red cent over some goddamn shawl,' Hogan said, laying down the law. 'The rule is that only high priority cases are to be taken.'

Naturally. Probably because too much money was spent by bigwigs flying to the Caribbean to sip drinks by the pool while discussing the endangered species trade. Meanwhile, hard-working agents were relegated to Kumbaya courses on *Hand Holding 101* and brainwashed into not making waves. 'And I suppose that murder doesn't qualify as high priority,' I sniped.

'That's right. Especially when it's not our jurisdiction,' Hogan promptly shot back. 'If your friend ever found any such shawl then it probably burned up in that fire along with her. In which case, the problem has been solved and good riddance.'

Hogan rubbed his hands together as if having cleverly disposed of an annoying inconvenience. That simple gesture totally infuriated me. I'd be damned if I'd let Magda's death be written off that easily. However, I also knew enough to keep my mouth shut for now.

No question but that Hogan would have my butt should he learn that the shawl not only existed, but had already been shipped off to the lab. I could only hope that it proved to be shahtoosh and had the makings of a good case. Otherwise, I'd be sent shuffling off to Buffalo in no time flat.

Hogan finished his donut and then slapped his palms on his desk, as if having come to a decision.

'You look like hell, Porter. Take the rest of the day off as sick leave and go home,' he ordered.

I had no problem with that. But first I went into my office and checked for any messages. There were five on my answering machine. Each was from Santou wanting to know where I'd disappeared to last night, and if everything was all right. I must have forgotten to turn my cell phone back on after retrieving it from the recharger. I called him now, not wanting to put it off a minute longer.

'I swear, you're going to make me crazy, chère,' Jake

swore, upon hearing my voice. 'You've got to remember to keep that damn thing turned on.'

'I'm sorry. My mind was elsewhere,' I apologized, guilty as charged. 'I had a call from Magda during dinner last night. She didn't feel safe in her truck, but refused to go to a shelter or let me come by and pick her up.'

'This is the same woman that I saw on TV in that field where von Falken was found?' Santou clarified.

'Yes. I couldn't get her out of my mind. Especially after Terri's phone call in the middle of the night.'

'Come on, Rach. Don't tell me that you let his psychic mumbo jumbo get to you,' Jake lightly scoffed. 'You know that's nothing more than a bunch of hogwash.'

'Maybe not,' I replied, as a legion of goosebumps broke out on my arms. 'Both he and Magda had a premonition, and they proved to be right. There was a fire at the port last night. Magda's truck was burned down.'

'And Magda?' Jake asked.

'She was inside,' I said, my voice cracking with emotion.

'I'm sorry, chère. But the fire could have been due to anything. Really. An accident, or even a robbery gone wrong,' he tried to console me.

It was as if Santou already knew what I was thinking.

'Don't jump to conclusions until you've learned more,' he warned. 'One other thing. Do me a favor and be careful out there. We've been intercepting vague threats concerning Newark Airport. Try to be extra vigilant and keep an eye out for anyone that's the least bit suspicious.'

Terrific. Like I hadn't heard that one before. It would include just about everyone I knew, along with Hogan, who ranked high on my list.

'You can stop worrying for the moment. I'm being sent home for the day. Apparently, Hogan wants me to get my beauty sleep,' I told him.

'He's right, chère. I hear that smugglers are more likely to cooperate with good looking agents than ones that are haggard and tired,' he joked.

Santou should only have known the lengths to which I would go to get someone to twist and turn.

'Oh, by the way. Gerda offered to take care of Spam while we're at work. That's where you'll find him now,' Jake added, before I hung up.

I grabbed my things and began the drive home. Magda's unworn coat lay on the back seat like a newly inscribed headstone. It chided me by its mere presence.

She wouldn't have been killed if you hadn't taken the shawl, but simply left her alone. It's your fault that the woman is dead, it seemed to say.

I wondered if that were true. Had my interference set a chain of events into motion? Possibly her death had been meant as a warning. Or had Magda known more than she dared to admit? In any case, it was yet another episode that fueled my ever expanding collection of demons.

I knew I wouldn't be able to rest until I finally managed to connect all the dots. Part of that involved giving Magda a proper send-off. I phoned Nunzio, as I sped along the Turnpike.

'To what do I owe the pleasure of this call?' he good-naturedly inquired.

What a surprise. The man was actually beginning to thaw. A former boss of mine once said that I was like having a case of flat feet. You eventually got used to me.

'I wanted to ask if I could have Magda's remains whenever the police are through with them,' I replied.

'What in hell for?' Nunzio inquired, seemingly puzzled by my request.

'She doesn't have any family over here. In fact, I don't believe she had any family at all. I want to make sure that she gets a proper burial,' I explained.

'Exactly how well did you know this woman?' Nunzio asked, a hint of suspicion creeping into his voice.

'Not well at all. She was just a casual acquaintance that I spoke to whenever I bought coffee,' I responded, playing down any connection.

'Uh, huh. First she calls you, instead of the police. And now you want to get hold of her bones. If you ask me, something doesn't add up,' he declared.

Any trust that had been building between us instantly

vanished. 'I don't know what else to tell you,' I said, not in the mood to quibble.

'Why do you care what happens to her remains, anyway?' Nunzio continued, refusing to let it go.

'Do you have any idea what it's like to be all alone? Think about it, Nunzio. The woman worked all day in the cold, and then slept on the floor of her truck, for chrissakes. She didn't have a home. I think the least she deserves is to have someone care about where her bones are laid to rest,' I retorted, surprised by my own strong feelings. 'So, will I be able to get her remains or not?'

'I'll have to get back to you on that,' Nunzio formally responded, having morphed back into his old official self.

'By the way, have you discovered anything more about the fire last night?' I inquired, deciding it was worth a shot.

'You're asking about a case that's under active investigation. I'm unable to comment at this time,' Nunzio responded, effectively shutting me out.

I hung up feeling more frustrated than ever. There had to be a way to put the jigsaw puzzle pieces together, in spite of both Hogan and Nunzio's maddening roadblocks.

Faced with a long stretch of tank farms and chemical plants, my mind began to wander. It's strange how some things in life change, while others remain the same. For consistency, nothing beats larceny, greed, murder, and the endangered species trade.

I flashed back to those shiny black limos that parked at the piers, sleek as well-fed seals, and immediately knew who might be able to provide me with answers.

I bullied my SUV into a small space in the parking garage, and quickly rushed home. I didn't stop to get Spam, but dashed into my apartment, took a fast shower, and then picked up the phone. I punched in a memorized combo of numbers, only to be caught by surprise as strange voice answered the line.

'Vincent Bertucci's residence,' announced a woman in a nasal tone.

'Excuse me, but can I speak to him please?' I inquired, wondering who it might be.

I'd never seen Vinnie with a woman in all the time that

I'd known him. So why was a female suddenly living at his house?

'He's not here at the moment. This is his answering service. Can I take a message for you?' she robotically responded.

I left my number, feeling both annoyed and perplexed at this turn of events. Since when did a Mob guy hire an answering service to screen his phone calls? If something was wrong, I wanted to know about it.

I'd met Vinnie ten years ago, but it seemed as if I'd known him all my life. We'd bonded in New Orleans where we were both proverbial fish out of water. Bertucci had been a body-guard for a smuggler, while I was a rookie agent with US Fish and Wildlife. Since then, he'd worked his way up the ranks of the Travatelli crime family, while my career had remained on a lateral path. We'd come to an understanding during that time. He didn't deal in the endangered species trade, and I kept my nose out of the construction and sanitation businesses.

Vinnie had put himself on the line for me over a year ago. He'd literally saved my butt in Hawaii, while nearly losing his own. For that, I still owed him big-time.

It only took a few minutes before Vinnie returned my call.

'Hey, New Yawk. What's up?' he asked, in his native drawl.

'I could ask the same of you. What's with the answering service?' I inquired.

'Oh, just the usual business,' came his noncommittal response.

Though I remained curious, I knew better than to ask any more questions over the phone.

'So did you call just to shoot the breeze, or is there something on your mind?' he queried.

I could nearly hear him drumming his perfectly manicured fingernails straight through the wire.

'A little of both. Have you got time to meet me for coffee?'

'Yeah, I think I can squeeze you in. But we'll have to do it pronto. My morning's pretty booked up and so is my after-noon,' Bertucci responded.

Well, wasn't he the social gadfly.

'Do you want me to come to Queens?' I asked, more curious than ever as to what was going on.

93

'Nah. I'm already here in the city. Let's meet in Little Italy. You know the spot,' he instructed.

I'd gotten used to Vinnie's fixation with verbal shorthand. He always figured any phone line that he used was being tapped. I didn't want to tell him the Feds were swamped with more important matters these days. Not only would it hurt his feelings, but it might spur him on to other illegal activities in order to regain their attention. He believed that being on their watch list was a lot like celebrities dealing with the tabloids. Once the press, or the Feds, lost interest, your career was pretty well shot.

'I'll see you there in half an hour. How's that?' I asked.

'I'll be waiting with bells and whistles on,' he wise-cracked.

Little Italy, as it had once been, barely existed anymore. Most of the area was now a front for the tourist trade. This was due to Chinatown which, much like an ink stain, had steadily spread and taken over.

Gone were the old Italian grandmothers that had cooked up storms in the cramped kitchens along Mulberry Street. The restaurants were now all Chinese owned and operated, though they still retained their *paesano* names. Only the waiters remained Italian in a ruse to draw in unsuspecting customers.

I parked near the corner of Elizabeth and Grand. That was one of the perks of being in law enforcement. I could park wherever I pleased. This was official business and I wasn't about to pay for taxis and subways out of my own pocket.

I placed my handy dandy parking placard in the window and then walked to a small café that was more or less a 'social club'. It was one of the few spots in the neighborhood that the Chinese didn't dare set foot in. I entered to find Vinnie already seated and sipping an espresso with his back to the wall. If I hadn't known it was Bertucci, I'd have thought I was meeting an Italian movie star.

Gone were the polyester leisure suits, as well as the pointy alligator shoes. Vinnie was decked out in an expensive Brioni number. A camelhair overcoat lay draped over his shoulders,

94

with a fedora perched jauntily on his head. His open-collar shirt revealed a perma-tan that would have sent Terri dashing back to the nearest salon in envy.

Bertucci still weighed in at three hundred pounds. However, my eyes were drawn more to his twenty-four karat gold chain than to his heft. Dangling from it was a medallion of St Anthony that was the size of a small spare tire. Vinnie barely lifted a finger before an ancient waiter came scurrying over.

'Give the lady a cappuccino and bring us a plate of pastries,' he ordered, without my having to ask.

I looked at him and shook my head, utterly impressed.

'I know it's been a while since we've seen each other, but what's going on? You look terrific,' I said, feeling a bit envious.

I was more aware than ever of my discount clothing fetish. Maybe Terri was right. Perhaps it was time that I threw caution to the wind and blew some money on a more stylish wardrobe.

'I've got a new sideline going,' Vinnie revealed, his lips curling up in a satisfied smile.

'You mean in addition to all your other business ventures?' I joked.

'What can I say? I'm a true blue American entrepreneur,' Vinnie replied, looking like a well-cured side of beef.

'So, are you going to tell me what it is? Or do I have to guess?' I asked, as the waiter placed a platter of biscotti, Napoleons, tiramisu, zeppoli, and cannoli before us.

'This one? He's the new Johnny Depp,' the waiter proudly said, in a thick Sicilian accent.

The old man broadly smiled, revealing blank spaces where there should have been teeth.

'Johnny Depp, my ass. I'm more of a Bobby De Niro,' Vinnie protested. But I saw him slip the waiter a twenty.

'I'm not even going to try and figure it out. What's going on?' I asked, not having the slightest idea what either of them were talking about.

Vinnie took a sip of his espresso, ever so daintily curling his pinkie. 'I was walking out of Sparks Steakhouse a coupla months back when this casting director spotted me. Next thing you know, I'm being hired to play a wiseguy on *The Sopranos*, and the networks are calling me about doing a coupla shows. I'm even appearing in movies.'

'You're kidding me,' I said, totally flabbergasted.

'They told me I'm a natural. I got, whaddaya call it? Oh yeah. Screen presence,' Vinnie informed me. 'And if they decide to use one of those big name actors instead? Then I'm hired as a character consultant. You know, it's so they can ask dumb-ass questions like, *Hey, Vinnie. Do I wear my ring on this finger? Am I walking OK? And is my hair all right?*'

He emitted a high-pitched giggle and swallowed a cannoli in one bite.

'I guess my life experience is finally paying off. To tell you the truth, it's not a bad gig. What the hell! I'm raking in enough moolah to get free dental and health insurance from the Screen Actors Guild. And you know what those premiums cost. That alone was killing me.'

'What!' I exclaimed, beginning to feel totally pissed off. 'You're already a member of the Screen Actors Guild?'

'Of course. How else do you think I'm doing all this?' Vinnie retorted with a snort.

Forget the tan. Blast the new suit. I was upset that he was getting free dental and health insurance. I'd never managed to do that the entire time I'd been an actress. Vinnie was already doing better than I ever had after years of studying acting and speech, to say nothing of Shakespeare and classical theatre.

'But my favorite thing is when the make-up girl comes on set to do our final touch up. *Fluff 'em and puff 'em,* as they say. I just love that stuff. My boys in the 'hood get a kick out of it too,' Vinnie said with a wink. 'Even Billy Crystal told me just the other day that I'm gonna be a big star.'

Bertucci puffed out his chest, looking like an over-inflated penguin, as he scarfed up a zeppole. I almost choked on my tiramisu, unwittingly consumed by jealousy.

'What can I tell ya? Life is good right now. In fact, my agent's even working on a cookbook deal for me. I'm gonna call it *Mangia with the Mob*. Whaddaya think?'

'You've got an agent?' I asked in disbelief.

'Sure. That's why I'm a little pressed for time today. I got two auditions this afternoon,' he divulged. 'I think Victoria Gotti wants me to be on her reality show. Or maybe it's a Victoria's Secret commercial. I tend to get 'em mixed up,' he said with a laugh.

I polished off a Napoleon hoping that it would provide me with some comfort.

'So, how's by you?' Vinnie asked, apparently through with his update.

'Obviously not as good as you,' I replied, still trying to quell my envy. 'Listen, I called to ask a favor.'

'What? Another?' Vinnie queried, and arched an eyebrow. 'I'm gonna have to start charging you at this rate.'

'I just want a little information,' I told him. 'A luncheonette truck was set on fire at the port last night. The woman that owned it was inside at the time. Is there any way to check if the local Mob was involved?'

'And why would you think that?' Vinnie inquired with a deadpan expression.

No wonder he was landing mobster roles left and right. You couldn't get any more real than the goombah that was sitting before me.

'From what I hear, pay-offs are part of doing business at the port,' I replied.

'I guess it would be fair to say that,' he concurred.

'My boss thinks that's why Magda's truck was torched. Because she refused to pay. But I tend to believe it was something different,' I revealed.

'Oh yeah? Like what?' Vinnie questioned, not one to be left out of any juicy gossip.

'You heard about the body that was found there the other day?' I asked.

'Sure. The rich broad with the Wall Street husband,' Vinnie replied, clearly keeping up with the news.

'Magda saw the body being dumped,' I explained.

'Did she get a good look at any of the faces?' he asked.

'No, it was too dark,' I reported.

But something struck me as not quite right. Perhaps it was the way his pinkie had involuntarily twitched.

'I'll see what I can find out,' he smoothly replied, his finger once again under control. 'But you gotta do me a favor and stay outta trouble this time. I already got you outta one scrape. I don't need to be picking up any body parts in Newark. It might cut into my screen time.'

'I'll keep that in mind,' I replied, suddenly aware that *I* was the one with my back to the door.

I stood up and turned sideways, no longer certain as to which direction was safer.

'Hey, I gotta joke for you, seeing as how you're working in the Garden State these days,' Vinnie said, as we walked outside. 'You know why New Yorkers are always so depressed?'

'No. Why?' I asked, willing to play the straight man.

'It's because the light at the end of the tunnel is New Jersey,' Vinnie said, punctuating his punch-line with a loud *badda bing*. 'Keep your head down and your eyes open,' he added, by way of a new sign-off.

I watched as he strolled down the block. He now had the life of which I used to dream. And all it took was being a mobster. I figured there was a lesson in there somewhere about show business.

I got into my Trailblazer and wondered what to do next. I had yet to check my cellphone for any messages from last night. That ought to eat up a good five minutes. Most likely, there'd be a barrage of scoldings from Jake about not having kept my cellphone on.

I entered my code and my blood immediately turned cold, causing the hairs to stand up on my neck. The first message to be heard was a voice from beyond the grave. Magda spoke to me once again.

Rachel? I've changed my mind. Would you please come and pick me up? You were right. I think I should go home with you tonight.

The Italian pastries curdled in my stomach at the gut wrenching sound of panic in her voice.

Had she heard something outside that had prompted a cry for help? Footsteps, perhaps? Or had she caught a whiff of kerosene as it splashed against her truck? How much longer had she lived after that? Long enough to feel sheer terror crawling inside her like spiders? At least long enough to have placed one final phone call.

I suddenly felt light headed, and feared I was about to be sick. Not just from the message, but from the odor of smoke that still clung to my skin from last night's fire. It was the noxious fragrance of death.

I silently vowed to track Magda's killer down no matter what. That's when it finally clicked. Why had Vinnie seemed to know that more than one person had carried Bitsy von Falken into the field that night? He'd specifically used the word *faces*. It was a bit of information that had yet to be released, and I certainly hadn't told him about it.

I now began to wonder if Vinnie was a better actor than I had possibly ever imagined. I also began to wonder if I was the biggest patsy alive.

Ten

I was too revved up to head home. If adrenaline were music, it would have been bugling through my veins right about now. Fortunately, I'd brought along the contact sheet that Joy from Haller Associates had so thoughtfully emailed me.

God, there were a lot of people that attended big money benefits, and Bitsy von Falken seemed to have known every last one of them. I quickly scanned the list, feeling like a kid in a candy store.

Skip the models. Save the actresses for later. I needed someone that might be impressed with the title 'Special Agent.' I settled on Muffy Carson Ellsworth as an appropriate target. She was a doyenne whose name was constantly in the society columns. I picked up my cellphone and promptly punched in her number.

'The Carson Ellsworth residence,' answered a man, with a killer British accent.

I immediately felt like a low class commoner.

'Is Mrs Carson Ellsworth at home?' I inquired, attempting to sound oh-so-proper.

'Whom may I say is calling?' he asked.

I was tempted to recite a sonnet, or break into Shakespeare. Instead, I came off sounding like a total idiot.

'Rachel Porter. This is in reference to Bitsy von Falken. It's a matter of the utmost gravity,' I said, hoping to hit the right note of authority.

I thought I heard a chuckle as the man cleared his throat.

'One moment, please,' he dryly responded.

Terrific. It's always nice to know that I've made a complete fool of myself. I couldn't wait for the day when I finally felt like a grownup. Until then, I'd just have to keep pretending to be one. I began to suspect I'd been cut off when a woman finally came on the line.

'This is Mrs Carson Ellsworth. I understand you're calling in regard to Bitsy von Falken. You're not with the media, are you?' she asked, her voice dropping like a lead weight.

'No, of course not,' I hurriedly assured her. 'I'm a Special Agent.'

'A Special Agent? And just what is it that makes you so special? Are you a female James Bond, perhaps?' my target sardonically inquired.

'No. It's that I work for a law enforcement branch of the federal government,' I responded, not yet wanting to mention Fish and Wildlife. 'Your name was passed on by someone that said you might be willing to help with my investigation.'

'Really? Who gave you my name? And help you exactly how?' she asked, sounding puzzled.

'I'm afraid I can't reveal my source at this time,' I answered, pulling an Officer Nunzio. I just hoped that she fell for it. 'However, my contact spoke very highly of you. I understand that Bitsy von Falken organized a charity event about a year ago at which some shawls were sold.'

'Oh, no, no, no,' Muffy firmly retorted.

My heart immediately sank. Had word already gotten out that I might call and should be stonewalled?

'Those weren't just *any* shawls. They're absolute treasures. No. Actually, they're much more than that. They're heirlooms, really,' Muffy said, waxing eloquent. 'To call them just shawls is to do them an injustice.'

Uh huh. I was fairly certain all the Tibetan antelopes that died to provide them felt exactly the same way.

'Well, Mrs von Falken might have gotten herself into a bit of trouble over them. Might I stop by and talk to you about it?' I asked, quickly glancing down at my outfit.

Ooh, yeah, my boots and jeans should really do the trick. With any luck, she'd simply take pity on me.

'Bitsy was in trouble? Does this have anything to do with her murder?' she asked, sounding intrigued. 'Or does it involve that slacker husband of hers?'

Jake had said that Gavin von Falken was about to be investigated for investor fraud. Was that what Muffy was referring to? Only how could she have known if it hadn't yet been made public?

'I'd rather not discuss it over the phone,' I hedged.

'I understand. Of course, I'll make myself available. I'm happy to help in any way that I can,' Muffy responded with barely concealed delight. 'When would you like to stop by?'

The sooner the better, I thought, knowing there was no sense in taking any chances. I needed to question her before she was advised not to talk.

'How about right now?' I asked.

'Right now? Why not? That would be fine,' she gaily responded, as though we were about to meet for tea.

Muffy gave me the address, and I headed once more to the Upper East Side.

I've always thought of Manhattan as a series of villages, each with its own distinct personality. Every street has a signature that makes it unique. I left the aroma of cannolis and cappuccino behind and traveled through an area of Latino owned groceries, their colorful awnings hanging heavy as metal eyelids over each little bodega.

Continuing on, I skirted past trendy and tired Soho with its hipper-than-thou air. I chose instead to cruise by the hot new shops of Noho and NoLita. Then it was on to the East Village before reaching Gramercy Park and Union Square. Once there, it was a straight shot up Madison Avenue, where I was able to catch a glimpse of the Empire State Building. Even now, I liked to imagine it being breached by King Kong.

Next came Midtown with its glamorous Art Deco landmark, the Chrysler Building. The edifice stood proud as an aging regent bedazzling the crowds with its stainless steel crown. A closer look at the façade revealed fancy brickwork designed to resemble automotive hubcaps. It was hard to believe this had once been the tallest building in the world.

It was here that I caught the fragrant whiff of grease

emanating from a group of pushcarts. Vendors sold hotdogs, souvlaki, and gyros sandwiches as the angry horns of taxis screeched past like a flock of hungry birds.

I left the hoi polloi behind, with all its noise and its traffic, and soon entered the privileged landscape of the Upper East Side.

Finding a space, I wrestled my SUV between a Mercedes and a Jaguar. Then I walked towards Fifth Avenue and Central Park East. Each step took me closer to a bastion of blue blood and old money. Truth be told, its roots could easily be traced back to robber barons and other assorted crooks.

I was surprised to find that Muffy Carson Ellworth's address didn't lead to an apartment building, but rather an elegant three-story townhouse. That's when I knew I was rubbing shoulders with really big bucks.

I rang the buzzer and my telephone buddy, Jeeves, promptly answered the door.

'Good day, Miss. May I help you?' he asked, in a most eloquent and sonorous tone.

If I hadn't known better, I'd have thought the guy came straight out of Central Casting. Not only did he look like a butler, but he had the role down pat. In addition, he'd referred to me as 'Miss' rather than 'Ma'am'. It didn't get any better than that.

'Yes, I'm Rachel Porter. I'm here to see Mrs Carson Ellsworth. She's expecting me,' I said, and flashed a smile.

Jeeves shot back a withering look as he glanced at my attire. So much for my natural charm and winning personality. He turned and I followed him inside.

'Please wait here. Mrs Carson Ellsworth will be with you shortly,' he said.

Jeeves took my jacket and gingerly held it before him, as though suspecting it might be toxic. Then he left me standing alone in an enormous room.

I figured this must be a multi-millionaire's idea of cozy. The drawing room had two burgundy velvet settees, the usual French cut-glass mirrors, and a large bureau of burl-wood. Atop it were numerous framed photos of Muffy at various stages of life, all neatly arranged in a stylish 'mess'.

The walls were a pale soft green and decorated with hand-painted murals; the theme, fat little cherubs gorging themselves on fruit. It was then I first became aware there was a cat in the room.

A Himalayan, soft and round as a chocolate truffle, came sauntering towards me. The feline idly rubbed its brown and cream fur against my pants, as though I were no more than another piece of furniture in its path, before heading to a loveseat. Hopping up on the settee, the furball circled three times and then nestled down in the folds of a beautiful blue shahtoosh shawl. I began to make my way over to check out the goods when Muffy Carson Ellsworth abruptly entered the room.

Perhaps *entered* wasn't the proper term to use. Muffy swept in with all the assurance of a *grande dame* coming to greet an adoring public. I turned to face her, quite aware that I was in the presence of a force of nature.

Muffy's hair was the same rich blonde sported by both Bitsy and Tiffany, though she must have been sprinting towards seventy years old. I had to hand it to the woman. She carried her age with style and class.

She stood adorned in a black Chanel suit and white chiffon blouse that was semi-transparent. An exquisite La Perla camisole flirtatiously played peek-a-boo underneath. Three heavy strands of pearls hung from her neck, each creamy globule nearly as large as the tip of my thumb.

The final touch was an enormous silver pearl encrusted with diamonds that dangled between her breasts. The gem perfectly matched the drop earrings that she wore. Not to be outdone was a diamond brooch in the shape of a snowflake. Its baguettes glistened like lethal slivers of ice on her lapel.

Muffy was one of those X-ray women that obviously believed you could never be too rich or too thin, and adamantly lived by her convictions. Which was to say, she was fashionably anorexic. Her cheeks didn't just sink into her face but submerged like a pair of deep craters, while her legs were the width of two sticks. I could see every vein, every bone beneath her paper-thin skin. The impression was that of a stylish cadaver. No matter. She still wore the latest Manolo Blahnik high heels.

'That's why you'd never make it as a socialite, Rach. Those women have got the iron will of Mussolini when it comes to eating,' Terri had once told me.

I could think of plenty of other reasons why I wouldn't have made it, as well. Such as the fact that I didn't have the necessary funds.

Muffy didn't come to greet me, but struck a pose in front of one of her French cut-glass mirrors. I took my cue and walked over to pay the appropriate homage.

'Agent Porter, isn't it?' she asked, and offered her hand as if she were the Pope.

I now knew who it was that Muffy reminded me of. She was a dead-ringer for the haughty actress Lauren Bacall.

'Yes. It's a pleasure to meet you, Mrs Carson Ellsworth,' I replied.

Her fingers barely touched my outstretched palm.

'Naturally,' she modestly retorted. 'Won't you sit down?'

I followed the languid wave of her arm to one of the loveseats. Muffy sat on the other, next to her perfectly coifed cat. Amazing. Even the little sucker was better groomed than I was. Muffy seemed to think so too as her eyes briefly flitted over me. I could almost hear myself being soundly dismissed.

'Is that shahtoosh, by any chance?' I asked, pointing to the wrap on which her cat lounged.

'Yes, it is,' Muffy replied, her voice oozing with pleasure as her hand tenderly stroked the wool. 'Beautiful, isn't it? I allow Everett to lie on one of my shawls whenever he's being particularly good. He just loves the feel of it.'

I couldn't say that I blamed him. I also couldn't help but think of all the homeless animals there were, and wonder how many bags of pet food the sale of just one shawl would provide. Everest was badly in need of a dose of reality, to my mind.

'*One* of your shawls?' I promptly chirped up. 'Are they all shahtoosh?'

'Of course. Once you own one, you immediately want more. They're so light, you can barely feel them. Everyone

I know has at least two, or three, or four,' Muffy responded, as if insulted that I might think otherwise. 'You mustn't view them as simply a fashion rage. Rather, they're an absolute necessity.'

True. What else could these women possibly drape over their bony shoulders, or use to swaddle their newborn babies?

'All except for Giancarlo Giamonte, of course. That scamp must have at least two hundred stoles in every color to match each of his sweaters, suits, and coats,' she blithely remarked, as though we were just two gals shooting the breeze. 'Then there's a certain socialite I know that had one made into a bedthrow, while Donna Karan swears that her shahtoosh shawl is her security blanket. For goodness' sake, even Queen Elizabeth, Blaine Trump, Christie Brinkley, and Patty Buckley own at least one.'

Muffy leaned forward, as if she were about to share a secret with me.

'Let me tell you. There was a mad dash on the shawls after British Vogue declared pashmina to be out and shah-toosh to be in. Of course, I already owned my stoles. I don't allow anything as base as a common magazine to rule my fashion taste. But there are others in my social circle that clearly do,' she confided, and raised a knowing eyebrow.

Whoa! Back up a minute. My mind was awhirl in a potent swirl of celebrity names. Obviously there was some serious shahtoosh lust going on out there.

'Excuse me. But exactly who is Giancarlo Giamonte?' I asked, vaguely remembering that Terri had once mentioned him. 'The name sounds familiar. Is he someone that I should know?'

'Well, that all depends. Anyone on the A-list would natu-rally be acquainted with him,' Muffy informed me, while disdainfully pushing back a lock of her hair.

Her eyes flickered in amusement, and a devilish smile licked at her lips, telegraphing that I had far less status than even a cockroach at the base camp of High Society. As if that was something I didn't already know.

I wondered what it was like to live Muffy Carson

Ellsworth's life, lunching on lobster salad at Le Bernardin and packing her Vuitton bags for a couture show.

'Would you mind giving me a bit more detail on him than that?' I asked.

As much as I would have liked to throttle the woman, I needed to keep it friendly for now.

'He's an up-and-coming designer and a very sweet young man. I show my support by wearing his designs whenever I can,' she replied. 'Giancarlo knows that if his fashions are seen on me, then others will surely buy them.'

Evidently, Muffy was more than just your average socialite. She was also a fashion stamp of approval.

'Giancarlo is such a perfect gentlemen that I often have him escort me to social events. It allows him to mingle with the right crowd, and I know he won't do anything to embarrass me,' she added.

A hint of color rose in her cheeks and I wondered if Muffy had a crush on him.

I held off on my next question as Jeeves entered the room with a silver tray. Balanced on it were two porcelain cups, a teapot, a creamer and sugar bowl, along with a small plate of cookies. He poured the tea and then left.

'How many shahtoosh shawls do you actually own?' I asked, my hands itching to snatch one of the buttery treats. However, I had no intention of doing so until Muffy did, and her fingers weren't moving.

'I have five. Of course, that doesn't include the seven stoles I bought at Bitsy's charity event last year. Those were for Christmas gifts. You should have been there. People were snapping them up as fast as they could,' Muffy said, and discreetly slipped a cookie crumb into her mouth.

As far as I was concerned, that was my green light to go. I plucked a chocolate cookie off the platter and began to munch.

'But you haven't yet told me what this has to do with Bitsy,' Muffy protested, with a slight pout. Then her eyes grew wide with fear. 'Oh, dear. You aren't suggesting that she was murdered for her shawl, are you?'

Her fingers wound themselves tightly around the shahtoosh wrap, as if daring someone to try and pry it from her cold, dead hands.

'Mrs Carson Ellsworth,' I began.

'Oh please, dear. We've already gone beyond that. Just call me Mrs Ellsworth,' she suggested, in what I could only assume was a sign of friendship.

'Mrs Ellsworth, remember I told you that I'm a special agent? Well, I'm with the US Fish and Wildlife Service,' I informed her.

'Oh, I see. Does that mean you suspect I'm abusing my cat? Or are you here for some kind of donation?' she asked, as if stymied.

For a moment, I wondered if Muffy might possibly be trying to bribe me.

'No, of course not. I'm here because shahtoosh shawls are illegal. They're made from a highly endangered species that's killed to obtain their wool,' I revealed.

Muffy looked at me as though I'd totally lost my marbles, and then laughed sharply.

'Don't be ridiculous. Of course they're not,' she brusquely responded, choosing to disregard my remark with a brush of her hand. 'Everyone knows that nomadic children and shepherds gather little tufts of their beard hair from off shrubs as they graze.'

It was my turn to gaze in amazement at the slightly addled fashion maven. Muffy Carson Ellsworth clearly didn't have the foggiest idea of what she was talking about.

'I'm sorry, Mrs Ellsworth. But exactly what kind of animal are you referring to?' I questioned.

'Well, toosh goats, of course. That's why the wool is so expensive. It's gathered strand by tiny strand until there's finally enough to make just one shawl. If you're *really* a wildlife agent, then shouldn't you already know all of this?' she asked, and began to regard me with suspicion.

I'd heard the fables before. The source of shahtoosh had been shrouded in secrecy and myth for years in order to make it more palatable to the 'beautiful people'. Dealers sometimes went so far as to peddle the tale that shawls were made from the feathers of a fictitious 'toosh bird' in a bucolic world where near-blind weavers spun them into jewel-colored clouds of gossamer.

'For goodness' sake, it's concerned women such as myself that help to keep those poor people alive by providing them with employment. And shame on you for thinking otherwise,' she scolded. 'No one would ever harm those dear little toosh goats. That's nothing more than a nasty rumor spread by those horrible animal rights activists. Oh yes, and by all those people that are envious because they can't afford to buy them.'

'Right. And the Three Bears had no problem with Goldilocks eating their porridge, either,' I couldn't help but snidely remark. 'Sorry to burst your bubble, Mrs Ellsworth, but that's nothing more than a fairy tale.'

'Mrs Carson Ellsworth to you,' she snapped.

'The truth is, you're wearing killer cashmere. Hundreds of Tibetan antelope are slaughtered each year to provide customers, such as yourself, with those shawls. The only way the animal gives up its wool is if it is killed,' I said again partly to educate her, but mostly to vent my frustration.

'God, but you're ignorant,' she declared with a defiant sniff. 'Friends of mine in the know tell me that no animal is endangered. For goodness' sake, how can they be when cats and sheep can be cloned, and Siegfried and Roy are able to rear three Siberian tiger cubs in the middle of Las Vegas? It's all just a ruse to give people like you a job.'

'In that case, humor me. Where did Bitsy obtain the shawls that were auctioned at her charity event?' I questioned.

'I'm sure I don't know. And even if I did, I'd have no reason to tell you,' Muffy huffily retorted.

If she was going to play hardball, so be it.

'Then I'm going to have to ask you to hand over all of your shahtoosh shawls. They constitute illegal property, and will have to be confiscated,' I replied, showing her that two could play this game.

'Over my dead body!' Muffy announced and, knocking the cat off her wrap, folded the blue stole tightly around her. 'They're precious works of art. Would you expect me to simply hand over a Van Gogh? A Renoir? A Monet? I think not.'

In reality, they were nothing more than frigging status symbols. Though by the way she was acting, you'd have sworn they were cocaine. Everett climbed on to her lap, as if also refusing to let me take his blanket away.

'Oh, and I'll need those shawls that you gave as Christmas presents, as well,' I added, purposely yanking her chain.

'And if I refuse?' she challenged, narrowing her eyes.

'Then I'll be forced to get a subpoena,' I replied.

Muffy Carson Ellsworth gasped in alarm. 'Well, I never! How dare you even suggest such a thing. That's simply impossible. I can't ask for those back. What would people say? I'd be called an Indian giver. Besides, the thought of never being able to wear them again is just too horrible to bear.'

Muffy clearly meant business. She glared at me and firmly clenched her jaw. 'Just who do you think you are, anyway? The closet police? I believe it's time that I give my lawyer a call.'

It was now my turn to scurry, painfully aware that I was treading on dangerous ground. One call from Ellsworth's attorney would not only bring the wrath of Hogan down upon me, but possibly blow a potential case and, perhaps, even my career. After all, I was secretly delving into this against his direct orders. The wisest thing would be to retreat and mollify Muffy for now. As much as I hated to eat my words, I quickly backpedaled with all the determination of Lance Armstrong.

'Perhaps you're right, Mrs Carson Ellsworth. The shawls *are* lovely, and I certainly wouldn't want to bring you any distress,' I concurred.

'I should think not,' Muffy replied, her voice filled with shards of reproach.

She looked as though she'd never forgive me. Even Everett seemed to glower resentfully.

'There is one thing, though. Would you mind if I run your shawl through my ring? It's a test to determine that the stole is really shahtoosh and not pashmina. I'd hate to think someone might have pulled the wool over you.' I was betting Muffy's ego wouldn't let her turn the challenge down.

'Oh, for goodness' sakes! Of course it's shahtoosh,' Muffy

bristled at the veiled insult. 'Don't you think I would know?'

'It's just that it's sometimes hard to tell what's fake and what's not. Sad to say, a number of women are conned every year,' I said, hoping to pull my own bluff.

I had no doubt Muffy could spot the real thing from the opposite end of a football field. The test was mainly to satisfy my own curiosity. Fortunately, Muffy Carson Ellsworth's vanity won out.

'Oh, all right. Go ahead if you like,' she finally agreed.

I reached for the shawl only to have the cat take a swipe at me.

'Everett is a very good judge of character,' Muffy quipped, and proceeded to lift the hairball off her lap.

I didn't respond, but removed my ring and easily pulled the shawl through the hole.

'There. I told you that it was shahtoosh,' Muffy victoriously preened.

Fish and Wildlife would have been smart to hire the woman as their resident shahtoosh expert.

'I'm sorry if I upset you,' I apologized, with all the fake sincerity I could possibly muster. 'But you'd be amazed at how many women are wearing pashmina, believing it to be shahtoosh.'

Muffy straightened her shoulders and pursed her lips.

'Hmm. I suspect there might be a number of them within my own social circle. I always thought that their shawls weren't quite up to snuff. To tell the truth, I don't believe they paid full price. It serves them right. That's what happens when you're cheap and try to get a bargain,' she loftily announced. 'Personally, I see it as a sign of bad breeding. Haggling is very low class. It reveals too much mixing of the gene pools, if you know what I mean.'

I understood perfectly. She was referring to mongrels such as me. If I'd had one wish at the moment, it would have been to dump Muffy in the middle of *Schmata Central* on the Lower East Side and let her fend for herself.

'I know exactly what you're getting at,' I replied, amazed at how bitchy a real snob could be. 'But we shouldn't let that distract us from the reason why I'm here.'

Muffy looked at me as though she were still waiting to find out.

'Bitsy,' I reminded her. 'I'm hoping that you'll decide to help me with this case.'

Muffy gazed off into space as though she hadn't yet made up her mind.

'You could be essential in helping to solve her murder,' I flattered, hoping that would do the trick.

'And why are *you* involved in this, again?' she asked.

'Because I'm a federal agent,' I replied, hoping she'd stop at that.

Muffy's fingers idly played with her large silver pearl, as she seemed to think it over.

'Yes, of course I will. After all, she *was* one of us. And I did offer, didn't I?' she said, after studying me. 'What say we just put this little misunderstanding behind us. Now, how can I help?'

I was astounded by the quick turn around, but wasn't about to let it show. The faster I tracked Bitsy's killer down, the sooner I'd uncover the person responsible for murdering Magda.

'Can you think of anyone that might have wanted to harm her and, if so, why?' I asked, prepared to hear that Bitsy didn't have an enemy in the world.

The corners of Muffy's lips curled up ever so slightly, though her mouth remained tightly pinched. 'Of course I can. A woman by the name of Tiffany Stewart for one.'

I stared at her in amazement. How had she managed to pick the very person that had contacted me about this case in the first place?

'I take it that you've already heard of her,' Muffy wryly noted, catching sight of my expression. 'But then again, who hasn't? The slut is notorious. She not only slept with Bitsy's husband – and heaven knows, there were plenty of women that did – but then had the nerve to openly flaunt it in her face. That's very bad form,' Muffy remarked, ever the Miss Manners of social etiquette. 'Sleeping with a friend's husband is one thing. But what goes on between the sheets should stay between the sheets. That only makes good sense.'

112

It struck me that Muffy was probably speaking from experience. This case was suddenly becoming a whole lot more interesting.

I wondered if Tiffany Stewart called me out of guilt for having done wrong by her friend. Or, if it had been part of a well-thought-out plan to throw me off track? Still, why had she phoned me at all, rather than the police?

'Tell me a little about Bitsy's husband,' I requested.

'Gavin?' Muffy asked and wrinkled her nose, as if having caught a whiff of something rotten. 'He's a very milk toast type of man. Sandy hair, pale complexion, very little backbone, and a handshake that's limp as a fish. I never had any idea what either woman saw in him.'

Perhaps it was what he had in his bank book. But Muffy quickly put that notion to rest.

'He made his money early on, and then lost most of it in the crash of 2000. It was clear at the time that he was a dud, but Bitsy was determined to hang on to him,' she revealed. 'Word had it that most of her fortune was tied up with his. Believe me, till death do us part generally involves finances more than love.'

Her skeletal fingers reached for a cookie, and then receded, as if having thought better of it.

I wondered if Muffy included herself in that cynical analysis. I looked around the room once more. There was no sign of a Mr Carson Ellsworth in the photographs, and the décor was resoundingly feminine. In addition, Muffy had yet to make any reference to a husband. The sole give-away was the diamond-encrusted wedding ring on her finger.

'However, Gavin turned out to be the poster boy for second chances,' she resumed. 'Hyde Barrow chose him to be the Chief Financial Officer of their firm soon afterward. I've always wondered about that. To my mind, he was rewarded for having taken down another company.'

'Then he lost more than just his own money?' I asked, not having realized that he'd been gainfully employed at the time. I didn't know what I imagined it was that rich people did with their lives. Well, that wasn't quite true. I usually envisioned them playing polo and drinking sherry.

'Oh my, yes. It was one of those dot com companies. Global Communications, or some such business. There were whispers about fraud, but they were never substantiated. And since Gavin's own money disappeared as well . . .'

Muffy shrugged her scrawny shoulders as if to say *que sera sera.*

'I've always maintained that conservative investments are the only way to go. None of that silly fly-by-night nonsense. Unless, of course, you're part of the grubby bourgeoisie trying to claw your way up from a lower social class. *That's* the difference between having old money and being nouveau riche. It all comes down to a matter of breeding and taste,' she concluded.

Maybe so. But Bitsy had conveniently hung on to enough dough to sponsor a charity event and plunk down twenty-thousand dollars of her own money on a shahtoosh shawl. And what about that big chunky diamond that Tiffany Stewart had told me about?

'So Gavin didn't come from old money, then?' I followed up.

Muffy gave a condescending laugh and waved her hand back and forth, as if driving away an annoying stench. 'Of course not.'

'And Bitsy? Was she new money as well?' I questioned.

'Bitsy was from a totally different class. Her father was Andrew Pierson, a highly respected man whose roots go all the way back to railroads and banking,' Muffy revealed. 'Bitsy's downfall was that she married outside of her station. She should never have given Gavin control of her money.'

I felt as if I were receiving a crash course in Manhattan's illustrious social stratosphere.

'And you really believe that Tiffany Stewart wanted Bitsy out of the way?' I asked.

I pictured Tiffany once more in her sequined top and skin-tight pants. No way could I imagine her knocking off Bitsy while tottering about in her Manolo Blahnik high heels.

'Tiffany's husband was a good deal older. My sources tell me that he left her very little in the way of financial assets upon his death. Most of the estate went to his two sons from his first marriage. Tiffany has been spending what little capital she has on contesting the will ever since,' Muffy revealed with a self-satisfied smirk. 'It seems that Mrs Stewart is scrambling about for money these days.'

Tiffany could have fooled me. It was then I realized that what *I* viewed as a lot of money, and what Muffy considered to be a tidy sum, were probably two very different things. I flash-backed to Tiffany's opulent apartment and drop-dead diamond ring. No doubt her paltry inheritance could have kept me living in style for the rest of my life.

'I hope that I've been of some help,' Muffy said in a sugary voice, while folding her hands in her lap with a saccharine sweet smile.

Who was she trying to kid? The woman was a blood-thirsty piranha. My only question was, what was her stake in all this?

Everett tried to snuggle his way on to her shawl once more, and Muffy coldly pushed him off. That was when I finally understood. She maintained her position at the top of the social food chain by using the proverbial carrot and stick. Tiffany had challenged Muffy's set of rules and was now being punished for it.

'Oh yes, you've been very helpful,' I agreed.

'Good. Then I don't expect to hear any more nonsense concerning my shawls,' she added, more as a stated fact than anything else.

Apparently, I'd received my carrot, and was now expected to roll over. I chose not to respond as she rang for Jeeves.

'There is one more thing. I take it that you and your husband didn't socialize much with either the Stewarts or Von Falkens,' I surmised.

I was hoping to find out whatever I could about Muffy's husband. Perhaps that would give me some additional insight into the woman.

'We did at one time, but Sterling passed away a few years ago,' she quietly responded.

The slightest quiver of her lips revealed that Muffy actually must have had feelings for him. She looked so forlorn that I almost felt sorry for the woman.

'Have you ever lost someone you loved?' she questioned, catching me off-guard.

'Yes,' I replied, thinking of both my mother and grandmother.

'Well then, you know what it's like. There's always a part of you that secretly hopes you might hear from them again,' she revealed. 'That they might contact you from the great beyond.'

I sometimes wished I were more in touch with my inner voice and knew when to keep my mouth shut. Instead, I heard myself speak before I could stop.

'I know this sounds crazy, but I don't suppose you've ever heard of *Psychics-On-Call*, have you?' I questioned.

Muffy sprang forward, as though she were coming in for a kiss. 'You know of Mr T? My dear, I've clearly underestimated you. The man is absolutely fabulous. Does this mean that you've called him also?'

Ohmigod. I'd apparently found her weak spot. Muffy was a psychic freak.

'No, I don't have to call him there. He's a good friend of mine,' I revealed.

Muffy looked at me with new found respect.

'I hate phoning that place, myself. It always feels rather sleazy. I'd much rather pay for a private meeting. Do you suppose that could possibly be arranged?'

'Hmm. He has a very busy schedule, what with all the important people that he sees,' I said, figuring that would whet her appetite. 'But let me speak with him and see what I can do.'

If nothing else, she'd owe me one and it gave me a reason to get back in touch with her. This time her hand firmly grasped mine as Jeeves appeared and I was shown out the door.

I left the cushy confines of her townhouse and hit the streets of the real world once more. Or, at least, as real as the snooty Upper East Side could ever possibly be. After all, I was now hobnobbing in a society where women paid six thousand dollars for bedsheets that boasted an eight-hundred thread count, and took up to a year to make in Italy. I daydreamed of how it must feel to sleep on something that soft and luxurious. The problem was, marinate too long in a rarified atmosphere and it becomes easy to lose all perspective.

Eleven

A friend had once told me the three rules for successfully living in Manhattan were money, money and
more money. He'd been right. I was roughly jerked back
to reality as I caught sight of my Trailblazer. Someone had
side-swiped the SUV where it sat parked. Hogan would
have a shit fit if I reported it and he learned what I'd been
up to. I'd have little choice but to pay for the repair myself.
That meant brown-bagging it the rest of the year. My only
hope for financial solvency would be to win the jackpot
playing lotto. I examined the damage and then slid in
behind the wheel.

More than anything, I was beginning to find these *über-
rich* people, and their petty problems, depressing. What in
hell did they have to complain about, anyway? The fact that
their bedsheets took a few extra weeks to come back from
a special drycleaner in Milwaukee?

*Oh for chrissakes, Porter. Suck it up. You've got rich
people-itis,* my pain-in-the-ass inner voice told me.

Unfortunately, my subconscious was correct. I felt like
Cinderella, doomed to scrub pots and pans forever after
having missed the ball. Maybe my fairy godmother would
be able to help me. I picked up my cellphone and called
Terri.

'Hi sweetie. Is something wrong?' he asked, upon hearing
my voice.

'What are you doing? Looking in your crystal ball?' I
dolefully joked.

'No. It's just that you sound like hell,' came his smart
retort.

'Well, I'm working on a case that's beginning to drive me

118

a bit crazy,' I admitted. 'But aside from that, I'm about to set you on the road to riches.'

'What are you talking about?' Terri asked, his voice crackling with excitement.

'Remember I predicted that all New York society would soon be clamoring at Mr T's door? Well, guess what? You just got your first appointment with a real honest-to-goodness socialite,' I revealed.

'Don't toy with me, Rach,' Terri warned. 'Not today. I'm feeling bloated, and I swear to God I have PMS.'

'Believe me, this is no joke,' I replied. 'I just came from a visit with Mrs Muffy Carson Ellsworth and she's a big fan of yours. In fact, she wants to arrange a face-to-face private reading.'

'Are you kidding me? That's unbelievable!' Terri yelped into the phone. 'I feel as if I've just died and gone to high society heaven. Do you know what this means? One word from her and all the crème de la crème of New York will be rushing to see me. How did you ever get in to her, anyway?'

'It's a long story,' I responded. 'But in return, I need something from you.'

'Just name it and it's yours. How about Eric's first born child?' he offered. 'God knows, I could use a break from Lily.'

'Actually, I was thinking more along the lines of information. Tell me what you know about a guy named Giancarlo Giamonte,' I requested.

Terri emitted a low, guttural laugh. 'I take it that you're referring to Mr Ralph Goldberg, formerly of Queens, New York.'

'Are we talking about the same fashion designer that's the darling of the moment with the Ladies Who Lunch?' I inquired.

'The one and only,' Terri confirmed. 'He changed his name from Goldberg to Giamonte not only because it sounded more exotic but – let's face it, you know how those waspy society women can be. They believe everyone should have at least a token minority in their circle – preferably one that works in the kitchen.'

119

'Yeah, I did catch a whiff of that,' I admitted.

What saved me time and again was my non-ethnic name and appearance. No one ever caught on to the fact that I was Jewish. It gave me access to any number of interesting conversations, some of which had been most helpful when it came to tracking down perps. The result was akin to working undercover without having to lie.

'But I don't get it. Giamonte is still ethnic. So, what's the catch?' I asked.

'Oh, but you haven't yet heard his lovely Italian accent. It was worth every penny he spent on it. And, of course, he isn't of lowly peasant stock but descends from a noble family,' Terri said with a giggle. 'He's not just some *schmo* from Queens, but rather the son of a Count with a castle in Tuscany. You know, it's sort of like *Ragu* versus *Prego* spaghetti sauce. They're both puréed tomatoes but with different labels.'

It was funny to hear Terri pepper his speech with Yiddish. 'I see your point. So what else can you tell me?'

'Plenty,' Terri disclosed. 'He's heavy into S & M, and has a thing for making videos of his sexual exploits. I hear he has quite the extensive DVD collection. Ralph is fairly notorious among the local gay scene. It's well known that you don't go home with him unless you want to star in his next movie. The only catch is he always makes certain that *he's* the one with the best lighting.'

I wondered how Muffy would feel if she learned all this about her fashion toy boy.

'Why hasn't word gotten out if it's true?' I inquired. 'I'm sure there must be more than a few people that would love to see him go down in flames.'

'It's because the guy is sharp,' Terri retorted. 'He's Ralph in his private life and Giancarlo when it comes to business. And he's smart enough never to mix the two.'

'Then how do you know about it?' I questioned.

'I'm psychic,' Terri replied.

I remained silent.

'Oh for chrissakes, Rach. I'm only kidding. I know the accountant that does his taxes.'

'You wouldn't also happen to know how I can contact him, would you?' I queried.

'Why? Do you have a secret sex life that I don't know about?' he teased.

'Very funny,' I responded.

However, part of me worried that Terri might have been right last night. Perhaps my personal life had become too staid. Spicing it up with a pair of handcuffs might not be such a bad idea – as long as I was the one holding the key.

'It has to do with that case that I'm working on,' I informed him.

'You mean the one involving the shawl stolen from a dead woman? Is that why you went to see Muffy Carson Ellsworth?' Terri inquired, fishing around.

'Look, please don't mention any of this to Muffy if you speak with her. She considers Giancarlo to be a close personal friend, and I'd like to keep it that way for now,' I warned.

'Got it. As far as I'm concerned, Giancarlo is as authentic as fettuccine Alfredo,' Terri assured me.

'Great. By the way, I also want to thank you for calling last night,' I added.

'Yeah, right. For waking you up from a dead sleep, you mean?' Terri asked with a snort. 'Sorry about that. Sometimes I let my impulses get the better of me.'

'No. As it turns out, you were right,' I told him. 'I only wish you'd called sooner. You're beginning to convince me, Terri. Maybe you really are psychic.'

'Why? What happened?' he warily asked.

'Remember you said that you envisioned the color red all around me? Well there was a fire,' I started to relate.

'And you're just telling me about this now? Damn it, Rach. That does it. You really have to move out of that miserable claptrack of a building,' Terri began to vent.

'No, it wasn't at my place. You remember Magda, the woman that called my cellphone during dinner last night,' I explained.

'The one that stole the beautiful wool shawl,' Terri said in a distant voice.

It was almost as if I could hear him begin to put the puzzle pieces together.

'I had an odd feeling about that call. I just couldn't quite put my finger on it. But it was as if a black veil were being drawn over me,' he related.

I shivered, even though the heater was on in the Trailblazer.

'Is she all right?' he asked.

But the tone of his voice betrayed that he already knew the answer.

'No. She died. Somebody purposely set her truck on fire while she was inside,' I replied, still haunted by the memory of those insatiable flames. They'd leapt into my brain, where they continued to burn with fierce determination.

'Oh, God. I'm so sorry, Rach. That's horrible,' he sympathized.

'I drove to the seaport shortly after you called. But it was already too late. I wasn't in time.'

I still couldn't forgive myself for having been irritated at Magda, and for not dragging her back to my place immediately. And for not having my cellphone on to receive her final call. The thought that I might have saved her was almost too much to bear.

'It wasn't your fault, Rach,' Terri offered, as if he were reading my mind. 'You can't beat yourself up over it.'

I only wished life were that easy.

'Is Giancarlo somehow involved in all this?' Terri asked, consumed by curiosity.

'I don't know yet. I just have to keep pulling at threads until something finally gives and begins to unravel,' I responded, not knowing any other way to work a case.

'OK, then. Here's his phone number,' Terri said and repeated it to me. 'Just be careful.'

'Why? Do you know something that I don't?' I asked, half jesting and half serious.

'You want the truth?' he queried.

'Absolutely,' I responded, though not really certain.

'Just knowing the chances you take would be enough to make me nervous. But there's more to it than that. I don't like what I'm feeling.'

That made two of us.

'Promise me that you'll keep in touch. And I'm not talking about calling in a few days. I mean, I want to hear from you either tonight or tomorrow.' He made me swear before he hung up.

Twelve

After that, I sat and stared at the phone number in my hand. Giancarlo Giamonte, or Ralph Goldberg. I didn't much care which persona I met, as long as one of them coughed up the information that I was after. I figured anyone owning two hundred shahtoosh shawls was bound to know the name of the supplier.

I quickly conjured my own cover story and then punched in Giamonte's number.

'Giancarlo Giamonte Designs. This is Giancarlo speaking. Who is calling, please?' demanded a man with an Italian accent as thick as pesto sauce.

'This is Miss Rachel Bush Porter. I was referred by Mrs Muffy Carson Ellsworth,' I replied in my best Texas drawl.

If Ralph was into playing name games with accents, so be it. I was more than happy to comply.

'I have a big affair coming up and I'll be needing a very special gown. Muffy said that you were the man for the job,' I told him.

'Dear, dear Muffy. How is she?' he asked, his tone instantly transforming from that of abrupt to obsequious.

'Aunt Muffy is just fine,' I replied.

'Ah? Then Muffy is a relative of yours?' he questioned.

'Well, no. Not legally. But she's a very close friend of my Auntie Barbara's, and I've known her since I was a child. When I told her about this event, she insisted I call you,' I improvised.

'Is she finally back home from her trip?' Giancarlo asked. 'I haven't heard from her for a while. Perhaps I should give her a ring.'

'No, don't do that,' I replied, consumed by a momentary

rush of panic. 'Aunt Muffy's out of town again for a few days. Auntie Barbara thought they could both use a rest, so they packed up and went off to a spa. But don't worry. She'll be back sometime next week. In fact, she mentioned there's a party coming up to which she'd like you to escort her.'

'Of course. I'd be delighted, as always,' Giancarlo said, nearly purring over the phone.

'In the meantime – I know this is short notice, but do you suppose I could stop by and discuss some designs for a gown with you?' I inquired.

'Please, there's no need to ask. It would be my greatest pleasure,' Giancarlo fawned.

It was amazing what money and social status could do. Giancarlo gave me his address and I promptly made a beeline for downtown.

I went from the East to the West Side. My Trailblazer traveled south along the Henry Hudson past the Seventy-Ninth Street Boat Basin, where New Yorkers too hip to live on land bobbed on the river in their houseboats. Soon after, pier after pier of cruise ships popped into view, each preparing to set sail for an exotic location. I had a momentary hallucination. What would it be like to chuck my old life and simply begin anew? The thought of taking on a different identity and starting all over again was surprisingly tempting.

What the hell's going on with you, anyway? my inner Mini-Me scolded. My restlessness had brought me all the way home. Even so, I was still feeling antsy. It was as if I had yet to make peace with the demons that chased me.

I continued down along the river, and then swung left on to Fourteenth Street. From there I entered the Meat Packing District. Once the stomping grounds solely of butchers, trans-vestite hookers and truckers, the area had now become *très chic,* transformed into the fashionistas' latest casualty.

Not only had it been prominently featured on *Sex in the City,* but even Stella McCartney had set up shop here. Her sleek clothing boutique shared the same block with other avant-garde designers and modern home stores too hot to dream of opening anywhere else.

I parked and navigated my way down the street, the uneven cobblestones turning my gait into that of a tipsy drunk. It was heartening to find that the area hadn't yet totally changed. Sure, there were upscale galleries and French bistros where toothpick-thin models posed like so much window-dressing. But there were also burly meat packers taking a break outside in their blood-stained smocks.

Exclusive nightclubs and bars had been lured to the spot by the neighborhood's old world charm. But the stench of decaying meat still wafted in the air where it intermingled with the scent of expensive pastry.

I headed over to Gansevoort Street where a few trannies huddled together in the cold. A blast of winter wind whipped at their vinyl knee-high boots, black fishnet stockings, and excessively short mini-skirts. They howled with laughter as a woman, in designer spike heels, stepped into discarded entrails lying outside a wholesale meat market. I dodged a small pile myself, while jumping across a gutter. No question but that this area had yet to lose the grittiness of New York's good old, bad old days.

I continued on to a warehouse that boasted a steel awning over its abandoned loading dock. Sharp meat hooks hung from the rafters above me. A check of the address verified that this was the abode of society's latest darling.

A static voice burst from the intercom after I rang the bell.

'Take the elevator up to the third floor,' it instructed, as I was buzzed inside.

I stepped into the hallway where my gaze was drawn to the concrete floor. Dried bloodstains formed a gruesome variety of abstract patterns. Either this had once been a meat market, or I needed to call in CSI.

I struggled with an accordion steel gate and entered what appeared to be the elevator. Actually, it was more of a death trap. It rose three excruciatingly slow flights accompanied by a disgruntled chorus of creaks, groans, and moans.

I was beginning to wonder if I was about to enter a designer house of horrors when the lift roughly jerked to a halt. It felt like forever before the elevator finally settled.

Only then could the door be opened. I found myself faced with a combo of all five men from *Queer Eye For The Straight Guy* rolled into one.

Giancarlo Giamonte stood in purple satin pajama bottoms and a tight white T-shirt, complete with plunging neckline, over which a long flowing robe had been thrown. If I hadn't known better, I'd have thought that Ralph Goldberg was a bad movie version of an Italian gigolo.

'Please come in,' he said and, taking hold of my hand, guided me over the threshold.

Giamonte's voice was as smooth and sensuously warm as a bowl of macerated cherries, his hair richly dark as a slick of premium motor oil. Giancarlo's eyes never left mine as he brought my hand to his lips and seductively kissed it. This guy had acquired more than just an accent. He'd also learned all the right moves to make.

Entwining his arm through mine, he led me down the hallway. Photos of Giancarlo accompanying an array of New York socialites, lined his walls. We entered a spacious room in which every piece of furniture, every exquisite accessory, had been ever so carefully placed. All the while, Giancarlo whispered a stream of sweet nothings into my ear – how nice my figure was, what lovely hair I had, and how much I resembled a younger, more vibrant, version of Muffy.

'No, truly. The two of you *must* be related,' he insisted, and gently squeezed my hand.

For a moment, I wondered if Terri had gotten it wrong and Giancarlo might actually be straight. Anyone looking on would have thought we were not only the best of friends, but possibly even lovers.

Then it hit me. Of course he was gay. No straight man would ever have been so thoughtful and attentive.

Giancarlo ushered me to a large leather chair where I sank into fabric as luxuriously soft as butter. Then, sitting across from me, he poured two cups of ginger tea sweetened with honey.

'Now tell me how it is that your aunt knows Muffy,' he quizzed, as if preparing me for an exam.

'Auntie Barbara and Muffy were roommates in college,'
I fibbed. 'They stayed in touch afterward and Muffy occasionally came and spent time at the ranch.'

'The ranch?' he asked, obviously yearning to know more.

'Yes, the ranch,' I teased. 'It belongs to Auntie Barbara
and Uncle George.'

'You aren't referring to *the Bushes*, by any chance, are
you?' he eagerly questioned, and intently leaned forward.

I opened my mouth to speak and then shook my head, as
if suddenly thinking better of it.

'Auntie Barbara doesn't like it when I brag,' I responded,
knowing the less I said, the more Giamonte would gobble
it up.

'Of course. And we wouldn't want her to be mad at us,
now would we?' he replied with glee. 'Not when you're
planning to order a fabulous new gown. So tell me – exactly
what sort of event it is that you'll be attending?'

'A gala in support of domestic oil exploration,' I said,
figuring *the Bushes, Texas* – it made sense.

'And will it be coming up soon?' he asked.

I watched as his eyes discreetly took note of my riff-raff
outfit. But he was smart enough not to say a word. That's
another thing about having money. You can get away with
wearing whatever you like.

'In about four months,' I replied, and took a sip of my
ginger tea.

'That's odd. I know all the comings and goings in this
city and I haven't heard a thing about it,' he remarked,
sounding slightly perplexed.

'That's because it's in Austin,' I swiftly responded, neatly
saving my rear end. 'I'm just here for a visit and to do a
quick bit of shopping.'

'What a shame. You'd make such a lovely addition to our
social scene,' Giancarlo oozed. 'But I suppose we'll just
have to enjoy your company whenever we can. Here, let me
show you my designs and see what you think.'

Giancarlo loosened the ribbon on a portfolio and began
to show me page after page of drawings. I thought they all
looked terrific.

'I particularly like this one,' I said, and pointed to a sleek strapless gown.

'Of course you would. What marvelous taste! That design is brand new. You'll look absolutely exquisite,' Giancarlo gushed.

'The only problem is that Austin gets rather chilly at night. What kind of wrap could I possibly wear?' I asked, allowing the slightest hint of frustration to slip into my voice.

'Don't you worry your pretty little head, my dear. I have the perfect thing,' he said with a wink. 'Just follow me.'

My pretty little head and I brought up the rear.

We entered Giancarlo's bedroom where I was instantly transported into an exotic new world. An explosion of shahtoosh shawls lay draped over every square inch of space, transforming the room into an Indian bazaar. Rainbow-colored clouds of fluff were tossed about everywhere.

'My goodness. What is all this?' I asked.

'The king of wools, the most exquisite material in the world. Here, feel it.' Giancarlo picked up a pure white shawl and gently rubbed the fabric against my skin. 'See? It's as soft as a lover's touch, as light as an angel's wings.'

'Is this pashmina?' I asked.

'Oh, my dear. Please, don't ever mention that word again. Pashmina is so *out* that the mere whisper of it will get you thrown off the best-dressed list. No, this is something far superior. It's shahtoosh,' he said, in near reverence.

Gotcha, I thought.

'Anyone can buy pashmina. But only the truly elite can afford shahtoosh,' he continued. 'It's like a fine work of art.'

Hmm. Now where had I heard those words before?

'You mean it's rather like a Lamborghini as compared to a Mini Cooper?' I ventured.

'Precisely. In fact, I'm surprised that you don't know about them yet. Everyone from Bel Air to Belgravia is wearing shahtoosh,' he remarked, and looked at me somewhat perplexed. 'Really, you must start spending more time in New York. It's all the rage among the most fashionable women in the world.'

He leaned in towards me, ever the trusted confidante.

'Truth be told, I know one society matron that takes her shawl to bed with her every night. Though, of course, even shahtoosh is no substitute for good sex.'

I quickly glanced over to see if he was serious. Giancarlo maintained a straight poker face.

'You're right. They truly are gorgeous. But will it keep me warm in winter?' I inquired, doing my best to appear naive.

'Absolutely. I've heard that an egg wrapped in one of these, and left in the sun, will cook in a matter of hours. In fact, the very best fashion magazines have declared shah- toosh to be *the* survival tactic of the season for getting through one's holiday parties. Here. Why don't you try it on?' he suggested, and placed a shawl over my shoulders.

Then he guided me towards a mirror.

'See how wonderful it looks? They drape in this special way that's extremely *luxe*,' he said, ever the perfect salesman.

I was once more on the verge of being seduced as I gazed at myself wrapped in something so exquisite. I couldn't help but wonder what my life might have been like had I been born a different person – one raised with tons of money. Would I also have felt that my wealth placed me above the law?

I'd never know. I glanced in the mirror again and this time saw the bloody pelts of five Tibetan antelopes slung across my back. I quickly removed the shawl.

'Do you own any of these yourself?' I asked, curious to know if what Muffy had told me were true.

'I'll let you in on a secret since we're becoming fast friends. It may seem a bit obsessive, but I own over two hundred of these scrumptious beauties. Each is specially dyed to match an article of my clothing. There's mauve, and cream, and periwinkle,' he said, and began to prance around the room.

I watched in bizarre fascination as, with each color named, Giancarlo plucked a corresponding shawl from off a chair, the bed, a bureau, as if it were a flower. But it was as he removed a loden green shawl that I stared in disbelief. Revealed was a stool that had been made from a severed elephant's foot. I continued to gaze at the amputated appendage in horror.

However, the revelation didn't end there. Giancarlo lifted shawls off what I'd thought were two poles on either side of his bed. Instead, they turned out to be enormous ivory tusks that looked to be six feet in length. Each was intricately carved from its base up to its tip and must have weighed close to eighty pounds apiece. The tusks stood lifeless as a pair of Egyptian mummies.

I now realized that my first instinct had been correct. I was indeed inside a little shop of horrors. Still, I couldn't help but walk over and run a hand along one of the ivory tusks.

My fingers slid across a series of elaborate designs that had been cut, smoothed and polished, telling the tale of endless herds that had once roamed the African plains. Those same savannahs now stood silent and empty. Perhaps it was because all the elephants had been sacrificed on the altar of vanity, fashion and greed.

My hand lingered on the ivory as though it might reveal a hidden secret: how long this particular elephant lived, and how it had died. And for a moment, I almost thought that I felt a heartbeat.

'I have plenty more ivory, if that's what you like,' Giancarlo declared, and flung open a closet door.

My breath caught in my throat upon catching sight of the exposed stockpile. Giancarlo's shelves were jammed with ivory jewelry and statuettes, each piece pale as a dollop of clotted cream.

Trade in ivory had been banned since 1990, after a decade of bloody poaching. Africa's herd of 1.3 million elephants were systematically gunned down and slaughtered during that time, until less than half their numbers were left. All the carnage had been carried out for a single purpose: so that hundreds of tons of ivory could be shipped to Hong Kong and Japan to feed a voracious annual multi-million dollar industry. Even now, I found it hard to believe that over one million of these magnificent creatures had been reduced in that time to nothing but trinkets.

Elephants are visible symbols of all that is wild in this world, not resources simply to be cut down like trees. Nor

131

are their tusks commodities to be hacked off and turned into chess sets and billiard balls. The ban may have slowed trade for a while, but black market demand remained insatiable. And, by the look of things, poaching was once again on the rise.

I tried not to shiver as Giancarlo slipped an elegant bracelet on to my wrist. The slender round of ivory felt cold and dead against my skin, all the life of its previous owner having been drained out of it.

The animal that died for this bauble had once swayed through tall savannah grass like a huge sailing ship, its life intertwined with a family unit of mothers, grandmothers, and aunts, all of whom shared enduring bonds of affection. They lived and played together, cared for one another in sickness and health and, like their human counterparts, were haunted by terrible memories. I'd heard them lift their trunks and rumble, the sound deeper than any church organ, the volume louder than thunder. The sight of all that ivory made me sick.

'I also have earrings and necklaces, along with any number of other articles,' Giancarlo assured me.

While that was clearly true, I didn't buy that Giamonte was the principle source for these items. He had neither the cunning nor the savvy to be a major player, much as he might have wanted to believe. Most likely, he was simply the middle man, a satin-clad conduit with ephemeral ties to the upper echelon of Manhattan society. That was fine, as long as it eventually led to the head honcho.

I continued to gaze in veiled disgust at all the booty in the room. Possession, in and of itself, wasn't a crime. Rather, I needed to prove that the importer knew he was trafficking in illegal goods. Then he had to be caught in the act. I was betting on the fact that Giancarlo hadn't the slightest idea concerning such pain-in-the ass legalities. With that in mind, I slowly began to weave my trap.

'My goodness. Where did you find all of these wonderful treasures?' I asked. 'Did you bring them back with you from trips?'

'No. I haven't much time for extensive travel. I'm far too

busy dressing beautiful women, such as yourself,' Giancarlo flattered. 'However, I'm fortunate to have found a very good source for shahtoosh and ivory.'

His fortune was about to turn into my field day.

'I have lots of friends in Texas that would kill for these sorts of things,' I said, taking in the array of carved Buddhas and geishas, fancy napkin rings and ornate walking sticks.

'Have them contact me and I'll be happy to sell them whatever they like,' Giancarlo eagerly replied. 'Of course, in return, you'd have first pick of my designs.'

'How kind,' I said, and coquettishly smiled.

I was impressed that Giancarlo was cocksure of having access to such a steady flow of illegal goods.

'Are you really able to obtain that much stock?' I pried, hoping to whet his appetite. 'You know Texans. They like to live large and spend big. I have no doubt that some of my friends would place hefty orders.'

'That's no problem,' he confirmed. 'My supplier is the largest of this kind in the world. He never runs out of ivory.'

How interesting.

'Really? And where do you get everything?' I asked.

'The shawls come from a company in Hong Kong,' Giancarlo disclosed, while shrewdly withholding the name of his source.

That information caught me off-guard. I'd assumed the stoles were imported from Europe.

'And what about the ivory? Does that come from Hong Kong, as well?' I asked, knowing that had to be the case. 'I'd love to buy a few large pieces for my home.'

I figured the more I used as bait, the more likely it was that Giancarlo would talk.

'As a matter of fact, yes,' he replied, and wrapped himself in a lovely pink stole.

'There's something I still don't understand. You said that you have only one source. Does that mean both the shahtoosh and ivory come from the exact same company?' I probed, while playing with the fringe on a shawl.

Perhaps I'd pushed too hard. Giancarlo's stole fell from his shoulders, his eyes grew wary, and his voice took on a rough edge.

'What's with all the questions, anyway? What do you want to know for?' he asked, his Italian accent starting to slip.

I pretended not to notice, but worried that I'd overplayed my hand.

'My goodness, Giancarlo. I didn't mean to upset you. Aunt Muffy would never forgive me, to say nothing of Auntie Barbara. In fact, she asked that I call later this evening and let her know how our visit went. All I meant was that it must make it so much easier for you to keep track of your orders if they all come from the same company,' I said in a trembling voice, as my eyes welled up with tears.

Ha! Let Vinnie try and beat that bit of acting, I smugly thought to myself.

Giancarlo's demeanor quickly reverted back to his former charming Tuscan self.

'My dear Rachel, did you think I was angry with you? Don't be silly. Of course I'm not. It's just that all these business questions tend to be so boring.' He kissed each of my fingers, and then began to stroke my hand. 'That's how we creative people are. But I'll be happy to tell you whatever I can, if it will help to put your mind at rest.'

Maybe so. But that glimpse into Giamonte's dark side proved enough to keep me on my toes.

'Here's what I know,' Giancarlo intoned, as if about to break into a lullaby. 'My source has ivory shipped from South Africa to Hong Kong where it's carved. However, he has businesses in both places. He's also recently begun sending ivory shipments directly to the US.'

I pulled out a tissue, while continuing to sniffle, and gently dabbed at my eyes. 'And why would he want to do that, if you don't mind my asking?'

'Of course not,' Giancarlo assured me, and held up a powder blue shawl. 'By the way, this is definitely your color.'

'Do you really think?' I asked, and allowed him to drape it around me. 'I'm sorry. Now, what were you saying again?'

'Oh, yes. Well, he's apparently decided to set up a carving factory here in New York. That can prove to be quite an advantage for my clientele.'

'How so?' I questioned, wondering what he was getting at.

'Say you decide to order a custom piece of ivory and there's some kind of problem. I can send it back right away to be fixed. See? Everything is working out perfectly for you and your friends,' Giancarlo explained, as though talking to a child.

That bit of information instantly set my mind awhirl. The fact that ivory was being shipped from South Africa made perfect sense. The country had long been a major smuggling route for everything from drugs and artwork, to forged stocks and bonds, over the years. It had also been a portal for ivory. So, why not still? As far as I could tell, the country remained hot, hot, hot when it came to dealing in contraband.

As for setting up a carving factory in New York, that was also totally logical. Once poached ivory slips into a country, and is carved, it becomes that much more difficult to prove illegal. Taken a step further, the US has one of the most active ivory markets in the world. American consumers, both at home and abroad, help to fuel the illicit trade. At times the situation seemed so futile that I wanted to throw up my hands and scream. Instead, I decided to focus my anger on nailing the law-breaking sucker in front of me.

'Didn't I read something silly about ivory being illegal?' I nonchalantly questioned.

'Yes. Absolutely ridiculous, isn't it? What else are tusks good for?' Giancarlo scoffed. 'But then so is shahtoosh. Can you believe it? What's a poor designer to do? To my mind, the fact that they're taboo only makes them all the more desirable. You know. It gives them that naughty but nice feel.'

'So then, it doesn't bother you at all?' I inquired, curious if he felt any remorse.

'What? That a bunch of elephants and antelopes are killed?' he asked, with a dismissive wave of his hand. 'Oh, please. Not the least little bit. That's what they were put on Earth for. To provide those of us that can afford it with beauty and pleasure.'

Funny how we defined those terms so differently. I viewed elephants and chiru as living, breathing creatures that should

135

be allowed to roam freely, while Giamonte saw them as nothing more than high-priced fashion accessories.

'Don't tell me that you're secretly one of those animal rights activists, are you?' Giancarlo playfully teased.

'Actually I'm a Special Agent with the US Fish and Wildlife Service,' I revealed.

'Very funny,' he replied with a burst of laughter. 'All right. You caught me. I suppose that now I'll *have* to give you a discount.'

'No, I'm dead serious,' I replied, and pulled out my badge to show him. 'I really am an agent.'

Giamonte's mouth fell open and his complexion turned pale as ivory. Then he slowly began to gather his wits.

'Does Muffy know of this?' he asked, still not quite certain if I was truly serious.

'She had no idea who I was when she mentioned your name,' I assured him.

'Ha! In that case, this amounts to entrapment,' he exclaimed.

'No. It just means that she never thought to ask,' I informed him.

'Then it must have been that bitch Tiffany Stewart that set me up,' he angrily spewed.

'Why would you say that?' I asked, surprised to hear her name again. Tiffany was turning out to be quite the pariah within her own community.

'Because that bitch is jealous of me,' he fumed.

'I find that hard to believe,' I replied with a chuckle, while taking in the scene.

Giancarlo looked as if he'd been hit by an out-of-control fashion tornado. He stood amidst a shower of shawls in his paisley robe and purple pajama bottoms.

'You find it amusing? She only wishes that she had my business. That skank actually tried to steal my clients away from me,' he nearly screamed.

'And how did she do that? Don't tell me. One day she decided to become a fashion designer and all your clients took her seriously,' I needled, hoping to obtain more information.

'No. The backstabbing bitch claimed that my shawls weren't really shahtoosh but pashmina,' he raged. 'But that wasn't the worst of it. She then had the nerve to announce she was setting up shop in her own living room. It was absolutely pathetic. She'd invite groups of women over and put out these horrid little *hors d'oeuvres* as if they were all attending some sort of Tupperware party. Tiffany would try to sell them cut-rate shawls in between serving New York State wine and Sara Lee cake.'

I raised a questioning eyebrow.

'Believe me. I have spies. Really. They told me. I swear, that woman doesn't have an ounce of class. Do you know she even had the gall to claim that what few shahtooshes I had came from slaughtered goats while hers didn't?' he accused.

'So then, the two of you are competitors,' I concluded.

'Fat chance. Naturally, her shawls were of far inferior quality. My clients aren't the type that have to shop for bargains. It wasn't long before they saw through her ruse and came running back to me,' Giancarlo said, and busied himself returning each shawl to its proper place.

'That's an interesting story. However, all that matters right now is that you're the one that got caught,' I retorted, and patiently awaited his next move.

'So, what are you going to do? Arrest me?' he asked, with feigned amusement.

'Now there's a thought,' I remarked.

It would serve him right to let him hang from his own shahtoosh for a while.

'In that case, you'd better have plenty of handcuffs because I'm not the only one in town that's doing this. Every two-bit divorcee and strapped-for-cash aristocrat is trying to sell shahtooshes from out of their apartments on Fifth and Park Avenues,' he disclosed. 'I happen to know of a doctor's wife, an art director, and a magazine editor that are involved, and they're making damn good money at it too.'

'Really? How much money are you talking about?' I questioned, curious to know.

'If I talk, will you let me go?' Giancarlo shrewdly asked, positioning himself to negotiate.

'That all depends on how good your information is. Tell me what you know and I'll see what I can do,' I replied, having no such intention.

'All right then. Scarves will sell for a thousand, good shawls for twenty, and specialty items, like throws, can command up to fifty-thousand dollars a piece.'

No wonder these people could afford to live such extravagant lifestyles.

'That sounds intriguing. I bet they also have a better clientele base than you,' I responded, attempting to reel him in.

'Like hell they do,' Giancarlo indignantly replied, neatly taking the bait. 'I'll have you know that my clients include princesses, dowagers, models, actresses, heiresses, and the very best trophy wives. Besides, those shahtoosh parties can get pretty ugly. I heard a fight broke out at the last one that Tiffany threw. Apparently, she didn't have enough good colors to go around.'

I wondered if Tiffany was really that strapped for cash? And if so, how low would she stoop?

'As you can see, I don't have that sort of problem,' Giancarlo announced, with a haughty sniff. 'Clearly, squealing on me was her idea of payback. She can't stand the fact that I'm such a success.'

Not anymore you're not, I thought.

'And what about ivory? Is she involved in that, too?' I asked.

Giancarlo tied his robe tightly about his waist. 'Well, I know for certain that Tiffany has been trying to worm her way into the market. She's gone so far as to approach my source about it. Who knows? Maybe she struck up a deal with somebody else.'

'Which brings us to the matter at hand. Just who is this source of yours?' I questioned, anxious to move things along.

'I'm afraid I can't tell you that,' Giancarlo said, and pinched his lips.

'Sure you can,' I replied, ready to apply whatever pressure was necessary. 'It's either that, or off to jail you go.'

'Journalists do it to protect their sources all the time. So I don't see why designers shouldn't, as well. Ooh, that *does*

138

sound catchy, doesn't it? In fact, I think that's the first quote I'll give to the press.' Giancarlo flashed a sly smile. 'Besides, you know perfectly well that I'll get off with no more than a slap on the wrist. And just think how good it will be for my business,' he gloated.

'While you're at it, why don't you contemplate how well Ralph Goldberg and his library of raunchy S&M videos will fly with the Ladies Who Lunch?' I countered.

Giancarlo's complexion turned two shades paler than before.

'Excuse me?' he asked, his Italian accent promptly biting the dust.

'You heard me. I also have my sources,' I loftily informed him. 'So, are you going to tell me what I want to know? Or do I spill your little secret?'

My Tuscan charmer angrily glared at me. 'You really are a bitch. You know that?'

'Don't try to flatter me. Now what's it going to be? Remain designer of the moment, or switch to a sad-ass career of making second-rate porn videos?'

I let the question dangle.

'Come on, Ralphie. You should know by now that women don't like to be kept waiting,' I prodded.

'All right,' he hissed. 'But this didn't come from me. And remember, I expect to walk away from this without any jail time.'

'Of course. I've already made a note of it,' I responded. 'Just give me the information.'

'I work with a company called Tat Hwong Products,' he revealed, while chewing on a freshly manicured fingernail.

'Who's your contact?' I pressed, refusing to let him off that easily.

'A man by the name of Lau Cheong. He's based in Hong Kong,' he divulged, and started to gnaw his way over to a cuticle.

'And exactly how are shipments of shahtoosh coming into the country?' I asked, determined to learn every little detail.

'Tat Hwong was paying airline stewardesses to bring them in with their luggage for a while. Nothing personal, but I doubt that your average Customs Inspector reads *Vogue* magazine. Besides, if a stewardess was stopped and questioned, she'd just say it was a Hermès scarf and walk right on through,' he disclosed. 'Only business grew too fast. They started packing shawls in boxes, marking them as children's clothing, and flying them straight into Newark Airport. That is, until 9/11 happened. After that, air freight began to be looked at more closely and their mode of operation had to change again.'

'So what are they doing now?' I inquired, unable to guess and dying to know.

'They're packed inside containers and shipped into Newark/Elizabeth Seaport where almost nothing gets inspected,' he told me.

Of course. I couldn't have come up with a better plan myself.

'And you deal with the same contact for ivory?' I asked, just to double check.

'Yes, until recently. But that's also changed with the opening of this ivory factory in New York. The big boss is here to make sure that everything is up and running smoothly. I've been told that I'm to deal with him for now.'

'And where's all the ivory being shipped?' I asked, though already certain of the answer.

'Into Newark/Elizabeth Seaport,' he confirmed.

Terrific. It had been happening this entire time right under my nose.

'What's the big boss man's name?' I snapped, taking my frustration out on Goldberg.

'I don't know yet,' he coolly responded.

'Don't screw with me, Ralphie,' I warned, not in the mood to be jerked around.

'I don't know because I haven't yet placed an order,' he petulantly retorted.

'Then go ahead and do so today. You're also to say that you want to meet with the big boss and would like a tour of the factory,' I directed.

'What are you – crazy? Why would I want to do that?' he questioned.

'You don't. *I* do,' I replied, setting him straight. 'When they call back with a time, tell them you've been unexpectedly called away but will send your trusted assistant, Cheri Taylor, in your place.'

'Cheri Taylor? That sounds more like a perky little candy-striper, not someone that I would hire,' he scoffed. 'Who is she, anyway?'

'You're looking at her. Just do it and don't ask questions,' I ordered.

'Fine,' he sulked, and casually began to close his closet door.

If he was hoping that I'd forget about his stash, he was sadly mistaken.

'Hold on a minute,' I said, and walked over.

'What are you looking for?' he apprehensively questioned, as I began to rummage through the shelves.

'I won't know until I find it, now will I?' I responded and, starting at the bottom, worked my way up.

I figured something good must be hidden, or Ralph wouldn't have been so nervous.

It was as I scrounged around the top shelf that my fingers finally struck gold. Pushed into a far corner was a box of DVDs. I pulled one from its container and read the title.

Fun and Games with Dick and Joe.

Whaddaya know? This was far more precious than if I'd actually found gold.

'What do you think you're doing?' Ralph exclaimed, as he saw what I held in my hand.

'Let's just call it an insurance policy,' I retorted, and stashed it in my bag.

'If that gets out it could ruin me,' he groaned.

'I know,' I assured him.

'Personally, I think this is all a big waste of time. Tiffany Stewart is the one that you should really be after. Believe me, that woman has her claws into more things than you can possibly imagine,' he said in an attempt to divert me.

'Oh, yeah? Then why don't you just tell me about them?' I suggested.

'Well, I'm not the one that actually has the details,' he

deftly sidestepped. 'But I know where you can find out. You should go and speak to Sy Abrams, her former boss. Word has it he's got all the dirt on her.'

'Does he own the club where she used to dance?' I inquired.

'If dancing is what you want to call it. But from what I hear, she didn't do all her bumping and grinding on stage,' he sneered. 'The place where she worked is a dive. It makes the clubs I hang out in look like the Ritz.'

'What's the name of this place?' I asked.

'The Beaver's Den over on Fortieth and Eighth. You can't miss it. There's a sign for Starburst Talent Agency on the second floor. That's where they book the strippers.'

'Maybe I'll check it out. In any case, I expect you to keep your mouth shut as to what went on here today,' I warned. 'Otherwise, Muffy and the rest of her posse will get their own private viewing of this tape.'

I patted my bag so there'd be no mistaking what I meant.

'Make that call to your ivory contact and I'll be in touch,' I instructed, and headed for the elevator.

I walked past the funereal web of shahtoosh shawls, through the picture perfect living room, and down the celebrity studded hallway to once more enter the rickety lift. It was as I pressed the button that Giancarlo seemed to think of one last thing that he wanted to say.

'So, are you really related to the Bushes or what?' he questioned, thrusting his head so far forward that I feared it might pop off of his neck.

Unbelievable. Even now the guy was fishing for more business contacts.

I didn't dignify it with a reply. Instead, I looked at him and smiled as the elevator emitted a long-drawn-out death rattle and the door slowly closed with a sigh.

Thirteen

Afternoon rush hour traffic was already in progress by the time I reached my Ford. The city streets were jammed bumper-to-bumper like an urban amusement ride. I wedged my way into line, figuring I might as well join in the fun. What the heck. My best thinking is usually done while I'm stuck in my car anyway.

However, my thoughts remained focused on only one thing – the carnage inside Ralph Goldberg's closet. I couldn't help it. Now matter how hard I tried, the vision remained.

For the life of me, I'd never understand how people could wantonly slaughter elephants. The largest creatures on land, they're also one of the most intelligent. They resemble human beings in so many ways. They have an intricate social life, love their families, and are led by the experience, memories, and knowledge of elders. Elephants are known to greet their family members with open emotion, racing towards them with rumblings and trumpetings as they happily flap their ears and tears stream down their face.

They shed tears for other reasons as well. Pachyderms rarely leave their sick and wounded but physically support them with their shoulders and trunks, bringing food and staying until they're no longer able to move. Neither do they desert a loved one once they've finally passed away, but linger in a ritual of mourning.

An elephant will sniff every inch of a fallen member's body while gently attempting to prod and shake them awake. Finally, they gingerly explore the remains in what can only be a deep comprehension of death. Eventually the herd files past, two and three at a time, as if to pay their final respects. Even then, elephants often return to the spot where a close relative has died.

They'll also carry the tusks and bones of other dead pachyderms that are found along the way, reverently passing them around to the rest of the herd. It's said that elephants suffer such trauma and distress over death that they sometimes die of grief themselves.

These whales of the land call to distant bands of elephants when they're being attacked and killed, either in warning, or as an anguished cry for help. What is known is that their faces are brutally hacked, their tusks cut off, and their flesh left to rot by poachers. Those few that manage to escape are forever scarred by such memories. It's why elephants are believed to have very old souls.

But the irreparable harm that's done goes even deeper. For poaching unravels the very fabric of elephant society. The older females, with their huge tusks of ivory, are more than just leaders of the herd. They're also repositories of accumulated knowledge. Deprived of that wisdom, orphans are left without any guidance when it comes to locating ancient migrating routes and distant feeding grounds. No one is there to teach them where to find springs during a drought, or lush meadows after early seasonal rains. Nor can they learn how to avoid being killed by poachers.

I was jerked from my own deep, dark thoughts as I finally approached Midtown. Much as I hated to admit it, Giancarlo had cleverly gotten me hooked. I had no choice but to pay Sy Abrams a visit.

It didn't matter how often I came through Times Square. I was still blown away by how much it had changed. No longer was it a carny version of Sodom and Gomorrah. Rather it had become a soulless shopping mall with a giant corporate grin plastered across its face.

Most of the porn theatres, adult video/bookstores, and fleabag hotels are now gone, replaced by Toys'R'Us, The MTV Store, Planet Hollywood, and The ESPN ZONE. Forty-Second street has been transformed into a Disneyfied version of its former self. One in which *The Lion King* reigns supreme and Madame Tussaud's Wax Museum sits on what had once been New York City's grittiest block.

What had formerly been Sleaze Central is now an equally charmless conglomeration of every giant chain store and super-sized restaurant that's laid claim to the US. The end result has been nothing less than death by fashion trend, family values and good old American commercialization. The only remnant of the prior Times Square is the interchangeable man that still stands on top a soapbox yelling about God and demanding that passers by repent.

I drove a few blocks west, toward the Port Authority Bus Terminal, and circled until I managed to find a parking space. Pulling my parking permit from the glove compartment, I stuck it in the window. Then I strolled down a stretch of city where a sprinkling of Triple X theatres still remain. It was there that I found The Beaver's Den.

A drab building, it stood lodged between a hole-in-the-wall greasy spoon and Joey's Cheap Peep Shots. My hand landed on something sticky as I pushed open the door and walked into the club.

I was greeted by billowy blue smoke that languorously curled and twisted around the forms of three topless dancers. They received little encouragement from the few men that listlessly sat at the bar and drank. Rather, their attention was focused on the basketball game being shown on TV. That night's free buffet of macaroni and cheese lay untouched in its tin pan, resting above a Sterno can, the contents having already begun to congeal. A topless waitress, with tired breasts and a puddle of caked make-up, sauntered over carrying an empty tray in her hand.

'What can I get for you, darlin'?' she asked. 'Why don't you go and take a table up front near the girls. They'll be happy for the company and maybe it'll even make them feel a little more like dancing.'

I found myself wondering how old she might be. The woman had stringy blonde hair that begged to be washed, and was so emaciated I could nearly see her ribs. The dim lighting did little to hide the track marks on her arms. I figured she could have been anywhere from a haggard twenty-five to a decimated forty.

'Thanks. But I'm looking for Sy Abrams,' I responded.

Only then did she give me the once over, as though sizing up new competition.

'He's up there,' she said, and pointed to a back staircase. 'But I've gotta tell you, this place is already fully loaded. We don't need any more waitresses or bartenders, if that's what you're thinking.'

Her features abruptly transformed from slack to ferret sharp as she jealously guarded her territory.

'No. I just want to talk to him,' I replied, hoping to put her at ease.

'OK. But don't say that I didn't warn you,' she advised, as I walked away and began to climb the stairs.

At the top stood a closed door with a sign that read Starburst Talent Agency. A gold star was pasted above it with a photo of a different topless dancer dangling from each of its five points. I wiped my hands against my pants and knocked on the door.

'Don't be shy. Come on in,' responded a voice that crackled and wheezed with age.

The door squeaked with the high-pitched squeal of a mouse caught in a trap. I stopped for a moment, and then pushed it open. Peering inside, I spied a wisp of a man barely visible behind a large wooden desk.

A pair of bushy eyebrows, wiry as two scouring pads, held reign over an ancient face There was as much hair growing out of his ears as there was on his head. My universal grandfather sat buried in a thick woolen sweater that was nearly as drab as his complexion. Only his piercing blue eyes appeared young for a man of his age.

'Excuse me, but are you Sy Abrams?' I asked.

'Yes, I am,' he cordially responded, and continued to dig into a take-out container of food with a plastic spoon.

Even from where I stood, the smell of greasy Chinese pervaded the tiny room. It was the kind that makes you hungry while turning your stomach at the same time.

'What can I do for you, sweetheart?' he asked. 'Though

146

I should probably tell you right off the bat that if it's work you're looking for, you're a little over the usual age.'

How nice to know.

'But then, of course, I haven't yet seen you without your clothes,' he added.

'And I can promise that you never will,' I pleasantly retorted. 'I'm a Special Agent with the US Fish and Wildlife Service.'

That response brought a smile to his lips. He smacked them a couple of times and then quickly ran his tongue over them.

'You don't say. So what brings you here? Are you after some of my beavers?' he joked.

Great. An old man that had a sense of humor, in addition to being a lech. What a coup.

'No. I'm looking for information about one of your former dancers,' I told him.

'Go ahead. Take your pick,' he said, and waved his hand around the room.

The dingy walls were covered with photographs, both old and new, of what must have constituted his past and present stable of topless dancers. Most were black and white cheese-cake shots of girls posed to show off their voluptuous goods. Each was signed *Love to Seymour*, their John Hancocks ranging from *Candy Kane* to *Scarlett Bottom,* to *Pussy Willow* in what was clearly an homage to the adult entertainment industry.

'I remember them all as if they were my very own daughters. Each is a lovely girl. By the way, feel free to take your jacket off. I promise that I'm not going to bite,' he added, and popped a piece of mystery meat into his mouth.

He must have noticed that I'd begun to break into a sweat. But then the room was hot as a sauna. I removed my jacket and immediately felt naked as his eyes brazenly focused on my chest.

Damn him, I thought, and nonchalantly crossed my arms across my breasts.

Then I continued to peruse the room until I found the photo that most resembled Tiffany Stewart.

'What about this one?' I asked, pointing to a woman that arched her back and stuck out her boobs.

'Ahh, the troublemaker of the lot. I should have guessed. That's Tiffany LaLou,' he replied, with a knowing nod of his head.

'Why do you say that?' I questioned. 'Exactly what made her so much trouble?'

'Are you kidding me? You name it. No matter what rule I'd put into effect, Tiffany would go out of her way to break it.' Sy put the cardboard container down and wiped the back of his hand against his mouth. 'OK, here's an example for you. I've never allowed the girls to have sex with the clientele at The Beaver's Den. So, what would happen? I'd go in the back room and catch Tiffany giving one of them a quickie. Can you imagine? They'd be *shtupping* right there next to the men's room. It was that kind of thing that drove me nuts.'

Understandable, I thought.

'Oh yeah. Here's another good one,' he said and slapped his palm on the desk with a laugh. 'I remember one time when I told all the girls there were to be no breast enhancements. I wanted everyone in the club to look *au naturel.* So, what did she do? Tiffany immediately ran out and got herself a giant set of knockers. I'm talking big bazoombas.'

Sy demonstrated by pretending to hold a large beach ball in each hand.

'I've got to give her credit though. She was always quite a girl. And so limber! You should have seen the things that she could do,' he fondly reminisced.

I wondered how much of this Muffy and the others already knew and when they had found out.

'Anything else that you can recall?' I pressed.

'Only that she got nabbed a couple of times for hooking, and I had to bail her out. That girl could never learn to hold on to money. Which was why I was surprised when she finally paid me back one day. Not only that, but she said I wouldn't have to worry about her any longer,' he revealed.

'Why was that? Because she'd married her husband by then?' I ventured.

148

'No, that came later. She went down South on a trip home. All I know is that Tiffany claimed to have met someone in law enforcement while she was there. She said she'd secretly begun to work for him, and swore that there wouldn't be any more trouble. Not while she knew someone on the job. And you know what? She was right. There wasn't a bit after that,' he reported.

'Do you know where it was down South that she went?' I asked, my curiosity having been roused.

Sy Abrams shrugged, his bony shoulders rising up like the round, knobby tops on a vulture's folded wings. 'Who can remember? Besides, all those states tend to blur together. The only thing I know about the South is that they have grits and cornbread. And I'm not too crazy about either one.'

'I heard that she met her husband here at the club. Is that true?' I asked, ready to move on to a different topic.

'You mean Andrew? Or Bippy, as he liked to be called. Yeah, she sure did. He was quite the whoremonger and Tiffany knew just how to play him. A little shake of the tush, a little feel of the rack, and she was leading him around by the nose. Or whatever other appendage she chose. Let me tell you, it's not every girl that leaves here having married a millionaire. But that's the thing about Tiffany. She has more than big tits. She also has smarts, and don't let anyone ever tell you differently,' he advised and patted my hand.

His skin felt as dry and thin as parchment.

'So what's your interest in her anyway? What's she smuggling? Exotic pussies?' he asked with a wink.

I chose to ignore the remark. 'I've heard that Tiffany is having money problems these days. You know that her husband passed away, don't you?'

Sy Abrams nodded, clearly miffed that I hadn't responded to his joke. 'Yeah. Bippy had the last laugh, all right. Tiffany thought for sure that she'd inherit his entire estate. But I guess that blood runs deeper than even the best lap dance.'

'I heard that she might be involved with dealing in illegal elephant ivory,' I revealed, and closely watched his reaction.

'Ivory shmivory,' he responded with a laugh. 'Tiffany wouldn't waste her time on anything like that. It wouldn't bring in enough money. At least, not the kind that she's after.'

The old man looked at me closely. 'Is that why you're here? Because you think I might know what she's involved in?'

I nodded.

'And what do I get in return if I tell you?' he slyly asked.

'How about I don't phone my friends at the Health Department and have them come and harass you?' I promptly shot back.

A smile flitted across his lips. 'Seems fair enough. I'm beginning to think that you're almost as smart as Tiffany.'

I decided to take that as a compliment. 'So what is she mixed up in these days?'

'All I can tell you is what I've heard. Word has it that Tiffany's dealing in hot rocks,' he confided, and crossed his arms on top of his desk.

'Hot rocks?' I asked, not quite sure what he meant.

'Yeah, you know. Ice. Diamonds,' he responded.

'What are you saying? That Tiffany's involved with stolen gems?' I questioned, finding it rather hard to believe.

All I could think of was Grace Kelly and Cary Grant in the movie *To Catch a Thief*. And Tiffany certainly didn't fit either of those roles.

'Nah. She's not a *goniff*.'

I looked at him thoroughly puzzled, having no idea what he was talking about.

'You don't speak any Yiddish?' he asked, peering at me askance.

'I do, but just a little,' I responded, knowing that I'd never be able to admit now that I was Jewish.

'She's not a thief, or a fence, or anything like that,' the old man said, with an impatient shake of his head. 'These are some kind of diamonds from Africa that aren't allowed into this country for some *facockta* reason.'

Though he didn't bother to translate, I got the gist of what he meant.

'Tiffany's the middle man of sorts. She's getting them to the right people to be sold,' Abrams explained and, reaching for a pack of Marlboros, lit up a cigarette. Then he began to wheeze and cough and spit.

'So, she's dealing in diamonds, huh?' I repeated, still having a hard time buying it.

'Sure. Why not? The girl knows plenty about them. God knows, she ought to. She has enough of them herself,' he declared.

'Do you have any idea who else might be involved in it with her?' I questioned.

'Sorry, sweetheart. But I'm afraid that's all I know. By the way, do yourself a favor and don't ever get breast implants. You don't need them. It looks like you already have a lovely pair,' he said, glancing at my chest again.

I quickly put on my jacket.

'Thanks for the information,' I replied and turned to leave.

I caught one last glimpse of Sy Abrams before exiting the room. His wrinkled face was wreathed in cigarette smoke, and he was digging out the last of the Chinese food with his plastic spoon.

I shut the door and went back downstairs.

'So, what happened? Did you get a job?' my friendly cocktail waitress asked before my foot hit the bottom step.

She must have been hovering there the entire time, anxiously waiting for me.

'No. You were right. Apparently, the club doesn't need any more help,' I responded, figuring that ought to make her night.

'Told you so,' she replied with a smile that barely dented her make-up. 'Better luck someplace else. Hey, why don't you try the Baby Doll House down in Tribeca? I hear they're looking for a few warm bodies.'

'Thanks. I'll do that,' I said, and walked past the three dancers. They seemed even more listless, having probably given up hope of making any decent tips.

I quickly walked through the exit door, not wanting to let in too much cold air. The weather outside was frigid, and the last vestige of light had been swallowed by night. Even so, my mind was beginning to wander. All I could think was:

151

what kind of diamonds wouldn't be allowed into the US? I'd never heard of such a thing before.

I pressed my arms tightly against my sides, and jammed my hands in my pockets. Damn! I'd forgotten my gloves once again. To make matters worse, I suddenly slid on a patch of ice, so that my arms flew out and my fingers clutched at thin air. I managed to catch myself only at the very last moment.

That did it. I promptly went into old lady mode. Hunching over, I kept my eyes glued to the ground and intently focused on each of my steps. Fortunately, there weren't many people around to bump into. The frigid weather must have convinced them all to stay indoors. Besides, this was a lousy part of town. I turned down a side street and began to head for my Ford.

Sy Abrams had been right. Tiffany certainly knew her diamonds. The woman could have worked in the business. Or perhaps she already did and it was just that most people didn't know.

My mind had started to wander once more, so that I wasn't paying attention to where I was going. That proved to be a mistake as my feet abruptly flew out from under me. Or so I thought. Only they never came back down to touch the ground. Instead, I felt myself being lifted, like a weightless length of shahtoosh, and swiftly carried through the air.

I began to frantically call out when a piece of tape was rudely slapped across my mouth. It was then that inexplicable fear set in. Though I tried to struggle and kick, it was all to no avail. At the same time, my purse was yanked from my arm. Naturally, my gun was in it. I realized that I was totally vulnerable and that this was the stuff of which nightmares were made.

I wildly glanced around for help, but none was in sight. That is, except for the two men whose identities were hidden behind face masks and caps. Each stood on either side of me, and held tightly on to my arms.

My heart beat wildly, and my breathing grew rapid and shallow, as adrenaline percolated through my veins. A whiff of something rancid hit my nose, and I could have sworn it was the same greasy Chinese food that Sy Abrams had been eating. The odor mixed with terror to form a noxious lump that twisted inside me like a giant clenched fist.

Though it couldn't have been more than a few seconds, it felt like forever as I was roughly dragged down a dark alley. Funny how in times of distress you focus on certain things while others slip by. All I could think of was that I'd be found like so much rubbish, thrown among the dumpsters and garbage, as rats skittered past. That was, until the pain began. Then all other thoughts receded from my mind.

I saw a fist coming at me and quickly turned my head. But that couldn't stop a set of knuckles from slamming into my jaw. The punch threw me up against a brick wall, whose rough surface and sharp edges callously bit into my back.

Defend yourself! my brain angrily screamed.

However, I couldn't even begin to try and use Krav Maga. It was as if the cold had insidiously penetrated my limbs and frozen every response.

That ended as a fist connected with my stomach and I doubled over as easily as a piece of origami. My head pounded and my eyes scuttled across the ground like a couple of severed crab's claws. My gaze stopped at the sight of an empty beer bottle that had been thrown nearby. Or at least, that's what I imagined it to be. I couldn't be absolutely certain since my vision was blurry. Not that it mattered. Whatever lay on the ground, I was bound and determined to go for it.

I threw myself down, grabbed what turned out to be a bottle of Bud, and viciously swung at the first set of knees. A loud grunt seemed to attest that I'd made contact.

The utterance of *You bitch!* verified it.

However, it also unleashed a new wave of ferocity from my churlish attackers. Though I tried to protect myself, two pairs of feet now began to fly fast and furious. They hit their mark as I rolled into a tight ball, grateful for what protection there was from my down jacket. Even so, kicks continued to rain on to my back and my ribs as I covered my head with my hands and just prayed that it would soon end.

I began to worry as to exactly what that ending might be

153

when a hand grabbed hold of my hair and roughly jerked back my head. The cold air nipped at my throat, its chill as sharp as a knife's blade.

'Stay out of things that don't concern you,' a voice harshly instructed.

The words slid past as I concentrated on absorbing the tone, the inflection and pitch, hoping to one day be able to identify my attacker.

'Did you hear what I said?' he asked, and savagely tore the tape off my mouth.

'Yes,' I croaked, wanting nothing more than to eventually have a chance for revenge.

'Good. Because otherwise your eyes and mouth will be sewn shut, just like your friend.'

That proved to be all the high octane fuel needed to set me on fire. This had to be the same man that had murdered both Bitsy and Magda.

Logic told me not to react. I paid little heed as my hand instinctively flew up and grabbed hold of his face mask. I pulled as hard as I could, trying to rip it off, and it slowly began to give way. The next thing I knew, a dull pain roared through the back of my neck, my arm fell to my side, and I was swallowed by a pool of darkness.

Fourteen

It was cold when I awoke, and my body hurt like hell. But the important thing was that I was still alive. Or at least, I seemed to be.

Then my attacker's last words came rushing back to me. I held my breath, afraid of what harm might have been done while I lay unconscious. Still, there was no other choice but to try and open my eyes.

A cry of relief escaped my lips to find that neither my mouth nor my lids had been viciously sewn shut. It was equally reassuring to feel all the loose pebbles and glass that cut into my hands around me. That simple detail revealed that I hadn't been dragged off somewhere else, but was still lying in the alley. For once, I didn't even mind the sound of rats scampering by. Instead, I continued to lie there for a while before finally gathering the strength to check out the rest of my body.

My arms and legs moved easily, and none of my limbs appeared to be broken. In fact, I didn't really ache until I tried to sit up. That was when I cursed out loud. No wonder I hurt. My torso had been used as a football.

I nervously took a deep breath. No trouble there. Thank goodness, at least my lungs hadn't been punctured. Then I gently began to poke around. There weren't any obvious bones sticking out, nor did I seem to have a specific sharp pain anywhere. With luck, the only problem would be a bad case of bruising, along with a jaw that was beginning to swell.

I slowly crawled on to my hands and knees and took a look around. There were two sets of footprints leading in from the street, along with a skidmark that ran between them.

I figured that was where my boots must have dragged through the snow. The same two pairs then headed back out, minus one unconscious redhead.

I glanced about to see if any evidence had been left behind. But the only thing in sight was the broken bottle of Bud that I'd slammed into someone's knee. Next to it lay a crumpled pack of Marlboros. I slipped the empty box into my pocket, and then slowly stood up.

That's when the pain near the back of my head sprang to life. I gingerly ran my fingers along the nape of my neck. A large tender bump had formed that hadn't been there before. But then, I supposed I shouldn't have complained. I was probably lucky to still be all in one piece. However, there was no denying the anger that was beginning to build up inside me. The son-of-a-bitch that had done this had also burned Magda alive like a piece of charred meat. No way was I about to keep my nose out of his business, whatever that might be.

I began to stagger through the alley, when I spied my purse tossed near a garbage can. Tottering over, I picked it up. Nothing had been taken, further confirming that this hadn't been a robbery.

Then I carefully made my way to my Ford. Unlocking the door, I crept inside, and slowly drove home. I felt so beat that I didn't even fight a Saab over the first available space in my garage, but instead settled for the next one to be found.

I wondered if this was how it felt to be eighty years old as I timidly walked down my block. My next thought was to ponder if I'd ever actually reach the ripe old age of eighty at the rate I was going.

I entered my building and stood facing three long flights of stairs.

How does Gerda do this every day at her age? I questioned and slowly began to pull myself up, all the while vowing that my next building would have an elevator.

I entered my apartment, glad to finally be home. The answering machine blinked hello, and I went over to see who had phoned.

'Hey, chère. I have to work late tonight. So don't wait for me to eat dinner,' Jake said.

His voice sounded tired and resigned, as though he were off fighting a war that couldn't be won. For once, I was glad that he wouldn't be home for a while.

I stripped off my clothes and headed into the shower. Standing under the water, I let its warmth beat down on me, wishing that it would wash away every bruise and unseen hurt as it coursed through my hair, streamed over my shoulders, and flowed down my back.

Who was it that set those thugs on me, anyway? I pondered, and mentally began to run down a possible list of suspects.

It had happened too fast for Sy Abrams to be involved. Maybe Giancarlo Giamonte had made a call, knowing there was a good chance that I'd head straight for the Beaver's Den. The other likely culprit was Tiffany Stewart. She had every reason to want to scare me away, based on what I'd learned so far.

I put that thought on hold as I toweled myself off, and began to inspect what bodily damage had been done.

Mirror, mirror on the wall, who's the fairest one of all?

It sure as hell wasn't me today. The sight of all those bruises certainly wasn't pretty. Besides which, my jaw was now swollen and turning various shades of black and blue.

I popped some Motrin, slapped on a couple of bandages, and applied a cold compress to my jaw. I'd have to hold it in place, which gave me a few minutes to kill. Fortunately, I knew exactly what to do with them. I picked up the phone and placed a call to Tiffany Stewart.

'Hello?' answered the same sexy voice that I'd first heard just a few days before.

'Hey, Tiffany. This is your good friend Rachel Porter,' I told her.

'Rachel who?' she asked, playing dumb.

'Oh, come on. You remember me. I'm the federal agent that came by to see you the other day,' I replied.

'Oh, yes. That's right. Now I remember. I gave you the name of a PR firm. So how'd that work out for you?' she inquired, with a studied note of indifference.

'Just terrific. Thanks for asking. In fact, after that I paid Muffy Carson Ellsworth a visit,' I informed her.

That tidbit was met by a moment of silence.

'How nice for you. Although, Muffy is a bit out of the loop these days. She still thinks that she's the Queen Bee, if you know what I mean,' Tiffany finally responded.

'Funny. She had something to say about you, as well,' I replied.

'Oh yeah? Like what? That she doesn't approve of the fact that I wasn't to the manor born?' Tiffany snidely retorted.

'No. More along the lines that you've been sleeping with Bitsy von Falken's husband,' I responded, dropping my first bombshell. 'Muffy doesn't seem to think that you were very discreet, but rather chose to flaunt the affair in Bitsy's face.'

'What does that old woman know, anyway?' Tiffany countered. 'For God sakes, she's in love with a fag and thinks that he's straight.'

'You must mean Giancarlo Giamonte,' I said, preparing to release my second nuke.

'What? You know him as well?' she sharply questioned.

'I sure do. In fact, I spent this afternoon with him,' I replied.

'Oh yeah? Then you must have had a hell of a time sitting around that tomb of his dishing about who does what to whom at which parties,' she sniped.

'Actually, he was nice enough to show me his collection of shahtoosh shawls,' I revealed.

'Get the hell out of here! You mean, he didn't know that you're a Fed? How delicious is that? What a complete moron!' she crowed, a bit too victoriously. 'So, did you arrest him, or what?'

'Why should you care?' I countered. 'Or is it that you want him out of the way so that you can try and set up your own shahtoosh shawl outlet again?'

'Where'd you get *that* idea from? Is that what Giancarlo told you? If so, he's a goddamn liar. For chrissakes, Giamonte's nothing but a jealous fag who wishes he had my boobs. Besides which, what would I want to do that for? I'm not one of those down-and-out stick-up-the-ass socialites that's been reduced to selling shawls from out of her Louis Vuitton luggage. I have far better prospects than that.'

It seemed to me the lady did protest too much.

'Let me try and guess. Such as selling illegal diamonds?'
I ventured, taking a stab.

'My, my. But you have been one busy little bee, haven't
you?' Tiffany nearly growled into the phone. 'I don't know
who you've been talking to, but they must have been smoking
some pretty strong weed. After all, I'm the widow of a very
wealthy man. Remember?'

'Yes, and from what I hear he left the bulk of his estate
to his sons,' I countered.

'Maybe you shouldn't believe all the gossip that's flying
around. It could prove to be dangerous,' she warned.

'To whom?' I asked, my jaw beginning to throb.

'To people who poke into things that are none of their
business. Let me give you a piece of advice. I have my
contacts. One word to them and you'll be told to leave me
alone,' Tiffany cautioned.

'Really? And who might those be? The two thugs that
jumped me tonight? Or is it your buddy that's "on the job"?'
I snarled, not in the mood for any more games.

'This is the only warning that you're going to get from
me, Porter. Don't call here anymore and stay the hell out of
my business,' Tiffany responded, and hung up.

I listened to the dial tone as if it might possibly reveal
something. Then I placed the receiver back in its cradle.

There was no question but that Tiffany had something to
hide. But if she hadn't wanted me to dig around, then why
had she bothered to call in the first place? I added that to
my list of questions yet to be answered.

By now the compress was warm and I threw it in the sink.
Then I slipped into a pair of sweatpants and a soft loose
sweater. A generous dose of concealer helped to hide some
of the black and blue marks on my jaw. After that, I rearranged
my long red hair as best I could to try and cover the rest of
it. Only then did I head over to Gerda's.

Spam began to bark upon my approach, as though he
instinctively knew my footsteps. I knocked and Gerda immediately answered the door. Her normally cheerful face
dropped in alarm upon catching sight of me.

'Oh my goodness! What happened to you?' she exclaimed

159

and, without waiting for a response, pulled me inside her apartment.

So much for my expert make-up job.

'It's nothing. I just took a spill on the ice. That's all. Don't worry about it,' I said, trying to slough it off.

But Gerda wasn't about to let the matter rest.

'If a fall did this to your face then I can only imagine what it's done to the rest of you. You must be hurt somewhere else,' she adamantly responded.

'I have a few other bruises, but it's no big deal,' I replied, determined to make light of the situation.

'Has Jake seen you yet?' she questioned, and eyed me suspiciously.

'No. He won't be home until later. I just stopped by to get Spam,' I responded.

'Oh no, you don't. You're not going anywhere in that condition. First I'll look at your bruises and then you'll stay for dinner,' she insisted.

I had to admit, the aroma coming from her kitchen was far too tempting to resist. Spam seemed to second the motion by jumping up and licking my face. It was clear that I'd never be able to leave without first letting her fuss over me. That being the case, I figured that I might as well stay and eat.

'All right. But I already cleaned myself up,' I warned, knowing there was little choice but to give in to the inevitable.

'I'm sure you did. But it's always good to have another pair of eyes. Most likely, you missed something,' Gerda said, and led me into the bathroom. She flicked on a set of bulbs that were bright enough to have lit up a city. 'Now let me take a look.'

I reluctantly removed my sweatpants and top.

'*Oy gevalt*!' Gerda cried out. She clucked her tongue and shook her head at the sight. 'If this is from a fall, then I'm a twenty-year-old showgirl. Rachel, what have you gotten yourself into?'

'Really, Gerda, it was due to my own clumsiness and stupidity,' I retorted, standing by my story.

And, in part, that was true. If I hadn't been such a klutz,

I wouldn't have slipped on the ice and kept my eyes glued to the ground, but have watched where I was going. Perhaps then I'd have had time to fend off my attackers.

'Is there any ointment under those Band-Aids?' she sternly questioned.

'No,' I admitted. 'But believe me, they're all right.'

'I believe that about as much as I believe that you fell on the ice,' she tartly retorted, and briskly ripped off a bandage.

'Ouch!' I complained.

But my protest fell on deaf ears as Gerda proceeded to remove every single one. Then she carefully cleaned each cut and applied a dab of ointment to it.

'Personally, I think you should go to the emergency room and have a doctor check this out,' Gerda said, her fingers probing for any other wounds.

'Absolutely not,' I obstinately responded.

However, I began to relax under her touch.

'You're a very stubborn girl, Rachel. But I love you anyway,' Gerda replied after finishing up. 'All right then, get dressed and come into the kitchen. At least you can eat some nourishing food.'

She was right about that. I sat down to a bowl of home-made matzoh ball soup. The rich chicken broth seemed to heal me from the inside out. My grandmother had always made it whenever I felt sick, calling each bowl Jewish peni-cillin. She must have known what she was doing because I'd instantly feel better, just as I did now.

'There's chicken roasting in the oven, and I'll heat up some potato latkes from the other night.'

Spam heard those words and immediately began to whine.

'Yes, yes. And you'll get some too, my little *meshugge*,' Gerda affectionately reassured him.

Spam must have understood Yiddish, for he patiently laid back down and rested his chin on my foot. I finished my soup as Gerda continued to bustle about the kitchen.

'Gerda, where did you learn to cook?' I asked.

She turned to look at me with a pot holder in her hand. 'Why, from my mother, of course. And she learned from her mother, who learned from her mother, who learned from

161

her mother. Just the same as your grandmother taught your mother, and your mother taught you.'

I started to laugh. 'I'm afraid that I dropped the ball on that one.'

Gerda sliced up some challah bread and set it on the table.

'Don't be silly, Rachel. You may not realize it, but there are lots of things your mother and grandmother taught you that you'll never forget. How else do you think we're able to carry on with our lives? You're here right now because this was your grandmother's home. Your mother grew up here, and now you've returned for a while. It's like a migration. Well, much in our lives works the same way. Who we are is based on what we learned as a child,' she explained.

'If that's true, then what about those children that lost their parents in the Holocaust? How did they learn to get by?' I questioned, my mind wandering back to what I'd seen today.

All that ivory still haunted me. Perhaps people had more in common with elephants than we realized.

'Many of them became lost souls who had to find their own way. That is, unless they had other relatives to turn to. But why are you asking me this?' she questioned, and began to carve the chicken.

I reached for a piece of bread as Gerda placed a plate with chicken and carrots and latkes before me.

'It's just something that I've been thinking about lately.'

But if what she said was correct, then my grandmother and mother had also been repositories of accumulated knowledge handed down over each generation, just as with matriarchal elephants. I'd grown up in a household of women. How much of what I learned had been unconsciously passed on? And what might I have never known if my mother and grandmother hadn't been around?

Perhaps it was collective wisdom, and ancient memories, that had drawn me back to New York. Though my family was gone, they'd always remain as much a part of me as New York City, where I'd been born.

'And what if there are things too painful to look back on?' I asked, remembering the sister that I'd lost.

'We can't escape our past. However, we can choose to

162

dwell on those things that we prefer to remember. The others, you tuck away and take out only once in a while,' Gerda wisely advised, and kissed the top of my head. 'Now eat.'

Every bite made me feel better, as though it were tonic for my soul – as long as I remembered only to chew on the right side of my mouth.

I tried to help clean up after dinner, but Gerda refused to hear of it.

'Absolutely not. You shouldn't be doing a thing for the next few days,' she commanded, as we finished our tea.

'By the way, there's something else I've been meaning to ask,' I mentioned.

'What? You want I should put salt on the sidewalk so that you don't slip again?' she questioned, casting a cynical eye my way.

I chose to ignore the remark.

'I've become interested in the diamond trade and was wondering if David would mind talking to me about it,' I replied, refusing to rise to the bait.

Gerda couldn't have looked more pleased. Perhaps she thought that her grandson and I might finally bond over precious gems.

'What? Are you thinking of maybe getting out of this crazy business you're in and going to work for him?' she suggested.

'No,' I calmly responded. 'It's just something I don't know much about and thought would be fun to learn.'

'Of course he'll talk to you. I'll give him a call right now,' she enthusiastically offered.

I wondered why I hadn't thought of this immediately. Surely, David would know why certain diamonds were illegal in this country. My pulse began to pound as she dialed his number.

'David? This is your grandmother. Rachel is here and she'd like to speak with you. It's something that I think will require the two of you getting together. Call her tonight as soon as you get home,' she instructed and hung up.

Oy veh. She'd cleverly made it sound as though I were fishing for a date.

'I left him a message. I'm sure he'll call you the moment he gets in,' she said, and walked me to her front door.

'Thanks, Gerda,' I replied and gave her a peck on the cheek.

My hand reached for the knob when she suddenly grabbed hold of my arm.

'Oh, my God. You aren't looking for an engagement ring, are you?' she asked with a worried expression.

'Definitely not,' I assured her.

'Good. Now go home and rest,' she ordered.

Funny. That's exactly what my boss had told me about twelve hours ago.

Spam and I walked down the hallway and entered my apartment. Though my body was exhausted, my mind wouldn't stop. To top it off, my nerves were raw and on edge. No way would Jake accept the half-baked story I'd just tried to pawn off on Gerda. I wasn't looking forward to the upcoming interrogation that I knew was bound to take place.

I slipped out of my sweatpants and into my pj's. Then I poured myself a glass of wine, knowing it was the wrong thing to do and doing it anyway. A couple more Motrin and maybe I could knock myself out.

No such luck. Having run out of options, I turned on the TV. I was still wide awake by the time that Jake came home. The glass of wine must have made me feel brave. I figured that I might as well just face him now and get it over with.

'Hey, chère. You here?' he called out.

'Come on, Spam,' I said, hoping he'd accompany me for moral support.

But the dog refused to leave the bed, like the coward he was. They say animals can predict when a natural disaster is going to happen. Spam must have felt that one was about to erupt in Manhattan. I was left with no other choice but to go it alone.

'I'm right here,' I said, and walked out the bedroom door.

Jake's mouth predictably fell open.

'Dear Lord. Are you all right?' he asked, and in two quick steps had his arms wrapped around me.

Maybe it's going to be OK, after all, I thought, momentarily deluded.

164

That illusion was promptly shattered as his hand brushed against the nape of my neck and I flinched. Santou quickly backed away.

'What in the hell happened to you?' he demanded.

Heavy bags held reign under his eyes that I hadn't noticed before, and the lines in his face had grown deeper. No longer were they merely etched with acid, but were now carved in granite. I could feel any wiggle room that there might have been begin to slip away.

The trouble was, I knew Jake all too well. I couldn't just tell him the truth. He'd insist I drop an unauthorized case, and that wasn't about to happen. Instead, I did what came naturally. I fibbed for the greater good.

'I was in the wrong place, at the wrong time, and got mugged,' I boldly lied through my teeth.

Actually, I thought that sounded darn credible. But Santou wasn't buying it.

'You? Miss New York? I sincerely doubt that,' he said, nailing me.

'I swear it's the truth. You know how I am on the ice. I hate the stuff. I wasn't watching where I was going, but kept my eyes on the ground. What can I say? I was the ultimate victim. It was my own damn fault,' I replied, prepared to take all the blame.

'Did you report the attack to the police?' Jake asked the logical question.

But right now, logic was simply getting in my way.

'No. I didn't bother. It wouldn't have done any good. They were wearing masks and I couldn't see either of their faces,' I responded.

'So then, there were two of them?' Santou continued his interrogation.

I nodded, my jaw beginning to throb once again.

'Well, I'm sure you went to the hospital to be treated. They must have had you file a report there,' he insisted.

'You know, I'm beginning to feel pretty tired. Maybe I should just go to bed,' I said, and began to turn around.

'Wait a minute. Are you telling me that you *didn't* go to the emergency room after this happened?'

Those damn eyes of his were as intense as two lasers. The man could see clear through to my soul.

'No, I didn't,' I admitted.

Right then and there, I knew that he had me.

'What are you, crazy? Who knows what kind of damage they might have done to you?' he asked, beginning to fume.

'I'm just badly bruised is all. Gerda checked me out,' I informed him.

'Oh, well, as long as Gerda says you're all right then I suppose everything's OK,' he retorted in exasperation. 'For chrissakes, chère. What are trying to do? Scare the hell out of me? I'm concerned. Don't you get it?'

That did it. He knew exactly what buttons to press so that my defenses instantly crumbled. He touched my face and my eyes welled up with tears. Not because it hurt, but because I couldn't imagine ever being without him.

'Where were you when this happened?' he inquired, his tone beginning to soften.

'I was on Eighth and Fortieth Street, not far from Times Square.'

'What were you doing there?' he asked in surprise.

'It involves a case I'm working on,' I revealed, knowing there was little choice but to tell him.

'I thought Hogan wouldn't let you do anything other than paperwork. When did he give you a case?'

'He didn't,' I admitted. 'It's something I started on my own. Remember I told you this morning that Magda had been burned in her truck?'

'Yeah. Go ahead,' Jake said with a nod.

'Well, she had another connection to Bitsy von Falken besides witnessing her body being dumped. Magda stole a shawl off her corpse before calling the police. The wool is from an endangered antelope. It's called shahtoosh and the shawls are illegal. I've been gathering leads on it ever since. Apparently, there's a booming black market for them here in the city,' I disclosed.

'So what are you saying? There's a ring of shahtoosh smugglers working out of Times Square, and they beat you up as a warning?' he cynically questioned.

166

The phone rang before I had a chance to respond, and Santou quickly answered it.

'Hello? No, I'm afraid Rachel will have to call you back. This isn't a good time for her,' he said into the receiver.

'Wait! Who is it?' I asked, before he could hang up.

Jake covered the mouthpiece with his hand. 'It's David. You know, Gerda's grandson.'

'Let me speak to him,' I replied.

But Jake kept tight hold of the phone. 'Don't be crazy. Whatever he wants can wait until tomorrow.'

'No, it can't. I need to speak to him right now,' I insisted.

Santou reluctantly loosened his grip, and I wrestled the phone from him.

'David, thanks for calling,' I said upon gaining control.

I turned my back to indicate it was a private conversation. But Jake stubbornly refused to leave the room.

Fine, I thought. *Santou now knows that I'm working on a case. Maybe he'll agree to help me with it.*

'I have some questions concerning the diamond trade,' I continued. 'I was wondering if we might meet and I could possibly pick your brain?'

'That would be fine,' David said on the other end of the line. 'Why don't you come by my office in the morning and we can discuss it then. Let me give you the address.'

His office was on Forty-Seventh Street, in the heart of the Diamond District. I couldn't have asked for a better location.

'Great. I'll bring the coffee. See you around ten,' I said in lieu of goodbye.

'You're meeting him tomorrow to talk about diamonds?' Santou asked, without missing a beat, as I hung up.

'Yes. It might have something to do with this case I'm working on, though I don't know for sure yet. I'm just following all leads,' I replied, knowing that Jake would do no less.

'I don't get the tie-in,' he said.

'Neither do I. All I know is that it's getting more complicated and is beginning to take some strange twists and turns,' I admitted. 'It started off with shahtoosh, expanded into ivory, and now seems to involve diamonds.'

167

'Explain this to me. How did diamonds come to be in the mix?' Jake questioned, sounding genuinely intrigued.

'Well, it all began with an anonymous call I received about Bitsy von Falken's shawl. I tracked down the informant only to learn that her motives weren't quite so noble,' I said.

'That makes sense. You know how these informants work. They're always in it either for revenge or monetary gain,' Jake retorted.

'You're right. Turns out my informant has been trying to sell shahtoosh shawls herself.'

'Naturally,' Jake chuckled.

'Anyway, one thing led to another and soon I flipped a fashion designer who's been selling not only shahtoosh, but also elephant ivory. The next thing I know, he's fingered my original informant as also being knee deep in dirty dealings,' I explained.

'What else is new?' Jake wryly observed.

'He suggested I talk to her former boss to get the lowdown. So, I went to speak with him this afternoon. I learned that Tiffany is now dealing in some kind of illegal diamonds. That's what I want to talk to David about,' I revealed. 'I'm trying to figure out what shahtoosh, ivory and diamonds all have in common. There's got to be a correlation between the three. I just have to connect the dots.'

'Tiffany, huh? That sounds like a stripper's name,' Santou commented.

'Good guess,' I said, wondering whether to be impressed or worried that Jake was spending his off-hours at T and A clubs.

'So what's her last name? Bling?' he asked with a soft laugh.

'It should be with all the jewelry she owns. She used to go by Tiffany LaLou, but her married name is Stewart,' I disclosed.

Jake's demeanor instantly changed from that of genial to Arctic cold.

'I want you to back off this case immediately,' he ordered, no longer the sympathetic listener.

'What are you talking about? Why should I?' I challenged, wondering what the hell was going on.

It had been a long time since Santou had tried to pull rank and we'd come to blows. Truth be told, I'd thought we were over this problem. Yet here we were again, bumping heads over cases and territory. Even so, I couldn't imagine what had possibly sparked his attitude. What was his stake in all of this, anyway? For a moment, I didn't think he was even going to give me an answer.

'You'd better have a damn good reason for asking this,' I warned, not in the mood to quibble.

Santou shot me an angry look as he shook his head, jammed his hands in his pockets, and began to rock back and forth.

'And just barking that you want me to back off isn't going to cut it either,' I added, egged on by the increasing pain in my jaw.

'The reason is confidential,' Jake retorted, clearly torn by whether or not to tell me.

'As if my cases aren't?' I brusquely replied.

'You're really going to push this thing, aren't you, Rachel? I guess my asking you to do so isn't good enough,' he responded, cleverly allowing a note of hurt to creep into his voice.

'Put yourself in my place. If I simply ordered you to, would you drop a case that you were working on?' I archly questioned and crossed my arms, indicating that I wasn't about to budge.

Santou fidgeted in place, as if he were about to burst.

'For chrissakes, all right. But you obviously can't reveal what I'm about to tell you. Tiffany Stewart is one of my informants,' he finally blurted out.

'What!' I exclaimed, my mind beginning to reel.

How was that possible? And then I remembered something that Sy Abrams had told me. Tiffany had stayed out of trouble ever since hooking up with a law enforcement agent down South. Most likely, whoever it was still had to occasionally bail her out.

I stared dumbfounded at the man before me. Could it be that person was actually Jake Santou? If so, he'd clearly kept her on his payroll even after moving over to the FBI. No wonder Tiffany had bragged about knowing 'someone on the job'.

'She provides information for ongoing cases, one of which I'm working on right now. Some of them involve national security,' Jake related. 'That's why you've got to stop whatever it is that you're doing.'

I started to laugh. 'Tiffany Stewart helping out with this country's national security? You've got to be kidding. This is some kind of joke, right?'

'No, I'm absolutely serious,' he replied.

I thought back again to the woman I'd met, bedecked in heavy-duty baubles, bangles, and beads, and still couldn't believe that Santou was actually on the level.

'What kind of information is Tiffany Stewart possibly providing?' I questioned, wanting some hard-core proof.

But Jake shook his head. 'You know better than to ask me that. But what I'm saying is the truth.'

'Fine. Then how long have you known her?' I shot back, surprised to find myself wracked by more than a tinge of jealousy.

'For years. In fact, probably longer than you and I have been together. I met her down in New Orleans. She'd gotten herself into trouble at a bar run by the Mob on the strip, and faced either doing jail time, or cooperating with me. Tiffany wisely chose the latter,' Santou said, with the hint of a smirk. 'She's a high maintenance informant, but well worth it.'

'Does Tiffany know about us?' I questioned, unable to shake this feeling of irrational jealousy.

'Of course not,' Santou replied. 'Why? Would you prefer that she did?'

Half of me wanted to scream, *Yes!*

'So if she's got you in her back pocket, then why would she bother to call me?' I angrily asked.

'You answered that yourself,' Santou responded. 'She probably wanted to knock off some shahtoosh competition. Knowing Tiffany, she thought that was as far as it would ever go. For chrissakes, chère. You're a Fish and Wildlife agent. Why would she think any differently?'

Just the way he said that rankled me. True, he was with the FBI. But I was still a federal law enforcement agent authorized to use all the power that implied. Most likely, that's why she'd called the Newark office rather than New York. She figured I'd be happy to nab a few shahtoosh shawls and the seaport and not take it any further. I'd be damned if I'd be cowed by Santou, or played for a fool by Tiffany Stewart with all her jewels and over-developed cleavage.

'By the way, I want you to call David back right now and cancel the appointment you made with him for tomorrow morning,' Jake instructed.

'And why would I do that? Is it somehow going to effect national security, as well?' I sarcastically inquired.

'As a matter of fact, it might. You're stepping on another agency's territory. That's all you need to know,' Santou tersely informed me. 'I don't want to call your boss, but I will if necessary.'

'And what territory would that be, Jake? The Diamond District, or all of New York City?' I countered. 'What is this? Some sort of punishment you've decided to mete out because I haven't played by the rules?'

'For chrissakes, Rachel. You have absolutely no idea of what you're stepping into,' he responded. 'How much do you even know about the seaport? Do you realize that it's a potential powder keg? Right now, that place is the number one target on the terrorists' hit list. Think of what could happen if you go mucking around in things that you don't understand.'

'What are you talking about? Of course I know the seaport. After all, that's *my* territory,' I possessively fought back.

'Oh yeah? Then I suppose you also realize just how easy it is to sneak highly enriched uranium through there,' Jake replied.

He had me on that one. I didn't know a thing about it.

'Should I tell you why?' Santou asked.

I wordlessly nodded.

171

'Uranium can easily be shielded with less than a quarter-inch of lead, making it likely to escape detection by passive radiation monitors. Just so you know, that's exactly what you have at the seaport. Those monitors can't distinguish between naturally occurring radiation, found in everyday items like ceramic tile, and something as dangerous as enriched uranium. Because of that, the devices sound so many false alarms that their sensitivity has been turned down. Naturally, that makes them even less effective,' Santou explained.

I kept my mouth shut, not having been aware of this.

'Think that's bad? It gets even worse. None of the cargo that leaves the port by rail or barge is ever inspected for radiation. Which means that someone could transport a nuclear bomb right through there,' he disclosed.

Terrific. How nice to know.

'But shipping containers aren't the only thing I have to worry about,' Jake continued. 'There are also trucks, planes, ferries, vans, tunnels, bridges, underground garages, high-rise buildings, anthrax, nerve gas, ammonium nitrate, chemical plants, nuclear reactors, subways and railroads, just to name a few.'

I now began to understand why Jake always seemed so pre-occupied of late.

'Just make the call, chère. I have enough to worry about. I don't need to add you to the list,' he said, his voice soft and low.

He kissed me, and I decided not to fight him on this one. I rummaged through my bag, pulled out my date book and looked up David's number. But instead of phoning him, I called my answering machine at work. It picked up on the first ring, letting me know there were other messages.

'Hi, David? It's Rachel again. Listen, I'm sorry but I'm afraid something's happened and I won't be able to make it tomorrow.'

I paused, as though he were speaking.

'Another time? No, I don't think that will be necessary. But thanks anyway,' I said to my machine and quickly hung up.

'You did the right thing, chère,' Santou said, as I turned around to face him.

He held my purse in one hand, and Terri's fuzzy red hand-cuffs in the other. 'By the way, is this what you're using for cuffs these days?'

He shook them and they playfully jingled.

Damn Tiffany Stewart or Tiffany LaLou, whatever her name might be. Maybe she had her tricks, but I had mine too. And I didn't intend to come in second to her in any conceivable way.

'No, those are special,' I said. 'Here. Let me show you.'

I reclaimed the cuffs and, taking Santou by the hand, led him into the bedroom.

'What are you up to, chère?' he asked, his lips close to mine as I pushed him down on the bed.

'Don't ask. It's top secret. National security,' I whispered into his ear.

He reached for me, but I deftly pulled away.

'Uh-uh. No more questions. Just do as I say. First, take off all your clothes,' I ordered.

Jake complied, never looking away.

'What do you think you're doing?' he asked again, breaking the rules when he was finally nude, his voice thick with desire.

I turned down the lights, to hide my bruises, and then removed my own pj's. Straddling him, I cuffed his hands to the bed.

'Anything I damn well please,' I told him.

Then ever so slowly I went to work, inch by inch, until my pain felt excruciatingly exquisite.

Fifteen

'You're taking today off. Right?' Jake asked the next morning, as he cupped each of my breasts and tenderly kissed them.

'Absolutely,' I agreed and then gasped for breath, as his fingers unexpectedly slid inside me.

He soon replaced them with something even better. I'd have to call Terri and thank him. I hadn't had this much sex since I could remember.

'Maybe you shouldn't carry those cuffs around, but leave them home,' Jake suggested, as he later rolled out of bed and headed for the shower.

I listened to the pounding of the water as the radiator began to hiss and spit. Then I watched Santou get dressed.

'I'll walk Spam and drop him off at Gerda's before heading off to work. I want you to get a full day's rest,' he instructed, and kissed me on the forehead. 'Just relax, watch soap operas, and catch up on your sleep. Who knows? We may be up late again tonight.'

'Promises, promises,' I said with a smile and stretched.

Then I waited until I heard the front door close, and slowly counted to ten.

By the time I reached twelve, I was already up and in the shower. After that, I quickly got dressed, picked up the phone, and placed a call to Jack Hogan. It wasn't that I'd deliberately lied to Santou. I had every intention of taking the day off, just not spending it in bed. There was too much to do, including a ten o'clock appointment in the Diamond District.

'Fish and Wildlife. Resident Senior Agent Hogan speaking,' answered a voice as gruff as if it had been dragged through a mound of gravel.

174

'Good morning. It's Rachel. Something's come up and I'd like to take a personal day,' I said.

'Well, good morning to you, too,' he responded. 'What's the matter? Didn't you get enough sleep yesterday?'

'Yes. I'm fine, thanks. It's just that I have to take care of a few things for my aunt. She hasn't been feeling well lately, and I'd like to get her to the doctor,' I lied, crossing my fingers and hoping that God wouldn't strike me dead.

'Yeah. No problem, Grasshopper. Go ahead. Just make sure that's all that you do,' he cautioned.

'What do you mean?' I asked, my stomach beginning to tighten.

'I mean that shit rolls downhill and I feel like I'm standing at the bottom these days. I just got off the phone with DC and they're warning that our budget's about to be cut once again. That's enough for me to deal with right now,' he complained.

I wondered if Santou had called him. But if so, Hogan would have been yelling at me by now.

'I'll see you tomorrow morning,' I said and swiftly got off the phone.

Then I immediately placed a call to Terri.

'Hello?' he croaked, sounding half frog, half human.

'It's me. Sorry to be phoning so early,' I apologized.

'What's this? Payback for my having called so late the other night?' he groaned.

'No. I ran into some trouble yesterday and need your make-up expertise. Do you think you could help me out?' I shamelessly begged.

The black and blue marks on my jaw seemed to be spreading and turning distinctly Technicolor.

'Sure. What are friends for? What time do you need me there?' he inquired.

'How about right now? I've got to be in the Diamond District in two hours,' I replied.

'Jeez, Rach. Nothing like a little notice,' he grumbled.

'Listen, if you can't do it, don't worry. I've got some concealer around and can probably patch myself up,' I said, taking another look in the mirror.

175

Who was I kidding?

'Is it really that bad?' Terri asked between yawns.

'Well, it's not too good,' I admitted.

'Oh, what the hell. I need to get up anyway. I'll be right there,' he responded.

'Are you sure?' I asked, feeling both grateful and guilty.

'Just have some coffee ready. On second thought, don't. I know what your coffee tastes like. I'll pick up a cup myself,' he replied.

'You're a lifesaver,' I told him.

'Don't I know it,' he retorted.

That done, I called and checked my answering machine at work, knowing there were messages. I punched in my code and listened to the first one.

'This is Mrs Charles Woodward the Third. I understand that you paid a visit to Muffy Carson Ellsworth and threatened her with a subpoena concerning her shahtoosh shawls,' said a woman's voice.

Oh shit! Was this some sort of attorney for the rich and famous that was about to take me down?

'I'll have you know I too attended Bitsy von Falken's fundraiser and bought a shahtoosh shawl. I'd like to arrange a time so that I can also be questioned. I'm certainly just as important as Muffy Carson Ellsworth. Besides, my shawl is of far superior quality. Please call me at your earliest convenience.'

I wrote down the woman's name and number, all the while wondering if it was some sort of prank, as the next message began.

'Hello? Agent Porter? My name is Mrs Barbara Andrews Sullivan and I spoke with Muffy Carson Ellsworth yesterday. I hear that you're going to be giving subpoenas to those of us with authentic shahtoosh shawls. Muffy had the nerve to say I needn't worry since mine is clearly pashmina. I'll have you know it's no such thing. I have the genuine article. She also mentioned there's some sort of test that will prove if a shawl is really shahtoosh. Would you please return my call as soon as possible? I'd like to make an appointment to have my shawl tested and receive my subpoena.'

I listened in amazement to the next message, and the next, and the next as the elite of Manhattan each demanded a subpoena as if it were the latest status symbol. All of the women insisted on being questioned, and having their shawls tested, apparently believing that would firmly secure their place in high society. Maybe this would finally convince Hogan it was time to open a case on the black market shahtoosh trade in New York City.

The buzzer rang and I let Terri into the building.

'Where's that maniac dog of yours?' he asked, upon entering my apartment and nervously glancing around.

'Gerda's watching him during the day,' I said, still unsure as to why the two didn't get along.

'Good. Then I only have to deal with your usual army of cockroaches. Now let me see your face,' he responded and took a gander. 'For chrissakes, Rachel. You didn't just run into trouble. It looks like you came up against The Terminator. What in the hell happened?'

'Let's just say I bumped into two guys who apparently weren't too crazy about me,' I replied.

'You've got that right. Let's go into the bathroom and see what we can do,' he said, and led the way with his makeup bag.

I watched in amazement as Terri pulled out concealer and foundation and began to work his magic.

'I still have it, don't I?' he sighed, upon finishing the job.

'You certainly do,' I agreed.

He'd touched up my jaw so well that there was barely the trace of a bruise.

'I know you probably don't want to hear this, but I'm beginning to get a little worried. I'm picking up bad vibrations closing in around you,' he warned.

His brow furrowed and the corners of his mouth turned down. Not a good sign. Terri was diligent about never doing anything that might create wrinkles.

'I'm sure it's just some residual bad karma left over from yesterday's skirmish,' I tried to assure him.

But I began to worry that I felt the same thing.

'By the way, thanks for the fuzzy handcuffs. I believe they

did the trick,' I said, hoping to steer him on to a different topic.

'I told you so,' he proudly crowed. 'I thought I caught the hint of a glow underneath all those bruises. Next time, I'll bring you another toy. You'll have that man of yours begging for more in no time.'

'That's the plan,' I agreed with a grin.

We left the building, and Terri went one way while I headed the other. I managed to catch a cab uptown by nearly throwing myself in the road. My taxi joined a sea of other yellow automobiles that were accompanied by the incessant honking and blowing of horns. The din sounded like a gaggle of pissed-off geese.

The Diamond District is one jam-packed block running between Fifth and Sixth Avenues on Forty-Seventh Street. I disembarked on a corner that boasted a streetlamp, its top the shape of an enormous diamond. This is the spot where tourists and out-of-towners come hoping to get a good deal. I joined the bridge-and-tunnel crowd to walk along a fantasy-land of shops that handle more than ninety percent of all diamonds sold in the US.

Each store window displayed a glittering array of gems. But that was just the teaser. For behind most doors was an entire floor laid out like a shopping arcade.

I entered one and began to count each of the separate booths. The tally came to twenty different jewelry shops from which to choose rubies and emeralds and diamonds. No doubt about it. This had to be one of the most interesting blocks in the world. Then I hurried on, not wanting to be late for my appointment with David.

I entered his building only to be immediately stopped by a security guard. The man ran my bag through an X-ray machine, found my gun, and nearly had a conniption until shown a gun permit and ID.

Having passed inspection, I then walked up two flights of stairs. David's door looked like every other in the non-descript hallway. The only difference was the plaque that read *Benjamin Isaac and Son*. Except, Benjamin had died a few years ago and now the son was the only one left.

A surveillance camera watched my every move as I rang the bell. It was promptly answered by a buzzer. I walked through a metal door and into a three-foot enclosure, fittingly known as a mantrap. On the right-hand side was a pane of bulletproof glass behind which David Isaac sat.

'How do you like my high-class security system?' he asked over the intercom, and buzzed me through a second metal door.

If I weren't with Santou, I might have actually been interested in the man. David was tall and lean with deep brown eyes, wire-rimmed glasses and a smile as sweet as honey.

'Very impressive,' I said, upon stepping into his office. 'Is it just for show, or is there really that much trouble in the building?'

'The Diamond District is a prime target for crime. It always has been. That's why there's a higher concentration of gun permits on this block than any other in the city,' he disclosed.

'Do you have a gun?' I asked.

'Absolutely,' he replied, and pulled a .45 from out of his drawer.

I wasn't certain if that made me feel safer or perhaps a little less secure.

'Just don't tell Grandma. I don't want to make her any more nervous than necessary,' he added.

'Of course not,' I agreed, and plunked a paper sack down on his desk.

David removed two cups of coffee and some donuts I'd bought along the way.

'Thanks. I can use this,' he said and bit into a glazed Krispy Kreme. 'I run on sugar all day. Now tell me what it is you'd like to know.'

'I'm looking into a case that possibly involves the sale of illegal diamonds in this country. Do you have any idea what they could be? I've never heard of such a thing before,' I replied, and took a sip of my coffee.

'I don't know. Are you talking about diamonds that have been stolen? If so, people usually pay cash for them. That ensures there's no record. Of course, there's also a way to change a diamond's identity,' he disclosed.

'What do you mean?' I questioned.

'Well, say somebody knowingly buys a stolen six carat diamond. All they have to do is take it to a diamond cutter. He puts it on his wheel and cuts it down to 5.97 carats. Presto. Suddenly, it's no longer the same diamond as before,' he explained.

'Interesting, but I don't think that's what it is. There must be other kinds of illegal diamonds,' I pressed.

'This is a strange business. It could be almost anything,' David responded, clearly reticent to say much more.

'David, your grandmother swore that you'd be honest with me and share whatever you know,' I replied, coolly stretching the truth and pressing the ever reliable guilt button.

David sighed, leaned back in his chair, and folded his hands over his chest. 'There is something called blood diamonds,' he finally said. 'Only people in this business don't really like to talk about them.'

'Why is that?' I asked, instinctively knowing this had to be it.

'Because it could be bad for business and tarnish a lot of reputations,' he conceded.

'OK. So what are they?' I prodded.

'They're diamonds from rebel held mines in Angola, the Congo and Sierra Leone, that are used to fund guerilla operations,' he revealed.

'You mean, uncut diamonds are sold to finance civil wars in Africa?' I asked, wanting to get it straight.

'Exactly. Though they can be used for that same purpose anywhere in the world. The money amounts to hundreds of millions of dollars a year and goes toward buying tanks, assault rifles, uniforms. Things like that. You name it. In essence, it's a diamonds-for-weapons trade,' he divulged.

My pulse began to thrum as some of the dots now became connected. It made absolute sense. Elephant ivory also came from Africa and had been used in the past to fuel bloody civil wars. Both offered money launderers a way in which to transform questionable cash assets into items that could be easily moved and sold elsewhere. Add shahtoosh to the mix and it amounted to a truly profitable industry.

Calm down, Porter, I told myself. *You're getting carried away and right now, this is all just theory.*

I tried to rein in my excitement, afraid that David might pick up on it and get spooked.

'Sorry, but I'm afraid that's all I know,' he said, as if having read my mind.

'Well, since I'm already here, I'd love to see what it is that you do. This seems like a very interesting business,' I said, in the hope of flattering him.

David smiled and reached for a second donut. God, but I wished that I had his metabolism.

'Actually, you're right. It is interesting. The Diamond District is a world pretty much unto itself. I suppose I could take you with me on my rounds. But first you should probably know something about diamonds. What can you tell me about them?' he asked.

'Absolutely nothing,' I admitted.

'Well, then, what say I give you a crash course?' he offered.

'That would be terrific,' I replied, figuring it might also help me gain his confidence.

'OK, then. Let's go into the back room,' David said, and led the way into a space about the size of a closet.

Inside was a table that held a small wooden box. David opened the lid and pulled out a handful of paper envelopes, each of which had something written in pencil on the front.

'I like to file my inventory of diamonds according to size, color and clarity,' David explained, while tapping a stone out of the first envelope and on to a piece of white cloth. From there, he picked up the gem with a pair of tweezers. 'This one is two carats and the color is *glace,* which is the very best. See how it matches the white fabric?'

I watched as he held the gem over a bright light. Then he raised a jeweler's loupe to his eye while dangling one end of his wire-rimmed glasses in his mouth.

'I next check for clarity. That means I'm looking for any flaws,' he said, and examined the diamond. 'OK. Now take a look and tell me what you see.'

He removed the loupe from his neck and handed it to me,

along with the stone. The diamond felt cold to my touch. Then I raised it to the light.

'I don't see any flaws. It appears to be perfect,' I remarked.

The stone dispersed sparks of light that danced about the room like fire. It was strange to think that lying in my hand was a gem that had been created under the Earth's crust over a hundred million years ago.

'There are also flashes of light all across its surface and very few dull spots,' I observed.

'Yes, diamonds are full of surprises. That's very good,' David remarked, and put the diamond back in its envelope.

I felt as if I'd just been given a gold star.

'Now take a look at this one,' he instructed, and placed a diamond that appeared to be six times as large in my palm.

'Well, the color is slightly yellow and there seem to be a number of flaws,' I noted, holding it up to the light.

'That's right. Although it's bigger, the stone is of inferior quality and not worth as much. I'll make you an offer. Come in every day, study diamonds for the next six months, and I'll make a dealer out of you,' David said with a smile.

'It's tempting,' I teased.

He put on his coat, slipped a handful of envelopes into his pocket, and locked the wooden box in a safe.

'You're going to walk around like that?' I asked in surprise.

David chuckled as he went to his desk, opened the drawer, and pulled out his gun. 'Most gem dealers carry at least a half million dollars of stones in their pocket while making rounds to cutters, setters, and retailers. Still want to come along?'

'Absolutely,' I responded, wondering if he knew that I was an adrenaline junkie.

The street was now bustling. It was filled not only with tourists and customers, but also Hasidic Jews in their broad fur-trimmed hats, long black coats, and beards as they rushed between stores. It was as though I'd been transported to Eastern Europe as I caught snatches of conversation, all conducted in Yiddish.

'The windows on the street are just for retail,' David related, as we passed by them. 'The trade workers and manu-facturers are all located on the upper floors.'

I gazed around at the old multi-story buildings on the block. None were spiffed up, but had a tired, depressed feeling about them. We entered one and took the elevator up to the fifth floor. Even the hallway felt musty and old. But that was nothing compared to what I found as we were buzzed through one of the office doors.

Inside was a space that had been converted into a small dark workroom, its every inch filled with wooden tables, benches, and equipment. Desktops were cluttered with pliers, screwdrivers and tweezers, along with lamps, microscopes, stained coffee cups and old cookie tins. Taped to the walls were cheesy girly calendars displaying beach babes dressed in nothing but thongs. Meanwhile the windows in the room were useless. Their panes were filthy and black, having become caked with decades of grime.

I spied a husky man that looked like a miner wearing a visor. Its band, bedecked with magnifying glasses and a miniature swivel lamp, encircled his head. He sat in front of a tray of diamonds with a flame torch in one hand.

'Ged, I need you to set these diamonds. You'll do a good job for me, won't you?' David asked, and handed him four of the small manila envelopes.

'Of course,' Ged said in a thick Romanian accent, while giving me the once-over.

Then the two men shook hands and, without another word, we left.

'What? That's it? No receipt?' I asked in astonishment. 'Aren't you going to get some kind of proof as to the number of diamonds that you left, along with their size and color?'

But David shook his head as we walked out of that building and into another.

'No need. Everything is based on a handshake in this business. The Diamond District operates on a strict honor code.'

I'd always heard that the diamond trade was secretive and mysterious, but this seemed ridiculous. It was as if I'd stumbled into an arcane, medieval world. No wonder there was so much crime, what with lax record-keeping, and piles of cash and loose gems lying about.

We next entered an office where an old man sat hunched over a revolving wheel, his fingertips blackened and bandaged. The wheel's hum filled the room with a continuous whir as he carefully polished a diamond.

David tapped some gems out of an envelope and placed them in the old man's hands. 'Izzie, you'll call me when they're ready?'

'Don't I always?' he responded with a smile, and then nodded to me. 'You hear that sound? Sometimes a stone will cry. But not this one. This diamond is singing to me sweetly.'

From there we stopped at a place called Red Sun. David left a two-carat stone with a Chinese diamond cutter, along with exact instructions as to how it was to be cut.

'Do you know everyone in the trade around here?' I asked as we left the room.

'Just about. It's a pretty close knit community. One in which we live and die by our reputations,' he said and, placing a hand on the small of my back, guided me into the elevator. 'All right. I know you have more questions about blood diamonds. So, go ahead. What are they?'

I felt as though I'd just been given a free pass.

'If blood diamonds are illegal, then how are they brought into the country?' I asked.

'Diamonds are easy to smuggle. Do you know why?' he quizzed.

'Because they're small?' I ventured a guess.

David slowly shook his head. 'It's something that few people realize. Diamonds can't be detected by X-ray, nor can they be uncovered by drug sniffing dogs. And once they're here, there's no way to tell where they came from. That's what's so fascinating about the stones. Diamonds are conducive to secrets. They're virtually untraceable, giving no clue as to where they originated.'

We entered yet another building and approached an ominous looking black door.

'OK, this next stop is a dealer who wants to buy some uncut diamonds from me. If he asks, you're my assistant. That way you won't make him nervous,' David instructed.

We were buzzed inside where a diminutive man, with

184

large glasses and small suspicious eyes, immediately pounced on me.

'Who is she?' he asked David, without so much as hello.

'Saul, this is my cousin Rachel. I'm teaching her the business. Not to worry,' David assured him and, pulling out a pouch, tapped five uncut stones on to the counter.

Saul quickly went to work placing a small digital scale, a sheet of white paper, and a clear glass plate next to them. Then using tweezers, he picked up one diamond at a time, placed it on the plate and held it over a bright light. He carefully studied each gem with his loupe.

'Their clarity is very good,' Saul finally pronounced.

But the transaction wasn't yet over. The diamonds were next transferred to the digital scale and scrupulously weighed, after which Saul's fingers pecked at numbers on a calculator. He handed it to David, who checked the total and then tapped in his own set of figures. I listened to the staccato rattle of calculator keys flying back and forth between the two men until they finally reached an accord. That done, they shook hands and said *mazel,* the Hebrew word for 'good luck'.

Then we walked back outside having concluded today's business.

'Now tell me. Would you have known where those uncut diamonds came from?' David asked.

I dodged to avoid colliding into a harried dealer, but to no avail. We silently bumped shoulders.

'No way,' I replied.

'Well, neither do I or my friends. The only one that knows is the original buyer,' he explained. 'And people that launder dirty money usually don't care if rebels mutilate and torture civilians to force them to work in their mines. By the time a diamond arrives at Tiffany's, its origin has already been changed or concealed. Just remember, nothing is what it seems to be in the diamond trade.'

That apparently was true, including a diamond's carefully cultivated image – that of romance and eternal love. Instead, the stones were stained with blood.

'Do you think blood diamonds are being traded and sold in the Diamond District?' I questioned.

David seemed to cringe. 'Anything is possible. There are disreputable people in this business, just as in any other. I've heard of jewelers that buy diamonds from shady characters. Most of the rumors involve drug dealers anxious to convert their cash profits into stones. No question but that diamonds are more portable than gold.'

I began to wonder if Tiffany Stewart might possibly be connected with a drug ring. However, that wouldn't seem to involve national security. Still, it was clear that behind the street's façade was a nebulous world of murky financial transactions.

'You have to realize it's hard to hide cash assets, while diamonds can easily be moved around the world. Word is that Al Qaeda has made millions selling diamonds mined by Sierra Leone's rebels. It would certainly be a smart way to sneak funds into this country. Their operatives could set up cells, buy weapons, and carry out terror operations without attracting any unnecessary attention,' he mused. 'And it wouldn't take much. Once the stones were smuggled in, all they'd need was a front man to sell the diamonds for them. Who would be the wiser?'

A chill grabbed hold of me, though I said nothing. What David had just proposed made frightening sense. Then I remembered something else I'd heard. Al Qaeda operatives had been caught using stolen South African passports. I feared this was beginning to turn into a spider's web of arms, diamonds and ivory.

I jumped as my cellphone rang, having become buried deep in thought.

'Excuse me, but I have to get this,' I told David.

Taking a deep breath, I tried to quiet my heart.

'Hello?' I answered.

'This is Giancarlo. I've arranged a meeting today with my ivory contact. He expects you within the next few hours,' he said, sustaining both his pitch perfect accent and charade.

'Hi, Ralph,' I responded, just to irritate him. 'Is it to take place at the ivory factory?'

'Yes,' he replied, maintaining his cool. 'It's in Chinatown. Here's the address.'

I rummaged through my bag and grabbed hold of a rumpled receipt and pen to quickly write it down.

'You're to tell them your name and say that you're there to pick up a blue ballgown,' he continued.

'Pick up a ballgown at an ivory factory?' I asked. 'Doesn't that sound rather strange?'

'Not at all. There's a tailor shop in front that serves as their cover,' he explained. 'The ivory factory is in the basement.'

Just hearing his voice made my blood begin to boil. I felt sure Giancarlo had arranged for my beating. However, I had to keep a lid on my anger until I'd obtained all the necessary information.

'Who should I ask to see?' I calmly inquired.

'I wasn't given a name. They'll tell you when you get there,' Giamonte instructed.

That was all I needed to know.

'So listen, Ralph. That was quite the surprise you had waiting for me yesterday afternoon. If I were you, I'd keep your windows and door closed and locked because you're going to be sorry,' I advised.

'What in the hell are you talking about?' Giancarlo responded, sounding confused.

'Oh, come on. Don't play dumb. I know damn well that you set me up. Those two thugs outside the Beaver's Den. They said it was you that sent them,' I lied, hoping to use it as bait.

'Thugs outside The Beaver's Den? You're losing your mind, Porter. Whatever happened, I had nothing to do with it,' he vehemently insisted. 'Those aren't the kind of people that I associate with. You should know that by now.'

'You'd better hope I don't get proof. In any case, try it again and you're a dead man,' I warned.

'How did I ever think that you were a socialite? You have absolutely no couth,' he retorted.

'Uh-huh. Unlike the polish and gentility that you display in those DVDs of yours,' I reminded him.

Giancarlo Giamonte, aka Ralph Goldberg, was silent for a moment.

'Do you still want to go through with this meeting? Or don't you trust me enough? I imagine that you think it's a set up,' he finally said, getting straight to the point.

Giamonte was right. I remained suspicious, but had no intention of backing out now.

'I'll take your word that you had nothing to do with the attack,' I said, knowing there was no way to be absolutely certain. 'In the meantime, don't mention this to anyone. I'll be in touch,' I told him, and hung up.

I turned to find David staring at me with a look that fluctuated between distress and horror.

'Rachel, is everything all right?' he asked in a worried tone.

'Sorry about that,' I responded, having momentarily forgotten about him. 'I'm afraid I have to deal with some skeevey people in this business. That's probably another thing that we shouldn't tell your grandmother.'

David gave an understanding nod, but I could tell that he'd never regard me the same way again. Then he headed back to work, as I took off for Chinatown.

Midtown traffic was crazy by now, and I didn't want to blow my life savings on a cab. With that in mind, I scampered down a set of stairs and into the bowels of New York.

Sixteen

The best thing about the subway system is that it's still a bargain, compared to the rest of the city, and operates twenty-four hours a day. I didn't have to wait long before a platinum eel of a train approached, its gleaming silver line cutting through the dark underground tunnel. I jumped on and became one more pinball jostled about in a car full of people. In no time at all, I arrived in Chinatown.

I emerged to join a crowd that snaked along torturously narrow streets. The sidewalks were filled with open-air fish markets, fruit stands, and sweet shops. My nose was amply rewarded with the delicious aroma of scallion pancakes, roast duck and fried dumplings as I made my way through the swarm.

If Yiddish is the official language of the Diamond District, then Chinatown also has its own vernacular. The only English to be heard came from Caucasians and tourists. Little did they know that behind exotic looking stores, Chinatown is still an area filled with gangs, protection rackets, drugs and sweatshops.

I left Tourist Central and headed down Oliver Street, eventually reaching the address that Giancarlo had given me. Just as he'd said, I spotted a sign that read *Black Star Expert Tailor Shop*. I opened the door and entered a room sparsely furnished with clothing racks, a floor-to-ceiling mirror, and a sewing machine. A bell rang, briskly notifying the owner that a customer had arrived.

The following moment, an elderly Chinese woman appeared from behind a heavy dark curtain. She looked to be frail as a delicate porcelain statue, pale as a ghostly new moon.

'Hello. My name is Cheri Taylor. I'm here to pick up a blue ballgown,' I told her, wondering if she knew what I was talking about.

The woman's face remained placid as a frozen lake as she nodded once and disappeared.

I waited, growing increasingly anxious, curious as to what was taking so long. My unease was partly due to a strange buzzing sound that I heard. It was as though a hive of bees were hovering all around me. The menacing noise reached deep inside and rattled my nerves. The old woman finally peeked from behind the curtain and motioned for me to follow.

Had Giamonte decided to permanently dispose of his problem by selling me into the white slave trade? I wondered, slipping past the curtain to spy a steep flight of stairs.

Suck it up, Porter. What are you, suddenly afraid of every little thing? Don't you remember? He told you that the ivory factory was in a basement, I sternly reprimanded myself.

I blamed it on the fact that my body was sore, my jaw ached, and the back of my neck continued to throb. Even so, my heart began to beat wildly as my foot hit the top step.

The buzzing grew louder as a spectral cloud of dust began to rise and fill the air. The tiny white flakes invaded my eyes, nose and mouth like gentle flurries of snow. The minute crystals tickled my lungs with each intake of breath as my stomach twisted and turned in anticipation of what I was about to discover. There was no doubt but that each step brought me closer to a unique sort of hell. I continued my descent into the equivalent of what was an elephant graveyard.

Little by little, I caught sight of a row of men in front of saws that whirred and lathes that turned. And everywhere there were containers filled with ivory.

Others worked by hand, plying their trade with chisels, awls and files. They carved tusks that had been ripped from mothers, grandmothers, aunts, brothers, sisters and babies. Fortunately, their deaths hadn't been for nought. They now made lovely cigarette holders, chopsticks and paperweights. Other elephants had been reduced to a large pile of newly carved Buddhas.

190

There was even a special table dedicated solely to the making of *hanko*s or 'chops' – personal finger-size signature seals used on financial contracts and other official Japanese documents. Their popularity and status has elevated them to 'must have' items.

I thought of all the elephants that had been mowed down. So, this was why they were being indiscriminately slaughtered – for knickknacks and curios in what amounted to a sickening display of man's vanity. It almost made me ashamed to be human.

But I had little time to dwell on such thoughts as someone began to approach. I found myself facing a Chinese gentleman that could have been anywhere from his mid-fifties to seventy-five years old. He was impeccably dressed in a tan tailor-made suit. The choice of color was wise. A shower of white clung like dandruff to everyone's clothes.

My contact moved with a sense of grace that was surprising, almost as if he floated on air. But there was an undercurrent of power in his walk, as well. My gaze was drawn to a face smooth as an ivory billiard ball, and track-marks left by a comb in his dark slick of hair.

'Miss Taylor, welcome to my factory,' he said, displaying two shiny gold teeth, and formally shook my hand.

I instantly knew that dealing with the man would be akin to sticking one's arm in a tiger's cage just to see what might happen. At the same time, he couldn't have been any more courteous.

'May I offer you some tea?' he politely inquired.

'Thank you. That would be lovely,' I replied.

The old woman silently poured me a cup. I took a deep whiff. It was the intoxicatingly sweet scent of jasmine.

'This is wonderful,' I said, after taking a sip.

'I'm glad you like. You'll notice a hint of orchid in there, as well. I have it specially made in Hong Kong,' he remarked.

The man was so proper, I found it hard to believe that he had yet to introduce himself.

'I'm afraid you have an advantage over me that needs to be rectified,' I mildly pointed out.

My host raised a questioning eyebrow. 'And what might that be?'

'You haven't yet told me your name,' I informed him.

He shook his head, chuckled, and gave a small shrug. 'How thoughtless. Please forgive me. I'm an old man and my memory isn't what it used to be.'

I nodded sympathetically, but somehow doubted that.

'My name is George Leung,' he pleasantly revealed.

It was as if a nuclear bomb had gone off, causing my legs to tremble and the porcelain cup to shake slightly in my hand. Standing before me was a living legend – the Godfather of the illegal wildlife trade himself.

Leung was notorious as the main mover and shaker of ivory. His front company, Africa Hydraulics, had been responsible for smuggling vast amounts out of Africa during the bloody eighties. He had led the charge that decimated elephant populations and helped to place them on the endangered species list.

But my connection to the man was far more ominous and personal than that. His son had been the sharkfin dealer that Vinnie Bertucci and I had been forced to kill in Hawaii.

Beads of sweat broke out on my forehead, although the room was cold, and I knew that he was watching me closely. If I didn't play this right, I might not make it out of here alive. Or perhaps my fate had already been decided, and Leung was simply toying with me.

'It's a pleasure to meet you,' I said, doing my best to appear composed.

But he surely must have noticed my pulse was pounding so hard that it was about to burst out of my body. And there was no stopping the train of thoughts that continued to speed through my mind.

Giamonte had said ivory was being shipped out of South Africa. It was common knowledge that Leung had been based there for decades. So why hadn't I made the connection before? After all, I'd heard about the man ever since my days as a rookie agent in New Orleans. He'd been the nemesis of my former boss, Charlie Hickok, his personal Moby Dick that had gotten away.

Charlie had claimed that Leung's protection came from high-level South African sources. He'd endeared himself during apartheid; when sanctions against the country were imposed, Leung had helped out by importing much needed electronics and computers from China and Japan.

There was no question but that he had plenty of money with which to grease the right wheels. Besides ivory, Leung had a hand in everything, from restaurants to a Mercedes dealership, Chinese medicinals and sharkfin, as well as maintaining luxury homes in Johannesburg and Hong Kong. Then there were his 'front' companies, dealing in timber, copper scrap and auto parts, that were used as covers for smuggling.

'Allow me to give you a tour of our humble facility. As you know, we only recently opened shop. But we hope to soon be up and running to full capacity,' Leung said, using the all-encompassing term 'we'.

I wondered if others were involved in this venture that I didn't yet know about.

'And what would that be?' I questioned.

Leung tilted his head, as though he didn't quite understand.

'What do you consider to be full capacity?' I clarified.

'Ah. Let me explain,' Leung said.

We walked over to where a man carefully chiseled an ornate ivory egg by hand.

'In the past, a worker might spend up to a year carving a single tusk, depending on the intricacy of the project. However, with the advent of electric tools, eight people can now produce enough jewelry and figurines to consume the tusks of three hundred elephants in just one week. It's a marvel of modern industry, wouldn't you agree?' he amiably questioned.

I gave a small nod in concession, but shuddered at the thought of all that collective wisdom being ground into dust.

'What are those?' I inquired and pointed to two large vats, ready to move on to another topic.

'I like to think of it as magic, but it's our antiquing method,' Leung replied, sounding pleased that I had asked.

I'd always been curious as to the process. It was a clever

ploy by which illegal ivory was sometimes brought into the country. The law declared that only ivory obtained before the 1990 ban could legitimately be bought and sold. Therefore, making ivory appear to be old was a common trick of the trade.

'Here. Let me show you how it's done,' Leung congenially offered.

He led me to a pot of boiling liquid as dark and murky as the water surrounding the seaport; the scent so acrid that it nearly jumped up and bit my nose.

'What you see here is a mixture of coffee, tea and tobacco leaves. Pieces of ivory are boiled in this concoction for two hours before they are carved,' he explained. 'The second vat is reserved for items that have already been sculpted. Those carvings are soaked in a cool form of this same liquid for nearly two weeks. After that, you have a lovely piece of 'antique'-looking ivory such as this one.'

Leung pointed to an elegant swan, so beautifully carved that every single feather was a work of art. Even I had to admit just how exquisite it was.

I was caught off-guard as Leung abruptly turned and stared at me.

'By the way, why was Mr Giamonte unable to make our meeting today? You're a welcome replacement, but it strikes me as rather odd. Especially since he repeatedly called Hong Kong and insisted on seeing the facility,' Leung pressed.

I took a deep breath and immediately became queasy. I couldn't be certain if it was the bitter smell of solution and all the dust, but it was as though I were surrounded by death.

'Mr Giamonte is terribly sorry and sends his regrets. However, there was an unforeseen emergency. That's why he asked me to come in his stead. He didn't want to let the opportunity slip by,' I replied, hoping the excuse would pass muster.

Leung lowered his chin, grunted, and seemed to accept the explanation. Then he raised his head and I caught sight of something cold and hard in his eyes. Whatever it was scared the hell out of me. So much so, that my hands grew clammy and my stomach tightened another notch. Once again, I couldn't help but wonder if Leung had any inkling as to who I actually was.

Snap out of it. You're falling prey to your own paranoia, I harshly scolded myself.

But there was no shaking the feeling that I was caught in a deadly game of cat and mouse.

'Mr Giamonte also asked that I order a large quantity of figurines,' I said, knowing a trap had to be laid if I hoped to catch Leung bringing ivory into the country.

'How odd, considering that he already placed a sizeable one only this morning,' Leung stiffly responded.

Damn. I hadn't counted on that.

'We must have gotten our wires crossed,' I tried to casually slough it off.

But Leung refused to let the incident go.

'How can you be his assistant and yet have no idea as to what is going on?' he brusquely questioned. 'That doesn't sound like very good business to me, but as if something were wrong.'

A tool clattered to the floor, fraying yet a few more of my nerves. Only I didn't dare look around. Instead I held Leung's gaze, hoping to convince him that I had nothing to hide.

'Mr Giamonte has been busy with other matters of late. However, he has a number of new clients that are eager to purchase beautiful items for their homes,' I responded. 'He must have decided to place the order himself instead of having me do it.'

Leung remained quiet for a moment, but it was as though he could see straight through to my soul.

'In that case, please inform him that a shipment is arriving at the port today and will be delivered to the factory tomorrow. The consignment contains many lovely artifacts that Mr Giamonte's customers might find of interest.'

'Thank you. I'll be sure to let him know,' I replied. 'Once again, I appreciate the tour. It was most informative. Now I best get back to work and not take up any more of your valuable time.'

Leung graciously smiled and gave a perfunctory nod.

I didn't take another breath until I was up the steps, out the door, and standing on the sidewalk. Then I brushed every tiny flake of ivory off me, and quickly rushed home.

Seventeen

A jolt of adrenaline raced through me as I picked up the phone and promptly placed a call to Fish and Wildlife.

'Hi, Connie? It's Rachel Porter. Listen, I just received a tip that a shipment of ivory is arriving from South Africa today. Is there any way we can get the container pulled and secretly inspect it?' I asked, the words rushing out on one stream of breath.

There was a deep sigh on the other end of the wire.

'I appreciate your zeal, Rachel. But that's like trying to find the proverbial needle in a haystack. Do you have any idea how many containers are offloaded at this port every day?' she questioned.

'A lot,' I ventured.

'Roughly about six thousand of them. That makes trying to locate your shipment nearly impossible. Especially if it's already been electronically cleared,' she explained.

'Please, Connie. You don't realize who I've got in my sights. I just came from a meeting with the head honcho of the illegal ivory trade,' I revealed.

'How did you manage that?' she asked in surprise.

'He thinks that I work for one of his clients, which makes this the opportune time to nab him. Believe me, this guy won't be happy until the very last elephant has been killed so that he can jack up the price of ivory. Isn't there some way we can find this container?' I continued to beg.

'Not without Customs' assistance,' Connie informed me.

My heart began to sink.

'Although I *do* have a friend there that might be willing to help us,' she slyly added.

'Oh, thank you, thank you, thank you!' I gushed, beginning to feel absolutely ecstatic.

'Hold on. He'll need the name of the company in order to run it through their system,' she told me.

'No problem. The name is Tat Hwong Products,' I cheerfully complied.

'And of course he'll also want the container number,' Connie said. Oh, hell!

'I don't have it,' I grudgingly admitted.

'Hmm. That's going to make tracking this shipment a whole lot more difficult,' she disclosed. 'It could take a while.'

'Terrific. Time is exactly what we haven't got,' I groaned.

'Well, all we can do is give it a shot and see what happens. Look on the bright side. This certainly won't be the last time that your friend brings in ivory,' she said in an attempt to cheer me up.

'Actually that's the dark side, Connie. I want to nail this bastard now, while we have the chance. Who knows when I'll get this kind of opportunity again?' I responded in frustration. 'By the way, don't mention any of this to Hogan.'

'The big boss man? Don't worry. I wouldn't dream of it. That would spoil all the fun. For once, I might actually get to do my job. I'll give you a ring as soon as I hear anything,' she assured me and hung up.

I immediately began to pace the apartment, search the shelves for cookies, and drum my fingers on the kitchen table. Patience has never been my strong suit. No question but that I'd lose my mind if I had to sit and wait much longer. Then I remembered, there was someone else I needed to call.

'Vincent Bertucci. You cast me and I shoot 'em. Bam, bam!' Vinnie answered his line.

'Hi, it's Rachel,' I replied, still trying to adjust to the idea of Vinnie being an actor.

'So, how do you like my phone greeting? Pretty catchy, huh?' he asked.

'Yeah. It's definitely unique,' I responded. 'I'm just calling to see if you found out anything else for me about Magda.'

'Who was that again?' he questioned.

Terrific. I just hoped that Vinnie was better at remembering his lines.

'You know. The woman that died when her luncheonette truck was torched,' I patiently reminded him.

'Yeah, yeah. Now I remember. Sure, I asked around, but none of the guys were involved in that hit,' he revealed. 'In fact, they were pretty pissed about it. They really liked the broad's pierogis and kielbasa.'

'I'm sure she would have been pleased,' I said, having suspected all along that my boss Jack Hogan was wrong.

I had no doubt but that Magda's death was somehow connected to Bitsy von Falken, shahtoosh shawls, and now possibly ivory.

'Listen, there's something else I need to ask you,' I began, knowing there was no way to tiptoe around the next topic.

'If you're thinking of trying to get back into acting, you should fugedaboudit. I can't help you there. In fact, my agent says that broads over thirty-five stand a better chance of finding a patsy to marry than breaking into show business,' Vinnie said in his own gentle manner.

'No, that's not it. I'm curious as to how you knew more than one person was involved in Bitsy von Falken's death?' I inquired, referring to our former conversation in Little Italy.

The question was followed by an awkward pause.

'Huh? What are you talking about?' Vinnie finally responded.

'I mentioned that Magda saw Bitsy's body being dumped and you asked if she got a good look at the men's faces. Don't you remember? What made you think that two people took part in the hit?' I asked again, hoping that Vinnie wasn't somehow linked.

'Just an educated guess. Idiots usually travel in pairs,' Vinnie smoothly responded.

'And why were they idiots?' I questioned.

'Cause otherwise they'd have checked out that luncheonette truck before dumping the body,' he said darkly.

I wondered if Vinnie knew this from experience.

'Listen, I gotta go. I'm shooting a scene later this week

with Bobby De Niro. It's only a few lines, but I wanna get it right. Talk to you later,' he said, and hung up.

I was left with an uneasy feeling about what Vinnie might possibly know and not be telling me. I dealt with it the best way I could – by polishing off a bag of Oreos. When the phone finally rang, it was Connie with news that I didn't want to hear.

'Sorry, but nothing came up under Tat Hwong Products. That's why it's so important to have the container number. It's the best way to find a shipment. Are you sure that you've got the name right?' she asked.

'Yes,' I muttered half to myself, knowing this could be the only chance I'd ever have to catch George Leung.

I couldn't let him slip through my fingers. Not when I was so close to nabbing him. There had to be something else I'd overlooked. I thought of Charlie Hickok and wondered what he'd do. That helped trigger a hunch.

'Have your friend punch in a company called Africa Hydraulics,' I excitedly urged.

'OK. But he won't be able to help us much after that,' Connie said.

'Just do it,' I implored, feeling as though I were betting my last dollar on a lottery ticket.

I anxiously waited as Connie put me on hold. I'd never forgive myself if Leung got away. One more minute of this and my head would explode.

'That's it!' Connie reported back triumphantly. 'The container's been offloaded at Starr Terminal, and its contents are listed as auto parts.'

'Terrific. How would you like to help me uncover a ship-ment of ivory?' I asked, knowing it would probably be the most fun that she'd had in years.

'I'd love to. There's just one teensy problem. The container is already stacked with others on the dock. We'll have to find a longshoreman that's willing to pull it for us and break the security seal,' she revealed. 'That won't be easy. The shipment's already been electronically released by Customs, and you know how those longies can be. They're not about to do us Feds any unnecessary favors.

They might even have been paid off to make sure no one touches it.'

What I knew for certain was that organized crime tightly controlled both the local longshoremen's union and companies doing business at the port.

Now who do I know with connections to the Mob? I mused, already aware of the perfect person.

'I might just be able to solve this problem. Give me a couple of minutes and I'll call you right back,' I mysteriously replied.

Then I quickly placed another call to Vinnie.

'Vincent Bertucci. You cast me and I shoot 'em. Bam, bam,' he answered his phone.

I wondered when he would finally get tired of saying that.

'It's me again,' I said.

'What's up? I'm tryin' to memorize my lines and all these calls are breakin' my concentration. Whaddaya suddenly got the hots for me or something?' he questioned.

'I need a simple favor,' I replied.

'Ain't no such thing in this life. Don't you know that by now, New Yawk?' he responded.

'I guess I'm a little slow in that department. But since you're already on the phone, why don't we give it a try?' I persisted. 'I want to have a container opened at the port so that I can inspect its contents.'

'Yeah. And what's that got to do with me?' Vinnie questioned.

'The container was electronically cleared before landing. That means it's probably already stacked up with a bunch of others at Starr Terminal. I'll need a longshoreman to pull it from the stack and break the security seal for me. And you know how sticky those union rules can be,' I responded.

'You're talking about one of those big forty-foot mothers?' Vinnie questioned.

'Yes,' I replied. 'The thing is, it has to be done on the QT. There's something else you should know. The shipment belongs to George Leung. I posed undercover and met with him this afternoon.'

'Holy shit! You gotta be kidding me,' Vinnie said in a

hushed tone. 'Are you talking about the Chinese Godfather? Michael Leung's old man?'

'The one and only,' I verified.

'For chrissakes! Whaddaya out of your mind?' Vinnie exploded. 'Did the old man have any idea who you were?'

'Of course not,' I said, though I couldn't be certain.

'Unbelievable, New Yawk. I can always count on you to shake things up,' he retorted with a snort.

'This is important, Vinnie. I really need to stop this guy. You know damn well that Leung's bad news,' I replied, trying to drive my point home.

'Like father like son, I suppose,' Vinnie responded. 'When do you want this done?'

'It has to be today. The shipment is being picked up tomorrow morning,' I reported.

Vinnie seemed to think about it for a moment. 'OK. I can probably pull a few strings and help you out with the longies. But it'll have to be after hours, and no way in hell are you going by yourself to the docks tonight.'

'That's no problem. I've already arranged to have someone accompany me,' I informed him.

'Yeah? Who's that? The Ragin' Cajun?' Vinnie questioned.

'No,' I answered a little too sharply.

'What's the matter? Trouble on the home front?' he asked.

'It's just that I'd rather Santou didn't know about this. I don't want to worry him,' I lied.

'If he doesn't like to worry, he's with the wrong chick. So, who's the chump that's going with you then?' Bertucci persisted.

'A wildlife inspector,' I revealed, hoping that would satisfy him.

'And what's the guy's name?' Vinnie continued to quiz.

'Connie Fuca,' I responded, figuring her first name could swing either way.

'Connie? Is that like in Constance or Constantine?' Vinnie demanded.

'All right, Vinnie. You got me. Connie is a female inspector. I'm going with a woman. OK?' I finally admitted, tired of playing the game.

'Another broad? What a relief. Now I can relax, knowing you'll be well protected,' Vinnie derisively retorted. 'Listen up, New Yawk. It ain't gonna happen. Not unless she's six foot three, is built like a refrigerator, and has hair on her chest. Other than that, I'm coming with you.'

Sometimes I wondered if Vinnie was my guardian angel, or a three-hundred-pound albatross. Part of me also couldn't help but wonder if this might not also be a set-up. For all I knew, Vinnie had been involved in Bitsy von Falken's murder. Still, I'd had no choice but to trust him in Hawaii, and he'd finally come through – though it had been touch and go for a while.

'Listen, I'll be fine. You don't need to worry about me,' I tried to persuade him.

But Vinnie wasn't buying it.

'That's the deal if you want my help, New Yawk. Take it or leave it. But I'm not gonna have this crap on my conscience,' he said, laying down the law.

There wasn't a shot in hell that a longshoreman would cooperate with me out of the goodness of his heart. I needed Vinnie's muscle and Mob connections, if I was going to see this thing through.

'Fine. You can come along,' I conceded.

'Oh, boy. Lucky me,' Vinnie said, as though he were insulted. 'All right, here's how it's gonna play. We'll have to go late when there aren't too many people around. I'll pick you up at your place around ten o'clock tonight.'

'OK. See you then,' I agreed, hoping that Santou wouldn't be home.

Rather than take a chance, I decided to call up and find out.

'Hey, chère. What's going on?' Jake asked, sounding distracted as he answered the phone.

'Have I caught you at a bad time?' I questioned.

'When isn't it bad these days? Things are a little crazy here right now,' he admitted.

'Does that mean I shouldn't expect you home for dinner tonight?' I asked, hoping for once his schedule would work in my favor.

'With the way things are going, you'll be lucky to see me for breakfast,' Santou retorted. 'What say we make up for it over the weekend? With any luck, maybe things will break and I'll get some time off.'

'All right. But I'll miss you,' I said, relieved that the coast would be clear.

That was it. I was now going to hell for all of my lies.

'Just keep those fuzzy handcuffs close by,' he added with a low growl.

'You've got a deal,' I replied, and felt myself begin to blush.

That done, I quickly phoned Connie.

'OK. Everything's taken care of. Let's meet in the Fish and Wildlife parking lot about ten thirty tonight,' I told her.

'Wow. I'm impressed What, do you know someone with the Mob or something?' she inquired with a laugh.

'I suppose you could say that,' I replied.

'Really?' she asked curiously.

'Well, he used to be. But these days he's an actor,' I disclosed.

Who knew? Maybe with the right case, and a little luck, even *I* would manage to get a movie deal one of these days.

'By the way, he'll be coming with us tonight,' I added, almost as an afterthought.

'Then this *is* going to be exciting,' Connie said, to my surprise.

Obviously, neither of us had a very thrilling social life.

The hours seemed to drag by as I waited, giving me plenty of time to think. I spent it trying to dredge up stories that Charlie Hickok had once told me.

Half the time, I hadn't bothered to listen as he'd prattled on. But there'd been one particular tale about Leung that I now tried to remember. What the hell was it, anyway? I swore it was floating around in there somewhere, playing hide-and-seek, tottering on the edge of my brain. I was just about to give up when I finally recalled the story.

Leung had once hidden ivory tusks in the false bottom of a truck, carrying copper scrap, that was traveling between Botswana and Zambia. The driver was stopped by a border guard, the truck searched, and the ivory found. As was routine, all the tusks were confiscated. However, that hadn't been Leung's main concern. Rather, he'd been desperate to recover the truck itself. So much so, that he'd offered a minor fortune for its return.

Perhaps Leung shouldn't have been so overly eager. His fervor prompted yet another search, and this time a second clandestine compartment was found – one that was packed, not with ivory, but a hidden cache of diamonds.

That was all Charlie had known. But it was enough so that another piece of the puzzle now began to fall into place.

I thought back to one particular place that David Isaacs had taken me to only this morning – a Chinese diamond cutting firm. Damn. What had been the name? Wracked my brain. It had something to do with the planets. Then my eyes landed on a jar of strawberry jam that had been left on the kitchen counter. That was it! Red Sun.

I wasted no time, but grabbed my notebook and located the home number for Bill Saunders, the other Special Agent at Fish and Wildlife in Newark.

Though he was Jack Hogan's buddy, the guy was more importantly a bona fide computer geek and that's exactly what I needed right now. Word had it he could track down a company's business records in no time flat. Calling him would be a gamble, but I knew that I had to take the risk. Either he'd choose to help, or he would sell me out.

'Hello?' a young boy answered the phone.

'Hi. Is your dad at home?' I asked.

The receiver was thrown on to a table with a loud thud that resounded in my ears.

'Hey, Dad! Some woman wants to talk to you!' the kid screamed.

Terrific. I'm sure his wife would be pleased.

'Hello. Who's this?' Saunders asked, as he came on the line.

'Hi, Bill. It's me. Rachel Porter.'

I suddenly felt tongue-tied, hoping that I was doing the right thing. Hogan could effectively shut me down if he got wind of what I was up to. But my curiosity refused to let me squirm out of it now.

'Rachel, this is an unexpected call. Is everything all right?' he asked.

'Fine. I was just wondering if you'd be willing to do me a favor,' I replied.

'I guess that depends on what it is,' Saunders tentatively responded.

What in the hell was I thinking? It wasn't as if I were his favorite person in the world. In fact, this was the most we'd spoken in the past week. Still I had no choice but to hope for the best, grab a deep breath, and take the plunge.

'I was hoping you'd check something for me. I'd like to find out if a few different businesses are owned by the same parent company. One is based in South Africa, the other in Hong Kong, and the last one here in New York,' I said.

'Sure. I can do that. Fire away,' Saunders congenially agreed.

'The names are Africa Hydraulics, Tat Hwong Products, and Red Sun,' I divulged.

'That sounds like some sort of exotic combo dinner,' he joked. 'Are you checking into something to do with hydraulics or traditional Chinese medicine?'

'It probably involves Chinese medicinals. Though I'm not really sure yet,' I lied.

'Fair enough. I'll call you back in a while,' he said and hung up.

My stomach performed somersaults as I waited, wondering if I could trust Saunders to get the information without reporting it to Hogan.

I was out of Oreos, there were no potato chips to be scrounged and, just like old Mother Hubbard, my cupboard was bare. I almost broke down and ate something healthy when the telephone rang and I lunged for it.

'Hello?' I nearly shouted over the wire.

'OK. I've got the information you wanted. Yep. Africa Hydraulics, Tat Hwong, and another company in Manhattan are all tied together, along with a number of other businesses. However, one of the names that you gave me wasn't correct.

The company in New York isn't Red Sun,' Saunders disclosed.

Damn! My hunch had been wrong and I was back to square one.

'Their official title is Red Sun Diamonds,' he revealed. 'So tell me, what does a diamond cutting business, a hydraulics company, and some sort of retail shop all have in common?'

'Probably nothing,' I said, though my heart was pounding. 'Thanks for the information, Bill, but I have to run.'

'Hold on a minute. Is this something you're working on with Hogan?' he asked, before I could hang up.

'No. I don't want to bother him unless it turns out to be worthwhile, and it's not looking very good at the moment,' I replied, hoping he'd leave me alone.

'That doesn't matter. Jack should probably know about it,' he lectured, ever the proper Fed. 'By the way, all these businesses are owned by one family, the Leungs. Any idea as to who they are?'

'Absolutely none. But I'll keep you posted on what I find out,' I fibbed, anxious to get off the phone.

'Thanks, I'd appreciate that,' he said in an odd tone.

I was willing to bet his next call would be to Jack Hogan. I decided not to take the chance, but turned off my cellphone and left the apartment, not wanting to hear Hogan's angry bellows over my answering machine. Instead I sat at a diner and drank coffee until it was time to meet Vinnie.

Eighteen

I was shivering on the corner, when Bertucci pulled up in a flashy black Cadillac Escalade. The thing was the size of a tank with Sinatra crooning inside.

'So what's the deal? You like freezing your ass off? Or were you afraid I'd come to your door and your boyfriend might see me?' he astutely questioned.

'Neither. I didn't want to be inside if my boss called,' I revealed.

'That's easy. Just don't pick up the phone,' Vinnie advised. 'Screen your calls on an answering machine like everyone else.'

I nodded, unable to explain to him a little thing known as Jewish guilt.

'So, aren't you gonna ask me how *my* day went?' he nudged as we hit the road.

'OK. How was your day, honey?' I joked.

'Terrific. There's gonna be a sequel to the movie *Goodfellas* and it looks like I might get a major role,' he reported. 'Of course, that is if it doesn't conflict with my shooting schedule for *Godfather 4*.'

My thoughts wandered as Vinnie prattled on about his latest accomplishments. Could Leung be buying blood diamonds through his company Red Sun? It would certainly be a clever way in which to launder all the illegal profits he made from shahtoosh and ivory.

The other question I had was: why didn't Santou want me snooping around the Diamond District? And what was Tiffany Stewart informing on these days?

My mind spun with endless conspiracy theories as we arrived at the port. We made our way into its heart where

I directed Vinnie to the US Fish and Wildlife parking lot. Connie was already there waiting in a beat-up blue Ford.

'Now *that* thing looks like it actually fell off a truck,' Vinnie said with a snort.

I motioned for her to leave the car and join us. Connie walked over properly dressed in her US Fish and Wildlife jacket and uniform.

'You know what? You're the only one here that looks official, so you should probably sit up front,' I suggested, and scrambled into the back seat.

I waited until Connie climbed inside and closed the door before making introductions.

'Connie, this is my friend Vinnie Bertucci. Vinnie, this is US Fish and Wildlife Inspector Connie Fuca.'

They looked at each other somewhat askance.

'Pleased to meet you,' Connie finally said, and offered her hand.

It swam in Vinnie's king-sized paw.

'Same here,' he added, and sat up a bit straighter in his seat. 'Make sure your seatbelt's on. I wouldn't want nothing to happen to a Fed in my car.'

The Escalade pulled out on to Fleet Street and we headed for Starr Terminal.

'So, where you from?' Vinnie asked, breaking the silence.

'Kearney, New Jersey,' Connie replied.

'No kidding? So's my mother,' he retorted. 'You know, they got the best pork store in that town.'

'You must mean Satriale's,' Connie guessed.

'Yeah, and that means you gotta be Italian,' Vinnie responded, beginning to loosen up.

'I also know a good place for cannoli,' she added.

Vinnie snuck another peak at her and smiled. 'Those are my favorite pastries in the world. I guess I'll have to try them.'

'I'll be happy to give you the bakery's address,' Connie replied.

'Or maybe you can just take me there yourself sometime,' he casually suggested.

Was I imagining it, or was Vinnie actually trying to hit on a Federal wildlife inspector? I put the thought aside for now as we arrived at Starr Terminal.

'Pull up to the gatehouse. I know the guard,' Connie instructed.

Vinnie did as told.

'Hey, Bobby. How you doing tonight?' she asked, and flashed her badge while leaning across Vinnie.

'Evening, Miss Connie. Everything all right?' he inquired, closely scrutinizing the hulk that sat behind the wheel.

'Everything's fine. We're just here to check out something on the pier. Don't worry. We won't be long,' she assured him.

'No problem. Take your time,' the guard told her and waved us inside.

Vinnie harrumphed as we passed through the gate. 'Did you see the look that guy gave me? What's his problem, anyway? What's he afraid of? That I know which container the big-screen TVs are in, and plan to hook it up and drive away?'

'Probably something along those lines,' Connie confirmed.

I was glad she was here to guide the way, as we drove through what could easily have been a maze. Starr Terminal is the largest facility on the grounds, comprised of four hundred and forty-five acres. Bordered by Elizabeth Channel and Newark Bay, Starr receives thirty percent of all containers shipped into the port.

Vinnie followed Connie's directions to an area that would have been bustling during the day. Tonight it was quiet as a grave, except for the sound of ships being loaded and offloaded in the distance.

Their industrial song conjured up visions of freighters, their rust-stained hulls continually attended by massive cranes that stacked containers as easily as if they were enormous toy blocks. The process continued around the clock. Time is money when the cost can run two hundred thousand dollars a day to dock and unload goods at the port.

Giant lamp poles cast a ghostly glow as snow began to swirl, lending the docks an otherworldly air. Rows of long metal boxes stood packed eight containers high, looking like over-sized coffins. Meanwhile other units sat loaded on chassis, where they patiently waited to be hauled away first thing in the morning. All I could wonder was how we'd ever find the right unit among this mountainous lot.

A frigid wind nearly took my breath away as we piled out of the Escalade and were instantly seal wrapped in a piercing sheet of bitter cold. The chill factor alone must have been fifteen degrees below.

'For chrissakes, it's bad enough out here to freeze my nuts off,' Vinnie grumbled, while slapping his arms across his chest to try and stay warm. 'Either way it's your fault if this weather makes me sick or sterile, Porter.'

I didn't reply but wrapped a flannel scarf around my neck and buried my nose in its wool.

'OK. What say we save ourselves a whole lotta time and trouble – why don't you just tell me exactly what it is you're looking for?' Vinnie advised.

'I can give you the name of the company and the container number,' Connie replied, and wrote the information down on a scrap of paper.

Vinnie took the slip from her hand and waved to a figure that appeared from out of the darkness.

'Stay here. I'll be back in a minute,' he said, and made his way toward the longshoreman.

'How'd you ever manage to get the container number?' I asked, as Vinnie trod away through the snow. He looked like the Jersey version of the Pillsbury Doughboy clad in a heavy down jacket.

'It pays to have a friend with Customs. Of course, now we owe *him* a humongous favor,' she retorted.

I glanced to where the longshoreman leaned against a bobtail that pulled container-filled chassis around the terminal. Vinnie stood beside him, his hands deeply entombed in his pockets, his feet stamping out a flamenco beat.

'He's really not with the Mob anymore?' Connie questioned with an upward tilt of her chin.

'Vinnie? No, he decided that he likes playing wiseguys better than being one,' I confirmed.

'In that case, he's doing one hell of an acting job over there,' she noted.

The longshoreman was practically scraping and bowing to Vinnie before springing to work. Jumping inside the bobtail, he backed up to a loaded chassis, fiddled with the connection, and drove the unit toward us. We watched as the longshoreman proceeded to cut the large metal bolt that served as the container's security seal.

'Thanks, Bobby,' Vinnie said, and extracted a wad of bills from his pants. Peeling off four fifties, he handed them to the man.

'No problem. Anytime for you, Vinnie. You know that,' the longshoreman responded and stuffed the money in his pocket.

Then he unhooked the chassis and drove the bobtail back to where it had originally been parked.

'It's all yours, New Yawk,' Vinnie said with a magnanimous wave of his hand.

The shipping unit stood a good five feet off the ground where it was stationed on the chassis. A close look revealed a pair of metal crossbars that hung from the bottom of its frame. I used them as stirrups to pull myself up and grab hold of the unlocked door handle. One hard tug and the container groaned open, exposing what amounted to a Chinese puzzle inside.

Though uncertain as to what would be found, I now stared at the sight in disbelief. The unit was packed from floor to ceiling, and wall-to-wall, with parcels that ran seven rows across and twelve cartons high. All told, there must have been at least eight hundred boxes consuming every available square inch of space.

'Well, I guess we'd better start unloading,' I remarked, not wanting to think too much about the impending task ahead.

But Vinnie had his own views on the matter.

'I didn't sign on to work here all night,' he gruffly replied.

Vinnie was right and I instantly felt like a jerk. He'd already done more than his share.

'Of course not. I meant the two of us,' I said, pointing to

212

Connie and myself in embarrassment. 'You've been great, Vinnie. Thanks for pulling strings. You've been great. I'm sure Connie won't mind giving me a lift home later on.'

'No problem,' she confirmed, her words gliding towards us on a hoary cloud of frost.

Vinnie glanced at her, and his expression immediately grew sheepish.

'Yeah, right. Like I'm gonna leave you two girls all alone here tonight. What the hell! We might as well get started,' he said, with a resigned shake of his head.

It was too cold, and there was too much work to do, to pretend to protest. Instead, I lifted the first box and handed it down to Connie, who passed it on to Vinnie in a rag-tag bucket brigade. The plan of attack was to remove one row at a time, cut the boxes open, and inspect them for ivory with the aid of our flashlights. Once that was done, the process would start all over again.

After an hour, my arms ached, my back hurt, and my fingers had grown numb. Still we'd barely begun to make a dent. To make matters worse, those boxes opened contained mostly auto parts, while only a few held African masks and carvings. Nothing illicit had so far been found.

'I've gotta take a break before some of my body parts begin to fall off,' Vinnie declared, and headed for his vehicle.

Connie and I dutifully followed, lured by the roar of its engine, seduced by the promise of heat. By now every ounce that I carried had grown heavy as a pound, and every pound had morphed into a ton. I needed to rid myself of all unnecessary weight if I planned to keep going. I removed my cellphone and gun, and placed them in Vinnie's glove compartment, while retaining my flashlight.

'What I wouldn't give for a shot of brandy right now,' Connie mumbled, while holding her hands up to the heater.

'To hell with a shot. We'll get ourselves a bottle of the best cognac,' Vinnie promised her.

'That sounds great. But first we've got to get through a few more rows of boxes,' I prodded, hoping to rally the forces.

Vinnie shot me a dirty look. 'You're already treading on thin ice, Porter. Don't push it.'

'That's OK. The faster we finish, the sooner we can get out of here,' Connie said, ever the loyal trooper.

We trudged back outside where Vinnie hoisted Connie up into the container. I wasn't certain if it was so he could gaze at her better, or was trying to keep her warm.

We worked our way through another two rows of boxes before Vinnie once again snapped.

'For chrissakes, isn't this crap ever going to end?' he vented as Connie handed him another carton. 'Are you sure there's anything in these damn boxes besides gaskets, and voodoo masks and carvings? Cause it's cold as hell out here.'

Glancing up, I saw that Connie's teeth were chattering and she'd noticeably begun to shiver. No way did I intend to stop, but neither did I want a mutiny on my hands.

'Connie, why don't you take a drive and find some place warm to get coffee?' I proposed.

She began to climb down before I'd even finished my sentence.

'Good idea,' she eagerly agreed. 'Only it's a hike back to my car.'

'Don't worry. I'm coming with you. Enough is enough. We need to get the hell out of this place for a while,' Vinnie said.

He emphasized the point by throwing the box in his hands on the ground.

It seemed I'd now officially become Captain Bligh.

'I have a better idea. Why don't the two of you go and I'll stay here,' I suggested, not wanting to let the container out of my sight.

'What are you – nuts, Porter? On second thought, look who I'm talking to,' Vinnie exploded. 'That does it. You're totally unbelievable.'

'Maybe so. But I'm still not leaving here. Go ahead. I'll be all right,' I replied.

'You're really pissing me off. You know that, Porter?' he asked, openly glaring at me.

'Yeah. I'm beginning to get an inkling of it,' I responded.

'This is silly. Don't worry. I'm a big girl. I promise I'll be fine.'

Vinnie sighed and took a quick look around. 'OK, it's your call. You're certain that you're a hundred percent all right with this?'

'Absolutely. The guard's right up front. There won't be a problem,' I said, doing my best to sound chipper. 'Just don't forget to bring me back a cup of coffee.'

But I knew, as I watched them drive off, that I was truly certifiable. What the hell was I thinking? That I could do this task all on my own?

The keen of offloading ships turned into melancholy cries as the night now swiftly closed in around me. I thought I spied shadows gliding among the containers and, for the first time, feared that I wasn't alone.

Don't be ridiculous. No one's here. The place is lit up like a friggin' Christmas tree, I scolded myself. *Now get back to work. After all, that's why you stayed behind.*

Hoisting myself up, I dragged out cartons until I'd managed to burrow a tunnel into the rear of the container. If any contraband were hidden, it would most likely be back here.

I grabbed one of the boxes, pushed it up front and slit the lid open with my knife. Nothing was inside but a bunch of scraggly African rag dolls. One stared with what seemed to be dark lifeless eyes. It took a moment to realize that each orb was a slash of black stitches. I couldn't help but think of Bitsy von Falken's fate and shiver. The doll's black gash of a mouth sinisterly smiled at me. Jumping down, I placed the box on the ground, and then climbed back up to repeat the process.

A few more hours of this and I won't ever have to work out again in my life, I tried to console myself.

But I was beginning to feel much like Vinnie. Perhaps Leung had been pulling my chain today just to screw with me. I could be sitting and drinking coffee some place warm right now, instead of climbing in and out of this container like a monkey. Even so, I still couldn't bring myself to stop.

Just one more box, I kept repeating over and over, until it had become my mantra.

It was then I spotted some cartons lodged against the back wall that were different in shape and size. Long and thin, these resembled crude cardboard coffins.

I dragged one up front and drew my knife down its middle, as if eviscerating a carcass. My pulse thrummed as my fingers clumsily pushed back the flaps, feeling certain that I had finally found something.

Damn! Inside was nothing but a collection of spears, each an elegant work of art. Kneeling down, I picked one up and examined it.

A decorative sheath of animal skin and coarse hair covered the metal spearhead on one end. This slipped on to a carved wooden shaft that terminated in a sharp metal stabbing tip. The spear appeared to be about five feet total in length.

I pulled out a few more spears and realized they were the same as those used by the Masai tribe in Africa. Only these days, formerly proud warriors carve them as tourist souvenirs.

I was beginning to put them away when something suddenly caught my eye. Hidden beneath the pile of embellished shafts was a cream-colored object that appeared to be cylindrical. It coyly peeked up as if wanting to play a game of hide-and-seek.

I tried not to raise my hopes. However, I couldn't help but be excited as spears flew out of the box and on to the floor in a cluttered heap. I didn't stop, my fingers growing more frantic, until I finally hit the motherlode. Eureka! This time I'd actually struck gold – or pieces of ivory, to be more exact.

Nestled on the bottom of the crate were large chunks of the stuff, as well as an entire tusk that must have been taken from a juvenile. I wondered if the youngster had cried as it died, and if other elephants had heard its pleas for help.

I picked up the tusk and closed my eyes, the imagined cry reverberating inside me like a mournful dirge. The tusk grew heavy in my hands, as though it held the souls of all those elephants that had crashed to earth, their lives reduced to trinkets, bracelets and other vanity items made of ivory.

I could almost feel the silence bearing down on me. But any peace that it held abruptly erupted into a menacing crack of thunder.

I swiftly laid the tusk back in its box and jumped outside, my feet thudding on firm land. Though I closely scanned the sky, it held no sign of a storm. Only the soft kiss of snow that continued to fall to the ground.

There was no question but that my imagination was too active by far. I'd obviously conjured the sound. Even so, a steady stream of adrenaline now began to rush through me.

I had no doubt that if ivory was in one box, there was bound to be more. I'd counted ten cardboard coffins lined up in a row. It constituted all the evidence that was needed. The next move would be to trail Leung's men once they picked up the shipment. Only after delivery had been made, and accepted, could charges kick in.

Just the thought of catching Leung in my trap made all the crap that I'd dealt with in Fish and Wildlife during the past ten years now seem worthwhile.

I wonder if I'll finally be given a promotion, I mused, knowing that such a move would make upper level management wild.

Perhaps it was the frigid cold, or the rush of anticipation, but I was suddenly hit by a wave of exhaustion. I gazed at all the stacked boxes that had been cut open. They'd have to be taped back up once more. But right now, I needed a break. The rest of the work could wait until Vinnie and Connie returned.

I spotted the bobtail and began to head over. Maybe the truck would have a comfortable seat, not to mention some heat. I climbed up its two steps, opened the door, and slid into the cab.

Whaddaya know? The key was still in the ignition. Perhaps Vinnie *did* have a plan to lift some TVs while he was here, after all.

I turned on the engine and waited to feel a blast of warm air, but the breeze that poured out was cold. Wouldn't you know? The heater was on the fritz.

A lot of good that does me. I better keep moving.

Otherwise, the temptation to lie down, curl up and sleep could prove to be far too alluring. And dozing off at this point would surely have deadly consequences.

Having little else to do, I decided to take a stroll around the rows of containers. I pulled out my flashlight, turned it on, and briskly began to walk.

This should help keep me awake, I thought.

Sometimes the best way to deal with demons is to confront them – and I'd begun to see the shadows moving again.

To make matters worse, I was cold. Though I tried to wiggle my toes, I could no longer feel them. It was as if the snow had cunningly crept inside my boots and turned my feet from merely raw to two lifeless clumps of flesh.

Think of something else, I commanded myself, while deliberately stamping my feet.

How easy it must have been for Leung to smuggle ivory into the Port of Newark all of these years. He simply didn't present any paperwork and Fish and Wildlife never bothered to question it. Nor did anyone actively search for ivory based on rumor alone. The message sent to agents and inspectors alike was not to be pro-active in their work. Rather the attitude had become one of: *what can we get away with? How much can we let slide by?*

I was speculating on what other contraband was probably slipping in when something unexpected caught my eye. A galaxy of tiny stars had fallen to the ground where they reflected their light in the flashlight's beam. I stopped to inspect the luminous phenomenon more closely.

Lying in the snow was a neat pile of fragments that glittered in the dark like an uncovered vein of gold. I removed a glove, bent down and picked up a few of the bits. They were pieces of metal as fine and thin as slivers of paper. Only these scraps were razor sharp. The single shard between my fingers smartly pricked my flesh, producing a drop of blood.

But that wasn't the only small mound of filings to be found. Others lay spread across the ground. Some were partially buried, while still more appeared to have been trampled by a flurry of footprints in the snow.

What I knew was that they must have come from somewhere close. The obvious answer seemed to be from the column of containers directly in front of me. Each was the

218

size of a schoolbus, and solid as a metal King Kong. I raised my flashlight and began to examine them, starting at the very top.

The beam bounced along rows of steel ridges uniform as crispy Ruffles potato chips. Nothing appeared out of the ordinary until my light reached the second container from the ground. Only then did I spot the jagged hole that had been cut in its side. The opening was just large enough for a person to squeeze through, and dangling from its puncture wound was a rope.

I'd heard of stowaways sneaking into the country this way. Word had it unscrupulous organizations charged illegal immigrants thousands of dollars for the service. For that, they received less than first-class accommodations. However, if they made it here alive, it was a good bet that they'd never be found.

Immigration and Customs rarely searches vessels for stowaways. Nor does a ship's captain generally find and turn them in. Rather, that job is left to local law enforcement agents with no legal authority over vessels coming into port, or the people that are legitimately – or illegitimately – on them.

I just hoped whoever had stowed away inside this particular container had already made it out. Otherwise, I had no doubt that I'd be tripping across a dead body.

'Anyone in there?' I apprehensively called, while directing my light toward the serrated hole.

The question echoed in my ears, even as the phantom darkness gobbled it up.

And for the briefest moment, I thought I heard a sound.

Then all grew silent once more.

Could someone still be alive inside? There was only one way to find out. But to do that, I needed something on which to climb, and there was no ladder around. Then I remembered the bobtail truck with its key in the ignition.

I ran back and scampered up the truck's two steps, their thin metal base clanging beneath my feet. Then, settling into the seat, I turned on the engine. There's a first time for everything. This was mine to play trucker.

Shifting into gear, I applied the gas and drove the bobtail between the steel rows. I searched until I found what I'd been looking for.

I carefully parked beneath the perforated container, climbed out the door, and scrambled on to the truck's hood. From there it was an easy shot up to its roof. That placed me directly in line with the punctured unit.

The adrenaline that sped through my veins now began to throb as I drew close enough to run my fingers along the hole. The gash had obviously been cut from inside with the use of a drill and a hacksaw blade.

'Hello?' I inquired again.

There was still no reply.

To say that I wasn't afraid would have been a lie. I could nearly taste my fear, sour and metallic, as it rose in my throat like Lazarus from the grave.

I expected to see a corpse, or two, or three, all huddled together in an endless state of sleep, having expired from either starvation or the cold. I nearly turned around, not wanting to know. It was my demons that drove me forward, leaving me no other choice.

I carefully aimed the flashlight's beam and stuck my head through the hole. The air inside was pungent and tinged with the odor of dirty clothes. I took a quick look around and breathed a sigh of relief. While something was inside, it clearly wasn't human remains. Pulling my head back out, I grabbed a gulp of fresh air and then squeezed my way into the container.

It appeared I'd been right; there was no sign of a corpse. However, the container's contents had definitely been human cargo. They'd left behind evidence of their stay, along with an overwhelming stench. The only way to keep from gagging was to hold a hand over my nose and mouth as I moved the flashlight about. I quickly pinpointed the source of the offensive aroma.

Four large plastic garbage bags had been used as toilets. But that wasn't the only sign of human habitation. Blankets, bedding, soiled clothing, and empty water bottles lay strewn about. Candy wrappers and a burial mound of chicken bones attested to the fact that the stowaways had been well fed, while a heater had assured they stayed warm.

But it was what I saw next that nearly brought my heart to a crashing halt. Detailed maps of Liberty International Airport and Newark Marine Terminal sprang to life under my light.

I picked them up and saw that a number of sites had been marked with red Xs, while others were heavily circled. In addition, three oil and natural gas pipelines had been scored, along with more than a dozen chemical plants.

I could barely control the shaking of my hands as the flashlight now illuminated a small sack that had been tossed in a corner. My breath came in short, sharp spurts as I quickly walked over.

I made sure my gloves were on tight and then, opening the plastic bag, began to rummage around.

Some sort of blueprints were inside. I removed them to find they were of four large chemical plants nearby. If they'd been picked as targets, their assailants couldn't have chosen more wisely.

A major campaign contributor, the chemical industry had fought vigorously against much needed safeguards over the past few years. They'd achieved their goal – thwarting Congress from passing laws that would make their plants more secure and, in the process, cost them more money. But the bag held a few other surprises as well.

I pulled out airport security badges, an airline mechanic's certificate, and Port Newark identification cards. I stared blankly at the ID passes, wondering why they didn't look familiar. Then it slowly began to sink in.

Homeland Security had talked about issuing them ever since the World Trade Center attack in 2001. Only it had never been done. The ID cards were obviously fake. The problem was, how many civilian employees at the seaport were even aware of that? If not, the bearers could easily pass through into secure and sensitive areas.

I stuffed everything back in the sack, knowing that it must have been left behind by mistake.

Was it possible the former stowaways in this container

were actually terrorists? The more I thought about it, the more it made sense. If illegal immigrants knew this was an easy way into the country, then surely Al-Qaeda had figured it out by now.

Another of these containers could very well hold enough ammonium nitrate to create a blast twenty times as strong as that which had rocked Oklahoma City. The only thing needed would be a truck to haul the unit to its intended destination.

A terrorist could easily bribe an exporter to turn a blind eye while chemical and biological weapons were packed in a crate, and slipped in a unit, carrying goods on a cargo ship bound for the US. If so, it might be hidden among one of the containers sitting on the pier right now. My heart began to race as I realized the implications of what I had just found.

But the sum of all fears was a 'nuke-in-a-box.' Should such a device arrive at a US port, it would already be too late. Perhaps that's what Santou had been pursuing during all his hours of working overtime.

I quickly squeezed out of the corrugated box, and climbed off the truck, knowing that it was urgent I call him.

Nineteen

My hand frantically searched for my cellphone while I raced between the rows of containers. What in the hell had I done with it, anyway?

Damn! That's when I remembered. I'd left my phone, and my gun, inside Vinnie's Escalade. I slowed down, knowing that nothing could be done until Bertucci returned. That is, unless I managed to find a way out of this maze and get to the guard at the gate.

Of course! I'd simply commandeer the bobtail truck. But first, I had to make certain that Vinnie wasn't already sitting here waiting for me.

I rounded a corner and nearly collided with George Leung. He seemed startled to see me, too. Only he was the one with a gun. I stared in horror as he motioned to someone behind him.

A thug materialized and came swiftly trotting towards me. The guy could have been straight out of a bad martial arts film, complete with a cigarette bobbing in his mouth like a drunken firefly.

Even Vinnie would have told this mook to update his look, I thought, as he deftly started to frisk me.

'Hey! What do you think you're doing?' I protested, having been caught completely off guard.

But Leung's expression stopped me cold.

'The question is, what are *you* doing, Agent Porter? I see you've been looking through my goods,' he said, pointing to all the opened boxes scattered around him. 'Were you able to find whatever it was you were searching for?'

I don't know which stunned me more – the fact that Leung knew my name, or that his body guard proceeded to roughly push me down on my knees. My body still hurt from where I'd been kicked the day before, and snow began to seep into my clothes as cigarette smoke curled noxiously about me.

Leung's guard removed the cigarette from his lips and flicked the butt at my face as he walked away. It hit my cheek and fell into the snow.

An empty pack of Marlboros had been tossed in the alley where I'd lain. Could this man possibly have been one of my attackers? Only that didn't make sense. For one thing, I hadn't yet met Leung.

'I had a feeling you would show up at the port tonight,' Leung continued, as though we were casually chatting at a party.

Things were happening too fast for me to process them properly. Or maybe I'd just grown sluggish from the cold. But I asked the one question that raced through my brain.

'How did you learn my name?' I inquired, and nervously bit my lips.

'Mr Giamonte told me,' he amiably replied. 'It's amazing what one can learn when a little pressure is applied. I thought it strange that he didn't attend our meeting after having gone to so much trouble to set it up. I decided to find out why.'

Leung had said nothing yet about his son. I took that as a good sign. Perhaps he still hadn't made the connection. I could only pray that was the case. Otherwise, what was about to take place would surely be an execution.

It was as if Leung had read my mind.

'Now remove your jacket and gloves, and place your hands on top of your head,' he ordered.

My only hope was to keep him talking until I thought of a way to escape. Or, until Vinnie arrived. Bertucci was turning into a regular savior. He was the one chance I had of getting out of this mess alive.

'This all began with Bitsy von Falken's death. I need to know. Were you responsible for her murder?' I asked, while doing as I was told.

The cold gleefully wrapped itself around me tight as a shroud.

Leung grudgingly nodded. 'Yes. That was done as a necessary favor.'

'A favor for whom?' I questioned, placing my weight first on one knee, until the pain became too great, and then shifting it to the other.

But nothing could fight the wet chill that had taken hold of my flesh and now worked its way into my bones.

'Why all these questions, Agent Porter?' he asked, hitting my name with undue emphasis. 'Do you really think that knowing the answers will somehow alter your fate?'

'You have me at a disadvantage. You know each step that led up to this point. You're the one in total control. It may not change anything, but I'd still like to know,' I replied, hoping to appeal to his ego.

'I believe you said something very much like that when we first met. I had the advantage over you then, also,' Leung mysteriously responded, as though he were the Cheshire cat. 'But since you ask, the favor was done for her husband. He and his mistress, Tiffany Stewart, have been selling me black market diamonds. Only von Falken put that in jeopardy when he stupidly stole money from his company. His wife found out, and threatened to call the police after learning of their affair. I couldn't allow that to happen'

So that's why Jake didn't want me snooping around the Diamond District, or questioning Tiffany. Then another realization hit. It also meant Santou must have known that Leung was in New York and decided not to tell me. Instead, he'd protected his case by trying to make sure that I didn't start one of my own.

'Gavin's arrest wouldn't have been good for business. And who knows where it might have led? Bitsy von Falken signed her own death warrant by threatening to turn him in. I merely eliminated a potential problem,' Leung explained.

I thought I heard a sound and involuntarily flinched. Leung noted my reaction and instinctively followed my gaze.

Oh, please don't let that be Vinnie, I prayed.

It wasn't that I didn't want him to come. I just preferred that he do it without his headlights blazing and the radio on, so as not to give Leung and his bodyguard any advance warning.

'Feeling a bit jumpy, Agent Porter?' Leung asked. 'It's certainly understandable in your case.'

I'd heard stories about Leung's sadistic streak in the past. Some I now tried to forget.

'Black market diamonds? Then that's how you launder all the money you make from shahtoosh and ivory,' I said, attempting to pick the conversation back up where we'd left off.

More than anything, it was imperative that I keep him talking.

'Exactly. And since diamonds have no certificate of origin, I'm able to buy them low and sell high. It's a win-win proposition all the way around,' he boasted.

Though I tried to block it out, there was no escaping the question that continued to haunt me.

'Why were Bitsy von Falken's eyes and mouth sewn shut?' I asked, unable to rid myself of the gruesome image.

Bitsy von Falken and the African doll coalesced in a macabre dance of death in my mind, their herky-jerky movements controlled by Leung, as they vainly struggled to open their eyes.

Leung looked at me in amusement.

'A tailor shop is the front for my new factory. The gesture seemed ironic. It serves as a warning of what happens to those that don't mind their own business. Having one's eyes and mouth sewn shut instills a certain amount of fear in people. Wouldn't you say?' he asked, his voice insinuating itself inside me. 'You can't see. You can't speak. And though you're alive, you might as well already be dead. In essence, your body has become your own coffin. Can you imagine how that must feel?'

My teeth chattered and my body began to shake, gripped by fear and the subzero cold.

'Mr Giamonte will be found in the same manner. And, no doubt, the police will set off in search of a serial killer. Who would ever suspect an elderly, mild-mannered tailor?' Leung mused, with a note of satisfaction.

My back had begun to ache, and I could no longer sit up straight. I was tempted to tell Leung to carry out his plans and just get it the hell over.

Don't be a fool. You still have time, a voice inside me urged.

Time for what? I wanted to scream, though I wisely held my tongue.

Instead, I asked the most important question of all: one for which I felt certain I already knew the answer.

'What about Magda?'

Leung raised a pair of barely discernable eyebrows and looked momentarily puzzled. Then his face relaxed.

'Ah, you must mean the woman that witnessed Mrs von Falken's body being dumped. Why? Was she a friend of yours?' he asked, sounding briefly intrigued.

I nodded while digging my fingernails into my palms. The skin had grown so numb that I could barely feel them.

'Don't worry. I did nothing so dramatic to her. We merely blocked the doorway of her truck and set the vehicle on fire,' he revealed. 'Obviously she couldn't remain alive.'

His callous response sent chills rushing through me that were far worse than those produced by the arctic air. My body began to sway and I feared I was becoming light-headed.

You've got to keep talking, I reminded myself.

However, even trying to think was becoming an effort.

'Do you know who is supplying von Falken and Tiffany Stewart with those diamonds you're buying, and how the money's being used?' I asked, mildly curious if Leung realized that he might be funding terrorists.

'Not really. Nor do I care,' he matter-of-factly responded. 'There are rumors, of course. But I believe in following my own advice. It's none of my concern. Now it's my turn to ask *you* a question.'

Leung brought his gun to my head, so that its mouth pressed into my flesh. I felt my soul being wrenched from its shell and sucked deep down inside the barrel.

'Why did you kill my son?' he asked.

And, for the first time, his voice was filled with emotion.

227

So he does know who I am.

I slowly raised my eyes to meet his, knowing that we'd finally reached the end game.

'Because I was left with no other choice. It was his life or mine,' I responded, the words turning sluggish in my mouth.

'Then you know exactly how I feel. You're getting off easier than you deserve, Agent Porter,' he replied. 'You're a lucky woman. I have no thread with me tonight, but you're still going to die.'

I closed my eyes, aware that Leung had already begun to squeeze the trigger.

Now I lay me down to sleep. I pray the Lord my soul to keep, I whispered to myself, just as I had as a child.

BOOM!

The blast resounded like a cannon shot in my head.

Only, I was still on my knees – alive.

'Throw your gun down, Leung!' Vinnie called out.

My eyes immediately flew open.

Leung's bodyguard lay on the ground near Bertucci's feet. However, rather than drop his weapon, Leung spun around and fired at the intruder.

I heard a grunt, and caught Vinnie's look of surprise, as the gun flew from his hand. It was as though the world had come to an end as Bertucci began to fall.

'No!' I screamed aloud.

Leung quickly turned back, his gun pointed at me, and I knew I'd already used up all my nine lives. Perhaps I deserved to die. I'd thoughtlessly removed my gun and, because of that, Vinnie had paid the ultimate price.

My body was ready to cave. It was my mind that refused to give in.

For chrissakes, you've got to do something! my inner voice shrieked.

Do what? I wanted to cry.

My heart beat so wildly, it felt as though I was about to be torn apart. At the same time, my breath came in short, shallow gasps. With Vinnie gone, everything moved in slow motion. There seemed no question but that all hope was lost.

The next moment, I miraculously heard his voice again.

'Hey, Leung. Did you know that your son cried like a little baby as I held him over the railing to feed to the sharks? He begged like the spineless coward he was,' Vinnie taunted.

Leung swirled to angrily face him.

'You son-of-a-bitch. Now I know who you are,' he furiously spat, and moved to where Bertucci lay sprawled on the ground.

Get up! Get up! Get up! my mind screamed, giving my body a verbal kick in the ass.

No way would I ever find Vinnie's gun buried in the snow in the short amount of time that was left. Instead, I scrambled to my hands and knees, forcing my legs to move, even though they vehemently protested.

I stumbled on to my feet and, summoning every ounce of will, began to lurch toward Leung's container.

'He was a weakling. That's the kind of son that you had,' I heard Vinnie spew with manic laughter.

Every muscle, every ligament shrieked, wanting to go back to sleep, as I pulled myself up on the metal crossbars and reached inside the container. My hand grabbed on to one of the spears that lay on the floor, knowing there wasn't a moment to lose.

I looked back just as Leung reached Bertucci and aimed his gun straight at him.

'Beg for your life as you made my son do,' he demanded in a strident voice

'Like hell I will,' Vinnie responded with a growl.

'In that case, your death will be slow and painful,' Leung calmly retorted.

Then Vinnie screamed as the gun went off.

I only hoped that his cry, and the snow, muffled the sound of my feet as I jumped back down and quickly headed towards them.

Run faster! I implored my legs.

But they were as weak as two worn-out rubber bands.

And then I saw Leung aim his gun again. Only this time, it was pointed directly at Vinnie's face.

I could no longer wait. It was now or never.

I pulled back my arm, took a breath, and swiftly threw the spear. The moment froze as the shaft silently flew from my hand and hurtled through space.

That was followed by a sickening thud as the spear found its mark, and Leung was impaled in the back.

Maybe Vinnie's still alive, I tried to convince myself.

Until Leung's gun went off again.

Bertucci struggled to move, but he wasn't fast enough, and the bullet caught him in the face.

All my resolve dissipated as I sank to the ground, overcome by nausea, as the snow turned to a crimson pool of blood.

The last sound I heard was the operatic rumble of ships unloading in a haunting lullaby, accompanied by the growing swell of sirens, as I closed my eyes and gladly succumbed to the beckoning night.

Epilogue

'Here. Look what I found,' Gerda said, and placed a heavy, leather-bound book in my lap. It was a photo album that I'd last seen years ago.

I pressed the treasure close to my nose and breathed in deeply, inhaling childhood memories. My fingers traveled over the well-worn cover; its color that of dried blood. Then I reverently opened the book, knowing that it held my history.

Inside were photos of Gerda and my grandmother. Their arms were linked together, as were their spirits, though one no longer trod this earth. They looked eternally young as they sat and happily smiled on a New York City bench. It was almost as though they hadn't been to hell and back.

I flipped a page and there was my mother at eight years old, her cheeks glistening from the cold, with a well-formed snowball in her fist. Life hadn't yet twisted her into what she would eventually become.

Next was my sister as I'd last seen her. How odd never to age, but forever remain a teenager. She ran away from home at the age of fifteen and I hadn't heard from her since.

I finally came upon an image of myself and stared in amazement. I hadn't realized the striking resemblance in all three generations. But there it was: the past and the present clearly converged in the nose, the eyes, and the mouth. Perhaps this was how the dead returned to life.

Fortunately, Vinnie had done just that after an ambulance had arrived on the scene and rushed him to the hospital. Leung's first bullet had barely missed his heart. The second had left a permanent scar on his face.

'I'm getting too old for this kind of crap,' Bertucci had

declared a few days later. 'That's it for me, Porter. I think you're gonna have to find yourself a new playmate.'

Vinnie instantly knew something was wrong when he'd spotted a Mercedes parked at the front gate, and saw that the guard had disappeared. He'd dispatched Connie to get help and promptly rushed to my aid.

'Do you know what a shot in the face is probably gonna do to my acting career?' he'd moaned while lying in his hospital bed.

What it had done so far was to launch him into semi-stardom. Taking two bullets proved to be the best career move he could ever have made. Not only was his heroism splashed across the news, but Vinnie became an instant darling on the talk show circuit, appearing on Letterman, Leno and Oprah. Even Donald Trump wanted in on the action. Bertucci had already been invited to participate in the next season of *The Apprentice*.

Meanwhile, discussions were underway for a TV movie after his story ballooned from having apprehended an ivory smuggler to taking on the entire Chinese Mob. It was amazing what a little good publicity could do.

It turned out my hunch had been correct. Santou *had* been tracking down a lead on terrorists. But like so many others before, once they snuck into this country they simply seemed to vanish.

The bombshell discovery I'd made of ID tags, blueprints and maps never hit the front page news. Rather, that bit of information was deemed too sensitive and kept tightly under wraps. Instead, the general public continued to be assured that all was well on the home front and spoon-fed pabulum.

The whole thing annoyed me to high hell. But Santou had offered up a simple explanation.

'Try as we might, there are no silver bullets to make us any more secure. So why cause unnecessary panic?'

It was good to know that Big Daddy government was doing such a bang-up job of keeping us all safe.

On the bright side, Gavin von Falken was being held for fraud and trade in illegal diamonds. He'd also admitted to hiring the thugs that beat me up. However, he continued to deny any knowledge of terrorists, while insisting that he was nothing but an innocent pawn in a dirty game.

Jake had laughed at that one, and said he hoped von Falken enjoyed his future prison accommodations. Personally, I hoped the guy ended up in a nice location – say somewhere like Abu Gharaib.

As for Tiffany Stewart, the woman was amazing. She'd managed to land on her Manolo Blahniks once again, having gotten off scot-free for all of her help. The last I'd heard, she was back on the prowl looking for another wealthy husband.

Most of all, I'd been surprised to find that I wasn't immediately reprimanded. The truth was that I hadn't yet heard from Jack Hogan. Instead, my fate was left to the powers that be – the big boys in DC, who had been gunning for me since Day One.

I'd finally learned of their decision only yesterday.

My punishment was severe – suspension from the Service for a litany of violations. Not the least of which was giving a damn about endangered species.

'Come on, chère. What say we take Spam for a walk?' Santou suggested, and gave me a kiss on the cheek.

I placed the album on the couch, knowing it would be there when I returned.

There's something magical about the city as it sleeps under a fresh blanket of snow. It's as though a spell has been cast over its soul. I could hear Manhattan's heart beating along with my own.

We walked to the river where a shaft of crisp morning light splayed across the waves, nearly taking my breath away.

'There's something we need to talk about, chere. I didn't want to bring it up until you were well on your way to recovery,' Santou informed me.

His tone immediately warned that the subject matter was serious.

Great. What was I about to be lobbed with now? I clenched my fists, not knowing how else to prepare myself.

'You lied to me, Rachel. You pretended to cancel your appointment in the Diamond District. You deceived me and compromised an active investigation,' Jake accused, his voice taut as a bowstring.

233

Every word that he said was true. Just hearing it made my heart ache. Still, Jake wasn't lily white himself. He'd had no qualms about doing what he deemed necessary in order to advance his case.

'You're right, and I'm sorry about that,' I agreed. 'But on the other hand, you clearly knew that Leung was in New York, what he was up to, and purposely didn't tell me. Rather, you insisted that I drop *my* case in order to protect your own.'

'OK,' Santou grudgingly conceded. 'I'll accept that. Only, you nearly lost your life on this one, chere. Maybe that's acceptable to you. But it sure as hell isn't to me.'

His voice broke, and he quickly tried to cover it with a cough.

'Yeah, but I didn't. I'm still here,' I responded lightly. 'Besides, you probably won't have to worry about that anymore.'

There. I'd said it aloud. Each word hung in the air like a tiny weight.

'What do you plan to do now, Rach?' Santou asked, as Spam chased after a flock of snowy pigeons.

'Oh, I don't know. Maybe take a trip to Disneyland,' I replied with a caustic laugh that couldn't disguise my pain.

But I knew what he meant. Did I plan to fight for my job? Or pick up my marbles and leave?

'I'm really not sure yet. I'll have to think about it for a while,' I finally said.

However, Jake wasn't buying my line.

'Don't take too long, chère. You're not one to stand idly by. I know you far too well. You have to be on the side of the angels,' he said and, placing an arm around my shoulder, drew me close.

That was true. The problem was that the angels had begun to elude me, and I no longer knew where they were anymore. Perhaps this would be a good time to find out. Meanwhile, I planned to spend some time with my family – Jake, Terri, Gerda and Spam.

As for the animals, I'd continue to be their voice in any way that I could.

The sun lit the city in an incandescent kiss as Santou, Spam, and I slowly began to walk home.

234